STONE LAKE

A Novel

By

Phil M. Williams

Printed in the United States of America

First Printing, 2015

Phil W Books

www.PhilWBooks.com

ISBN: Print: 978-1-943894-05-5

Cover design and interior formatting by Tugboat Design

Contents

Chapter 1

What You Deserve

Jon sits on the edge of a single wooden bed, bare chested, exposing his chiseled build, wearing only boxer briefs. His baby face is hidden beneath two days of stubble and topped with dark disheveled hair. The one-room cabin is chilly, the wood in the stove vanquished many hours ago. He massages his left knee, running his fingers along the four-inch scar. He grips the knee, grimacing as he pulls it to his chest, straightens it, and stands with a groan. He grabs his grease stained khaki canvas pants off the floor and pulls them on, his belt buckle clanging against the zipper.

Along the wall, milk crates double as a makeshift bookshelf, overflowing with worn paperbacks. Jon walks barefoot across the wood floor to a dented metal filing cabinet. From the top drawer, he pulls out a gray T-shirt and a pair of socks; from the bottom, a faded black hooded sweatshirt that reads Stone Lake Excavating.

He takes a few strides, and he's in the kitchen. White paint is peeling off the wooden cabinets, and faux wood is peeling off the laminate countertops. The refrigerator hums loud enough to annoy. A wood stove sits in the corner for cooking and heat. Jon leans on the counter with one arm, as he brushes his teeth in the kitchen sink. A dish rack sits to his right with a single plate, glass, and fork. He pulls a small cooler from the refrigerator, walks to the back door, laces up his work boots, and heads outside.

Dim morning light illuminates his backyard, enclosed by a sun-beaten board-on-board fence. Against the cabin, a wooden enclosure with a hose and showerhead hangs from the roof. Fruit trees and coppiced alders grow along the fence, with berry bushes and pruned silverberry growing underneath. Mushroom logs are propped up in the shadiest corner. Two beehives face the sun, atop cinder blocks protected from the wind. An annual garden mulched with wood chips sits dead center. Peas climb a teepee made from fallen branches. Jon opens his cooler and pulls out a faded Cool Whip container. He picks sugar snap peas, broccoli, and lettuce, filling the plastic tub, and shoves it back into the cooler.

He exits the garden through the far gate. He uses the outhouse, not bothering to shut the wooden door. He washes his hands in the outdoor spigot on the way to the driveway. The door of the old two-toned Ford F-250 creaks as he opens it. Pockets of rust scar the unlined bed of the diesel truck. He turns the key, the glow plugs light, and the ignition fires. From the dash, he grabs a black baseball cap adorned with CAT in white letters and pulls the brim low. He retrieves a travel-size container of mouthwash from the center console and takes a swig. He spits out the window, and turns to back out of the gravel driveway, that's more compacted clay than gravel.

Not long afterward Jon drives past the chain link and barbed wire gate into the industrial park, greeted first by a tow and scrap yard with junked cars stacked ten high. Two landscaping companies sit beyond the tow yard, with mountains of mulch and rows of container plants set out in the sun. A skid steer loads mulch on the back of a stake body truck. Jon pulls into the next gravel parking lot and parks in front of Stone Lake Excavating's one-story office with a twenty-foot-wide garage door on either side. Fifteen trucks are parked here, with trailers attached. One garage bay is open, a Ford F-450 idling in front. He walks by the truck into the shop. Three excavators, three skid steers, and two ride-on vibratory compactors are parked along the wall. An older Latino man sharpens a shovel on a bench grinder, and a younger man reads a sheet of paper on his clipboard.

"Good morning, Victor," Jon says.

"*Hola, el patron*." The old man nods and offers a brief grin, exposing a mouthful of silver.

"Good morning, Oscar," Jon says.

Oscar is Bolivian, with dark brown skin, jet-black hair that covers the back of his neck, and a smooth young face. He is considered a campesino in his home country—a term used for the darker-skinned, perpetually poor farmers.

"Morning, Jon. Is Chad coming in?" Oscar asks.

Jon smiles. "What do you think?"

Oscar frowns and shakes his head.

"I thought you guys were gonna finish yesterday," Jon says.

"Me too … lots of rocks. Now the client wants us to do more than what's on the work order."

"What did Chad say about it?"

"I called him on the radio yesterday, but he never picked up."

"Do you want me to come by and talk to the client?"

"If you can,"

"Would it be okay if I come by in a couple hours? I've got some bids that I need to finish up."

"If you can get there before lunch."

"I'll swing by around 10:30."

+++

Jon parks at the curb in front of a brick-faced McMansion. He walks past Oscar's rig in the circular driveway, striding uphill, alongside the house. A shrill female voice fills the air. At the crest of the hill, Jon sees the sunlight glistening off the lake below. Running down the steep embankment are perfect exposed-clay terraces, which Victor is fine-grading with a rake and a laser level. A cigarette hangs from his mouth. An elderly woman—in tennis shorts and a white polo shirt with orange clay clinging to the bottom half of her bright white shoes—lectures Oscar.

"Ma'am, I would be happy to do the extra work," Oscar says, "but I need to talk to my boss about it."

"It's not extra work. It says right here that the terraces should go to the bottom." She points a dark red nail at the contract.

"Hi, Mrs. Hensley," Jon says as he approaches, holding a metal clipboard.

"Are you who I need to talk to, to get this done the way I want it?" she says with her hands on her hips.

Oscar walks toward Victor, leaving Jon with the client.

"I think we can fit in another terrace at the bottom, if you want to, but I don't think it's needed. We will have slowed the water down enough that it won't cause erosion. I noticed that we're not planting the terraces." Jon double-checks his copy of the contract.

"My landscaper is doing that."

"Okay. Well, he needs to plant it immediately, just in case a big rain comes."

"He's coming on Monday."

"Great. Do you want us to put in one more terrace?"

"That's what I've been saying."

Jon opens his metal clipboard and pulls out a contract.

"This is a change order for the additional work," Jon says.

"I'm not paying extra for this. It's supposed to be in my original contract."

"The original contract allowed for five terraces built twenty feet apart, which Oscar and Victor built to spec."

She crosses her arms and glares at Jon.

"Here's the thing, Mrs. Hensley. I would normally just eat the extra labor and do this, but we are already a day and a half over on this job because of all the rocks they ran into."

"That's not my problem."

"Well, it's both of our problems, because, per the contract, we have labor and materials to be added for that extra time spent digging out large rocks, which we didn't charge for. How would you like to proceed?"

She purses her lips. "Then Chad should have told me as soon as they found the rocks. My husband is not going to like this … not one bit."

"It's up to you. Do you want to sign the change order, or do you want us to leave it as is?"

She snatches the change order from Jon's hand. He hands her a pen to sign the contract and holds out his clipboard as a makeshift writing surface.

"Thank you, Mrs. Hensley. I appreciate it."

She stalks away.

Jon approaches Oscar and Victor, checking the grade of the terraces with a laser.

"How's the slope?" Jon says.

"Pretty good. It's 2 percent back and about 2 percent toward the drains," Oscar says.

"She's gonna pay for the extra terrace. Do you think you guys can finish it today?"

"Maybe," Oscar says.

"I don't want y'all working on Sunday, especially on this dog. I'll give you a hand for the next six hours, then we can all go home."

+++

With the afternoon sun waning, Jon pulls up his driveway, the front of his cabin concealed by old growth forest. His cell phone rings. He glances at the caller ID, and exhales.

"Hi, Mom," he says.

"How's my favorite son?" she asks.

"I'm your only son."

"Still my favorite."

"I'm doing okay. How about you?"

"You know. I'm gettin' by."

"Can I give you a call tomorrow? I just pulled into my drive-way. It's been a long week."

"Oh, sure, honey. It's just my leg's still actin' up from when I fell. Those pills ain't worth a damn. I just need help with a couple things. Won't take long. I hate to bother you with this stuff. I know you probably got better things to do than help your broken-down old mother on a Saturday night."

"It's fine. … I'll be right over."

Jon tosses his phone to the seat next to him, flicks on the Ford's headlights, and reverses into the street. He puts the truck in Drive and presses on the gas. The gravel backwoods road turns into asphalt, and hunting cabins give way to luxury homes, as he comes down from the mountain. After a hairpin turn, he stops for a rafter of turkeys. Hundreds of turkeys make the late afternoon crossing to their nesting site. Some run across the road; some walk, and some fly, afraid of their feet touching the asphalt. He hears the screeching of tires, and the crunch of metal and plastic. His truck lunges forward a few feet. Turkeys squawk and fly haphazardly away from the scene. He steps on the parking brake, exits his truck, and marches to the rear of the vehicle, shaking his head.

The front end of a black Acura Integra is connected to his hitch. A young woman sits stunned in the driver's seat. She has straight dark hair, cut just beneath her chin, porcelain skin, and blue eyes. He taps on the window.

"Miss, are you okay?" He taps again. "Are you okay?"

Her eyes blink. She turns and sees Jon's body in front of her window. She opens her door and steps outside.

"I'm really sorry," she says, her hand over her mouth as she surveys the damage.

"No need to be," he says. "My truck's fine. Your car's a different story."

"I didn't see you after the corner."

"A rafter of turkeys was crossing the street."

"A rafter?"

"A group, a flock, a gaggle, whatever you wanna call 'em."

Her facial features are soft and symmetrical. Her build is athletic, toned. She stares at the crack in her front bumper and radiator, already leaking radiator fluid on the asphalt.

"Are you sure you're okay?" he asks.

"I think so." She exhales and purses her lips. "Do you think it's drivable?"

"Not sure. Put the emergency brake on. I'm gonna pull forward."

After separating the truck hitch from the Acura's front end, Jon surveys the damage.

"You could probably get it to the shop about two miles from here on Evergreen, but I wouldn't drive real far. You run the risk of the engine overheating."

"Are you going that way? Could I follow you?" Her eyes search the ground. A solitary tear spills down her cheek.

"It's not that bad," Jon says. "I'm sure your insurance will cover it."

She wipes her eyes with the cuff of her sweater, while shaking her head. "Sorry, it's just been … a long … week."

"Why don't we get going before you run out of radiator fluid? Keep an eye on the temperature gauge. Just honk if it starts to get into the red."

The two vehicles are moving again. Jon glances at his rear-view mirror to see the Acura chugging along behind him. A few minutes later they pull into a dark, deserted gas station and garage with a sign that says Stu's Service, Domestic and Foreign. Jon hops from his truck and taps on her window. She powers it down only a few inches.

"I'm sorry. I thought he'd still be here," Jon says, glancing at her temperature gauge running into the red. "You should cut the engine. It's overheating."

She turns her key, cutting the engine.

"Do you need a ride somewhere?"

"I'll call my fiancé to pick me up," she says.

"My name's Jon, by the way."

"Morgan … my name's Morgan. You can go now. I'll wait for my fiancé here."

+++

Jon takes the concrete steps two at a time to the vinyl-sided split level. Barking ensues. Inside, the smell of pizza, sour milk, dog shit, and BO permeate the air. He climbs the steps to the upstairs living room. Two black labs circle him with tails wagging. A big screen TV booms against the far wall with a little blond kid onscreen who thwarts crooks on Christmas Eve. A three-hundred-pound mass of a woman lies lengthwise on a brown couch, her head propped up by a pillow, her eyes closed, and her body covered by a blue-and-white flowered muumuu nightgown. The coffee table is riddled with gossip and entertainment magazines. A couple dog turds dot the off-white carpet like land mines.

"Mom. … Mom. … Mom!" Jon says. He reaches over the couch and shakes the sleeping form.

She turns her head. Her face is round, with three chins. He can almost imagine the beauty that once resided under this fat suit she can't seem to take off. Her unkempt hair is dyed blonde, and her nails are decorated with red, green, and silver glitter. Her nails are well cared for, like expensive tires and rims on a jalopy.

"Hey, honey," she says, barely audible.

"How are you feeling?"

She grimaces. "My leg's killin' me. This is the *only* position I can lay in without too much pain."

"What do you need me to do?"

"The dogs been messin' in the house, 'cause I ain't been able to let 'em out."

Jon exhales. "I'll take care of it, but I can't keep doing this. It's not that hard to let them out a couple times a day."

She frowns. "It is when you can't hardly walk, when everythin' hurts all the time. You just don't know what it's like."

"I'm sorry, you're right, I don't know what it's like."

"It's okay. I don't wanna be no burden." A tear slips down her round cheek.

"You're not, Mom."

She wipes the corners of her eyes with a fatty fist. "Why don't you sit down and talk to me? You never know how many more of our talks we're gonna have."

"Come on. Don't talk like that." Jon steps over the land mines and sits on the edge of the recliner.

"What are you doin' workin' on Saturday?"

"I had a few bids to finish up, and one of the crews needed a hand finishing a job."

"Where was Chad?"

Jon shrugs his shoulders.

"I thought so. Makes me sick, what they done to you."

"It's over. I really don't wanna talk about it."

"You deserve better. If I see either of 'em, they gonna get a piece of my mind."

"Leave it be, Mom. What you deserve and what you get don't always align."

"Well, did you hear the latest about Grandma and your aunt Claire?"

"I'm afraid to ask."

She picks at her scalp and slips the scab in the corner of her mouth with the tip of her finger. "My mother told me yesterday that Claire opened a joint account for her, so she can 'help' with the bills. *Help*, my ass. She's gonna help herself."

"If it's a joint account, Claire can use that money however she wants," Jon says. "I learned *that* the hard way."

"That's exactly what I told your grandmother. She don't listen to me though. Claire will have her cleaned out by the time she dies. As usual … nuthin' left for me." She sighs.

Jon stands, glancing at the piss-stained carpet and dog turds. "I should probably get this cleaned up."

Chapter 2

Friends?

Jon drives past Stu's gas station, toward the lake. The black Acura is parked in front, empty. His eyes feel heavy as he navigates the deserted two-lane road. The curvy road is tight, without a shoulder on either side. He sees a flash of white out of the corner of his eye. He slams on the brakes. The tires screech, and the truck dips forward, as it comes to a halt. His headlights illuminate Morgan walking along the road. She looks back briefly and continues to walk. Jon pulls up alongside her, with his window down.

"Morgan, you need a ride?" he asks, hanging out his window.

"I'm fine," she replies, not making eye contact.

He creeps alongside her, his truck matching her pace. "You're gonna get run over out here."

"I don't know you."

"I'm Jon, remember? From earlier?"

"I know *that*, but it's not exactly safe for a young woman to get into a car of a man she doesn't know. You're kind of creeping me out."

Jon rolls his eyes. "What happened to your fiancé?"

"It's none of your business."

"Morgan, I get that it's risky to accept a ride from me, but it's also risky to walk here, especially in the dark."

She stops walking. He stops the truck.

"Fine, but I'm going to get your license plate number, and send it to myself and my fiancé in an e-mail. So if something happens to me, you're screwed."

Jon laughs. "Fine by me."

She walks to the back of the truck and punches the license plate into her Blackberry. She strides to the passenger door, pausing with her hand on the handle. She studies Jon through the window. He smiles at her. She climbs in the cab.

"Where to?" Jon asks.

"Lake Landing. Do you know where that is?"

"Yep. You woulda had a long walk."

She glares at Jon. He looks over with a grin.

"Look, I'm sorry for scaring you. It wasn't my intention."

"I'm sorry. I don't mean to be so bitchy. I'm just used to guys trying to *help* me." She puts up air quotes when she says *help*.

"What? They're usually trying to help themselves?"

"Exactly, so please don't be one of those guys."

"All right." Jon laughs and takes his hands off the steering wheel in a show of surrender.

"Eyes on the road." She points ahead.

Jon puts his hands back on the wheel. "Just wondering … what's it about me that's so creepy?"

"I don't mean to be mean, but you look a bit rough. Your clothes are stained with … What is that? Dirt or grease?"

"Probably both."

"You have a face full of stubble, and you're wearing a black hoodie. A dirty guy with a hooded sweatshirt and an old pickup truck is exactly how you'd imagine a murderer to look."

Jon grins. "I don't know about that. Maybe if I drove an old van with dark curtains covering all the windows. I might also need to pick up some coke-bottle glasses and grow one of those copstaches."

She laughs. "*Copstache*?"

"You know, like the mustache all the cops wear. It makes 'em look like they fell out of a 1970's porno."

She shakes her head. "You're getting creepy again."

He grins. "Sorry. Let's try a safer topic. Do you like living on the lake?"

"It's nice, but I don't really live there. It's my dad's place. I just came up here to get away for a while, clear my head."

"I figured you weren't from around here." He glances at Morgan, then back to the road. "You don't look much like a local."

"How can you tell?"

"Not creepy enough."

"I'll have to work on that. Maybe buy some Aqua Net, tease my hair, take up smoking, and get myself a handful of unemployed baby daddies."

"Ouch. Is that what you think of us?" Jon frowns.

Morgan looks down. "I'm sorry. … I was just joking."

Jon laughs. "It's nice that you care about hurting my feelings."

She smiles and shakes her head. "You're such a jerk."

Jon pulls up to the gated street, reaches for the keypad, and types in 5424. A chain slides open the gate.

"I guess you've been here before?" Morgan asks.

"I've done a lot a work here. Which one's yours?"

"It's the last one on the cul-de-sac."

"The Anderson place?"

She raises her eyebrows. "How'd you know that?"

"I helped put in your dock a few years back. It's a beautiful place."

Jon stops the truck on the gray paver driveway. The stone mansion sits majestically on top of the bluff. The home looks modest from the front, with only one story exposed above the hillside. Jon remembers that, lakeside, the house is three stories of panoramic glass with a gigantic wraparound deck. Endless wooden steps allow access to the dock and the boathouse.

"Thanks, Jon. I appreciate the lift."

It occurs to him that it's the first time she uses his name. He reaches into the center console. She watches his hand. He pulls out a white business card.

"If you need a lift to Stu's, gimme a call. My cell's on the bottom."

She takes the card and frowns. "You know I have a fiancé."

Jon smirks. "I get that. You've mentioned him a couple times. It's a ride, not a marriage proposal."

She climbs out of the truck.

"It was nice to meet you, Morgan."

+++

A handful of guys wait outside the office as Jon opens the door. The alarm beeps, and he punches in the key code. He holds the door open, and they file in with coolers and brown bags in hand. Jon enters his office, sits down at his desk, and powers on the computer. The crew foremen go over the route sheets Jon prepared for them and grab their truck keys from the wall. A few come to Jon with questions.

Oscar knocks on his open door.

"Morning, Oscar."

"Thanks for helping us on Saturday. My wife gets mad if I miss church."

"No problem."

"I got another Chad job. Is he gonna be here today?"

"I would hope so, although it may not be until nine or so. Lemme take a look at that."

Oscar hands Jon the route sheet. Three guys stand behind Oscar, all with clipboards.

"This will take you a while to get the equipment and materials to the site. I would do that, then radio him."

+++

Jon grabs his clipboard and heads for the door. He walks by the reception desk, where Karen checks messages from the weekend. Jon gives her a wave and steps outside. A shiny black Range Rover pulls into the space closest to the office door. Jon cringes and walks toward his truck. He hears a cackle through the tinted windows. A young, curvaceous woman with curly blond hair bounces out of the SUV. She's freshly tanned, wearing short shorts and a tank top, her bra straps exposed. She sees Jon out of the corner of her eye and turns away. She shuts her door and skips toward the office, smiling at the driver stepping out.

"Jon! Hey, Jon, hold up," the driver says.

"I'm late, Chad," Jon says in monotone.

Chad is six feet tall with a muscular build and a chiseled jawline. His facial features are wide, almost Neanderthal, but handsome. His brown hair is cropped short. The women of Stone Lake flock to him, like flies on shit. He stands, holding his stainless steel coffee cup.

"I just wanted to find out how we did while I was away," Chad says.

"I thought you were supposed to be back on Friday?"

"We needed some time to decompress."

Jon frowns and crosses his arms. "A vacation from your vacation?"

Chad shrugs. "I thought maybe we could get together and have lunch later."

"I brought my lunch."

"Put it in the fridge. It can be on the company."

"I've got back-to-back consultations. I'll be eating in my truck."

Chad frowns, his jaw set tight. "Tomorrow then."

+++

Jon sits in his truck, a sandwich in one hand, punching digits on a calculator with the other. He hears a tapping on his window. He looks over with a mouthful of turkey and cheese to see Morgan with a broad grin on her face. He rolls down his window, chewing his food.

"Stalking me?" she asks. "I need to get that code changed."

She's wearing running shorts and a T-shirt, showing off toned arms and legs. Her dark hair is tied up in a ponytail. Her hairline and shirt are wet with sweat.

Jon swallows and takes a drink from his water bottle. "Me? You coulda run by, and I woulda never noticed."

"I think you would have noticed." She purses her lips.

"I thought you had a fiancé," he says.

"We're just talking. It's not a marriage proposal." She smiles. "What are you doing anyway?"

"Writing up a contract for installing some riprap."

"*Riprap*?"

"It's just large rocks that we use to stop shoreline erosion."

She nods. "Is this how you always eat lunch?"

"Most days."

"I'll make a deal with you. If you can give me a ride to Stu's tomorrow afternoon, then I'll take you out for a proper lunch."

"Sounds like a date."

"I can't have friends?"

"So we're friends now?"

She grins. "Maybe … So, can you give me a lift tomorrow?"

"Only if you let me take you to dinner on Friday. I have a standing lunch date with my old truck."

"Dinner as friends?"

"As friends."

+++

Jon sits at the laminate table with a burger in front of him. He takes a bite. Chad sits opposite, dipping his fries into a vat of ketchup. His face is tan, and his arms are ripped. Matted chest hair pops out from the collar of his tight T-shirt.

"So how'd the week go?" Chad asks.

"You mean the *two* weeks that you were on your honeymoon with my ex-wife?" Jon replies.

"Come on, dude. Don't be a prick."

Jon smirks and shakes his head. "So you wouldn't be pissed if the situation was reversed?"

"So we're gonna do this right now?"

"Fuck if I know. Nothing's up to me."

"I wouldn't be pissed, because I wouldn't wanna stay in an unhappy marriage. If my best friend could be happy with that person, then he's doin' me a favor, and I'd be happy for my friend."

"Wow, that's some serious rationalizing."

"I'm tryin' to be civil—for our business. Shit, man, you're my best friend. We've known each other forever."

"It's barely my business anymore."

"I didn't have anything to do with that."

"No, you just capitalized on it."

"I didn't betray you, if that's what you think."

"Interesting choice of words."

"We didn't get together until after you were separated."

"That's really noble of you."

"You gotta move on. You can't walk around so fuckin' miserable all the time. Why don't you take a vacation?"

"Are you gonna do my consultations and run my jobs while I'm gone?"

"Take your radio with you. Reschedule your appointments."

"That's what I thought. I'll end up more stressed from taking the vacation."

"You gotta find a way. That's what I do."

"No, that's not what you do. If you don't have any real responsibility, you don't have to do any work. Then it's easy to take a vacation."

Chad shakes his head. "The employees feel like they have to walk on eggshells with you. You're miserable, and you're miserable to be around."

Jon rubs the stubble on his chin with a smirk. "Who?"

"What?"

"Who? … Who told you that they have to walk on eggshells around me? Please tell me, so I can apologize to them."

"Well, I told them that I wouldn't tell."

"Oh, bullshit. I'm not buying it."

"Do you ever wonder why she left?"

Jon's eyes narrow. "Because she's a shallow, gold-digging bitch."

Chad stands up and pushes away his chair. "I'm not gonna sit here and listen to this. This is why she left, because you're an intolerable asshole."

"Fuck you."

Chad's cheeks redden. "I hope you can be civil at the company picnic. It's not fair to everyone else. I really wanted to find some common ground. She's pregnant. I wanted you to be the godfather."

Jon's smile is crooked as he shakes his head. He claps his hands—large, loud, slow claps, the opposite of a golf clap.

"Well, *congratulations*."

"Fuck you, Jon."

Chapter 3

Succubus

Jon sits alone at a white-linen-covered table for two. He looks through the window at the lake illuminated by the restaurant's dock lights. He's clean-shaven, wearing a light blue button-down shirt, the sleeves rolled halfway up his forearms. His wavy dark hair is tousled, brushed with water and his fingers. His face is tanned, his eyes hazel, his face proportional, except for an angular nose. Every few seconds he glances from the lake to the door. He nurses a glass of ice water.

A young waitress approaches. "Are you ready to order?" she asks, holding a pad of paper like an old-school detective.

"I'm still waiting for someone," he says. "Can you give me a little more time?"

The waitress presses out her bottom lip and smiles. "Take your time. I'll check on you in a bit."

Jon looks at the door, thinking if not for the off-season dinner crowd, he might slip out unnoticed. He stands and pushes his chair under the table and strides toward the front door. The waitress watches him as he puts his hand on the door handle. Through the window he can see Morgan running through the parking lot in chunky heels, a white sweater, and a sundress. He opens the door and holds it for her. She smiles wide when she sees him.

"I am so sorry, Jon," she says. "I went the wrong way. I was totally lost. I would've called but I forgot my cell."

Jon nods and gives a small smile. "I could have picked you up."

"You've done enough chauffeuring."

"We're this way." He shows her to the window table. "How's the car?"

"Good as new."

He pulls out her seat. She sits down, her breathing elevated.

Jon sits opposite her. "You look great, by the way."

She frowns. "I have a limited clothing selection with me." She looks Jon up and down with a grin. "You shine up really nice, like a new penny."

"That's about what I'm worth."

"You really do look nice, you know."

"Thanks."

"I like that you went without grease stains. That was a good choice. I'm surprised you didn't pick up a couple baby mamas while you were waiting."

He stares, his face expressionless. "I've already got a handful of those. I'm halfway to a flag football team."

Her eyes widen. She sits silent.

He laughs. "I'm joking. I don't have any kids."

She breathes a sigh of relief, laughing. "You do that on purpose to upset my uppity apple cart?"

He grins. "Uppity apple cart? I like that." He takes a sip of water. "I do have a pregnant ex-wife."

"Is it yours?"

"No."

"When did you get divorced?"

"Why don't we talk about you?"

"There's not much to tell."

"I don't believe *that* for a second."

The young waitress approaches. "Are you ready to order?" she asks.

Morgan looks down at the menu. "I haven't even had a chance to look." She eyes Jon. "Do you know what you want?"

"I was gonna get the special, local catfish, but take your time."

"That sounds good." She looks at the waitress. "Could I also have the special?"

Her eyes narrow at Morgan. "Anything to drink?" she asks.

"A glass of white wine."

"Do you need a wine list?"

"The house wine is fine."

"And for you, sir?"

"I'm gonna stick with water."

Jon hands the waitress the menus. She smiles at Jon and looks at Morgan with a blank stare.

"I think you have a fan," she says.

"Ya think?"

Morgan nods.

"So where were we?"

"You were telling me about your ex-wife."

"Isn't that exactly what you're not supposed to do on a first date?"

Morgan frowns. "Date? I thought we were just friends, having dinner together."

"I guess I just thought—"

"I'm not trying to lead you on. I really just need a friend right now. I like you. Can we keep it simple?"

"Of course. You've been clear. This was my fault." Jon stares through the window.

Morgan shakes her head. "No, it's mine. I should have stuck to my guns on an informal lunch. Look at us. We're all dressed up in a nice restaurant, overlooking the lake. I mean, it's a date place. I'm sorry."

Jon turns from the window, looking into Morgan's blue eyes. "It just so happens that I have an opening for a friend in my life."

"Friends then? No strings?"

Jon smiles. "That means I get to wear my grease-stained pants."

Morgan grins. "Okay, but I get to wear my sweaty workout clothes with no makeup."

"That's good, because I wasn't gonna be able to keep this up anyway."

"Keep what up?"

"These are my only clothes that haven't seen a job site. So it would have become my going-out-with-Morgan uniform. I'm pretty sure, if we were dating, you might have been disgusted after the fourth or fifth time in a row, seeing the same clothes."

Morgan laughs. "I know I have an uppity apple cart, but I'm really not that judgmental. I have a friend at work who wears the same three outfits over and over again on a perfect rotation. Brown pants and a short-sleeved button-down shirt, then black pants and a short-sleeved button-down shirt, and—for the finale—a brown sweater and khakis. The kids are merciless about it. He doesn't seem to care. He just cares about teaching. I'd be mortified. I'm way too superficial when it comes to clothes."

"I was wondering if you had a job. I figured you just lived off your trust fund."

"Do I not look like a working girl?"

Jon grins and shakes his head. "No, definitely not a *working* girl."

Morgan's face reddens. "I mean, do I not look like a woman

with a job?"

"I was the one being judgmental. You know, poor little rich girl with the resources to hang out at a lakefront mansion to find herself."

"Is that what you thought?"

"Not anymore, but it crossed my mind when we first met."

She grins. "If we were on a date, I might walk out on you."

"Good thing we're not."

Morgan gazes at the dock lights illuminating the lake.

"It really is beautiful here."

Jon nods. Morgan looks at him, smiles briefly, and looks back at the dock.

"What do you teach?"

Morgan turns to face Jon again. "English … twelfth grade."

"May's a bit early for school to be out."

She looks down. "I'm on sabbatical. I needed—"

"To clear your head?"

She nods.

"About this head-clearing … Anything you wanna talk about?"

"About as much as you want to talk about your ex-wife."

"Speaking of the succubus—"

"Succubus?"

"Didn't you ever watch *South Park*?"

"My students talk about it all the time. I've never seen it though. I think my TV's been stuck on CNN for the past four years."

"You like the news?"

"Oh, God, no. I can't stand it. David loves it. I prefer to read. You know, English teacher and all."

"David's the fiancé?"

Morgan nods and tucks a loose strand of dark hair behind her ear.

"What does he do?"

"He's a lobbyist at my dad's firm."

"Where'd you guys meet?"

"Can we go back to the succubus?"

Jon grins. "Of course." He takes a sip of his water. "So a succubus is a demon who drains the souls of men by having sex with them while they're sleeping."

Morgan laughs. "So that's your ex?"

"I think that's a pretty good description."

"Don't they say you should be wary of men who bash their exes?"

"Doesn't count for friends."

She grins. "You're really pushing the friend privileges."

"Speaking of friend privileges, I have a company picnic tomorrow. Would you go? You'll be able to check out a real live succubus up close."

+++

Jon parks in front of a sprawling two-story brick-faced McMansion with a four-car garage. A couple dozen cars litter the circular stone driveway. The lawn is a deep green, striped with a checkerboard mowing pattern. Ornamental shrubs are shaped in neat balls. Pointed blue juniper trees, pruned in a swirl, guard either side of the double doors.

Morgan sits in the passenger seat wearing shorts, a T-shirt, flip-flops, and a baseball cap, with her ponytail sticking out the back.

She looks over at Jon. "You weren't kidding about the grease-stained pants."

Jon smiles back. "I had to work this morning."

"On Saturday?"

"Just a half day. What about you? You look like you just finished running."

"That's because I did."

"You look good like that."

Morgan blushes. "You ready to do this? Face the succubus?"

Jon grins. "Thank you for doing this."

Jon and Morgan stand next to the truck and gaze up at the McMansion.

"I thought my dad's lake house was ostentatious. Your business must be doing well," Morgan says.

"More like the bank is doing well. That and my business partner got a pretty big raise."

A Honda Civic pulls up.

"I want you to meet someone," Jon says.

Oscar and a short young dark-skinned woman step from the car. She opens the back door and picks up the infant from the car seat. The baby kicks the air and coos as he's lifted.

"Oscar, Claudia," Jon says, "I have someone I want you guys to meet. This is my friend Morgan. Morgan, these are my friends, Oscar and Claudia."

"It's nice to meet you, Morgan," Oscar says.

Claudia smiles at Morgan and Jon. "It's about time," she says.

Morgan blushes.

"He's one of the nice ones," Claudia says.

"Who's the little guy?" Morgan says, changing the subject.

"Oscar Jr. Wanna hold him?"

"I would love to."

Claudia passes the infant, and Oscar Jr. holds out his chubby little arms toward Morgan. She holds the child tight to her body and smiles at his round face.

"Jon's wearing *his* work clothes," Oscar says to Claudia, his hands held open at his sides.

"My husband's not going to show up at a family picnic looking like he just fell out of an excavator," Claudia says. "No offense, Jon."

Jon smiles.

"It makes no sense. I'll be dirty again an hour from now," Oscar says.

Morgan hands Oscar Jr. back to Claudia. They walk down paver steps alongside the house toward the backyard. An expansive irregular stone patio, with a knee wall, is connected to the house. A stone walkway from the patio leads to a gazebo, where Chad mans the grill. The succubus collects burgers and hot dogs from Chad for the guests. Beyond the gazebo is a flag football field. The turf is perfectly clipped, numbered, and lined with white paint denoting sidelines and end zones.

The smell of grilled hot dogs and hamburgers hangs in the air. Men, women, and children sit eating and talking on rented rectangular picnic tables. Despite the camaraderie, a clear divide exists. The white employees sit together and speak English. The brown employees sit together and speak Spanish. Oscar and Claudia greet their friends in Spanish. She passes little Oscar around to the women, who fawn over him.

"Are you hungry?" Jon asks.

"I'm starving," Morgan replies. "I woke up late and skipped breakfast."

Jon grabs a plate for himself and Morgan. They add potato salad, apple wedges, carrot sticks, bell peppers, and hamburger buns with everything but the meat. They move toward the grill. When Chad spies Morgan, his eyes widen, and his mouth hangs open. The succubus glares at Morgan, strutting behind Chad—her tanned, toned, shapely figure busting out of her short shorts and V-neck T-shirt. She puts her arms around him and presses her body against his back. She stands on her tippy toes and kisses the nape of his neck.

"We just need two burgers," Jon says.

Chad smiles wide. "And who's this?" He wriggles free from the grasp of the succubus, still staring at Morgan. "Honey, could you let go for a second?" Chad says over his shoulder.

"This is Morgan."

Chad puts down the spatula. His nipples show through his tight white T-shirt, highlighting his athletic build. Dark hair grows dense on his thick calves. He glances over Morgan's body and grins.

"I'm Chad." He extends his hand, holding Morgan's a bit longer than necessary.

The succubus steps in front. "I'm Heather."

"Nice to meet you Chad … Heather," Morgan says.

"So how long have you two been dating?" Heather says with her hands on her hips and a smirk on her face.

"We're friends," Jon says.

Chad chuckles, still staring at Morgan. His muscles flex.

"I really like your shirt, by the way," Jon says to Chad. "What is that, an extra small?"

Chad scowls at Jon. "You gonna play today?"

"Not dressed for it."

"And if you were?"

"Not interested."

Chad gazes at Morgan. "Just friends, huh? And why is that?"

"I'm engaged," she says.

Chad nods with pursed lips. "Want some meat?" He holds up the spatula.

Jon and Morgan balance their plates as they search for two empty seats. The white employees stare and whisper, as the two make their way past. Jon sees Victor, sitting toward the end of a table with space around him.

"*Hola*, Victor. *¿Podemos sentarnos?*" Jon asks.

"*Por favor, el patron*," he says, motioning to the table.

"*Gracias. Esta es mi amiga* Morgan." Jon motions toward Morgan.

Victor tips his cowboy hat. "*Mucho gusto.*"

Morgan smiles blank-faced at Victor.

"He said, it's nice to meet you," Jon says.

"Oh, it's nice to meet you," Morgan says to Victor.

Victor smiles, showing off his silver. He returns to his burger. Jon and Morgan sit next to each other, talking between famished bites.

"So Heather's the succubus?"

"Didn't you see her suck Chad's soul right out the back of his neck?"

Morgan laughs. "I have the feeling she doesn't like me much. I'm guessing Chad's her husband."

"Yep … and my business partner and former best friend."

"Ouch." Morgan winces. "I can see why you didn't want to come here alone. And you have to work with him?"

"Yeah, *and* her. I'm out in the field most of the time though, so I don't see them too much."

"I think you can do better."

Jon takes a bite of his burger.

"What did Chad mean when he asked if you were going to play today?" Morgan asks.

Jon swallows. "The guys all get together and play one soccer game and then a flag football game. It's more like a race war, if you ask me."

Morgan shakes her head. "What are you talking about?"

"I guess that's a bit of an exaggeration. They pick teams, and the teams are usually pretty divided by race. So the Latino team beats the crap out of the honkies in soccer, then it's the other way around in flag football."

"That is so crazy. Does anybody get mad?"

"Not usually. The guys are pretty good sports. Chad can be a bit competitive. I think he's still trying to relive his high school glory days."

"Did you know him in high school?"

"We played football together."

"And Heather?"

Jon frowns. "She was a cheerleader."

Morgan giggles. "Jon, you have to play. I mean, you couldn't set the stage any better." Morgan speaks like she's introducing monster trucks. "Two former teammates, former friends, now sworn enemies, fighting for the love of a woman and the respect of a company."

Jon laughs. "You read too many books."

"No, seriously, you should play. It'll be fun … for me."

"I can't." Jon shakes his head. "I blew my knee out in high school."

"Didn't you get it fixed?"

"Yeah, but the doc recommended I stay away from football."

"It's *flag* football."

"You still plant and cut."

"Were you any good?"

Jon shrugs. "I was okay."

+++

Jon and Morgan stand on the sideline with the families, watching the guys play flag football. One side, quarterbacked by Chad, is predominately white; and the other, quarterbacked by Oscar, is predominately Latino. Chad throws a couple touchdown passes; Heather jumps up and down, her bra barely containing her breasts. White people, 2; brown people, 0.

Chad intercepts a pass from Oscar and streaks down the sideline. Oscar has the angle. He tries to grab the flag, but Chad stiff-arms him. Chad spins the football like a top in the end zone. Touchdown, white people. Oscar staggers to his feet, shaking his head, with Claudia looking on. Victor walks to the sideline.

"Victor, *que pasa*?" Oscar asks.

Victor waves his wrinkled hand. "*Estoy cansado.*"

"*Necesitamos uno más,*" Oscar says to the sideline.

Chad jogs to Oscar. "What's the problem?"

"We're short one."

"You can take one of our guys from the bench," Chad says. "We only need one more score."

Morgan leans to Jon and mouths *Help him.*

Jon takes one step onto the field. Oscar smiles broadly, showing bright white teeth.

Victor smacks Jon on the back. "*Bueno, el patron.*"

Jon walks over to Oscar and Chad.

Chad looks at Jon's work boots. "Don't be makin' excuses about footwear."

Jon stands in the huddle with his six teammates. Oscar looks at him, eyes wide.

"What play do you want?" Oscar asks Jon.

"You're the quarterback. You call the shots."

Oscar tells his receivers where to run by drawing a diagram on their chest.

"Can you catch?" Oscar asks.

Jon nods.

"Can you run?"

"I think so."

"Run deep. I'm gonna throw it up."

Jon lines up on the line of scrimmage with one foot forward and one back. Chad moves over from his safety position to cover him.

Instead of *hut* or *hike*, Oscar says, "*Corre!*"

Chad tries to jam Jon off the line. Jon plants hard inside, then swims outside, his feet moving like he's on hot coals. Chad bites inside and gets off balance. Jon blazes downfield, open by ten yards. Oscar puts the ball on the money. White people, 3; brown people, 1. The sideline jumps up and down screaming, "*Goooooooooooaaalllll!*" as if they just won The World Cup. Jon flicks the ball to Chad, who grins and nods his head.

"You've been holdin' out all these years," Chad says.

"Maybe you're just getting old," Jon says.

Chad drops back to pass. He throws a tight spiral toward the sideline. Jon steps in front for the interception and takes it back for another score. White people, 3; brown people, 2. On the subsequent drive, Chad gets frustrated and overthrows three passes in a row. On fourth down his receiver drops a perfect pass.

"You gotta catch that!" Chad says.

With a short field, Oscar tries to force the ball to Jon, but he's double covered. One pass is thrown into the dirt, and another is knocked down. On third down, Oscar hits Jon on a quick slant. Jon catches the pass over the middle and turns upfield, where he meets a wall. Chad lays a shoulder into Jon's solar plexus. Jon writhes on the ground, the wind knocked out of him. Chad bends down and unceremoniously snatches the flag off his belt and tosses it to the ground. The sideline is quiet, while Jon's teammates help him up.

"You have a play?" Oscar asks.

Jon nods. "Send everyone to the right corner of the end zone, except Julio. Send him to the left corner. You roll right, then throw it across the field to Julio."

Oscar smiles and explains the play in Spanish. On *corre* the receivers streak to the right corner of the end zone. Oscar rolls to the right, looking at the mass of receivers. He plants his foot, looks left. Julio's wide open. He throws a strike. The ball thuds off Julio's chest, but he cradles it tight. White people, 3; brown people, 3. The sideline erupts, and both teams congratulate Julio, even Chad.

On the ensuing drive, Jon intercepts another of Chad's passes near the sideline.

"Fuck!" Chad says.

A few parents frown at Chad.

A few Latino guys from the sideline laugh and say, "*Chinga.*"

Jon is still double covered, but he catches a few passes and pays for each, being tackled first, then having his flag removed. With only twenty yards to the biggest football upset in company history, Oscar tosses it up to Jon in the front corner of the end zone. Jon jumps and turns his body inside to adjust to the ball. Chad puts a shoulder into the side of Jon's bum knee. The ball slips through Jon's hands into a defender's. Jon lays on the ground in agony, watching the defender take it back the length of the field. Touchdown. Game over. White people, 4; brown people, 3.

Chad races down the field, pumping his arms like muscle-bound pistons. The guys on both sides shake hands and pat each other on the back. Jon sits up and slowly straightens his leg.

"You all right?" Oscar asks.

"I'm good," Jon replies.

Oscar offers his hand and pulls his friend to his feet.

"Sorry about that last one."

"You're a pretty damn good quarterback. Where'd you learn to throw like that?"

"I used to be a pitcher in Bolivia. My coach loved Nolan Ryan, so we practiced throwing a football, like Nolan did in his workouts."

Morgan saunters toward Jon, smiling. "You okay?"

"I need to get some ice. Can you help me to my truck?"

She furrows her brow and lets him put his arm around her. Chad walks up, holding the football in one hand, like a loaf of bread.

"Good game," he says.

"Fuck off, Chad."

"What?"

"You know what."

"You always were injury-prone. That's not my fault," Chad says, glancing at Jon's knee.

Morgan and Jon ignore Chad as they shuffle to the truck.

Chapter 4

Purgatory

"You want me to drive?" Morgan asks. "I can do it."

Jon adjusts his left leg with his arms before putting the truck in gear. With the midafternoon sun pouring into the cab, he puts down his visor to shield his eyes from the glare. They drive over a rusty suspension bridge toward the curvy mountain lake road.

"You and Chad … and Heather?" Morgan says.

"Yeah?"

"There's a lot of history there, huh?"

"You could say that."

They drive in silence, sun rays punching through the tree branches dangling over the road.

"You were pretty great today," Morgan says.

Jon chuckles. "We weren't exactly playing the Redskins."

"I used to run in high school and college,"

Jon raises his eyebrows, looks over at Morgan, and back to the road. "Oh, yeah? I could see that. Lemme guess. Middle distance?"

"The eight hundred."

"I bet you were fast. You certainly got the legs for it."

She smirks. "I was fast for high school, not so fast at Georgetown. I was pretty mediocre there."

"Still ... mediocre at D-one track is pretty damn good."

"I know running, and I've never seen anyone run like you in work boots and long pants. You must have been quite an athlete."

Jon shakes his head, keeping his eyes on the road. "Not really. I couldn't even get through a single football season ... in *high school*."

"I find that hard to believe. What happened?"

"I was a skinny kid, late bloomer. I lifted weights, ate like a horse, but it didn't seem to do much. As a tenth grader, I was a buck thirty-five, but I could run, so I was moved up from the JV a couple games into the season. My first game on varsity, I was playing defensive back, and I made this hit on this kid that outweighed me by damn near a hundred pounds. I came in low, and I was in a full sprint. The guy's knee hit me perfectly, breaking my collarbone. One game and I was done. My junior year, I was a little bigger. I made it to week five. I jumped up to catch a pass and got speared. I had three broken ribs. It hurt for a month just to breathe."

"What about track? Did you run?"

"For about a minute. It didn't interest me, running without a purpose. The track coach talked me into running winter track to get back into shape, after I recovered from the rib injury. I ran the fifty-five and the two hundred. I hated it at first, but I started winning, you know." Jon glances over at Morgan. Her eyes are on him. He looks back to the road. "I actually made it to state in the fifty-five. I was a tenth of a second faster than my closest competitor. Then I did what I always do. I choked. I was in the middle lane of the finals, and I got disqualified for a false start. It was pretty humiliating for a kid, you know?" Jon turns to Morgan.

She nods and purses her lips.

He focuses back on the road. "I grabbed my bag and sat on a bench by myself behind the bleachers and just cried. It wasn't only about the race. I felt like I was cursed, like I was bound to fail, no matter what. I didn't realize that some reporter took my picture. I ended up on the front page of the local paper here. The article was actually … I don't know. You would probably call it poignant, but, around here, I was just a crybaby with no heart."

Jon shakes his head.

"I'm really sorry, Jon."

"It was a long time ago."

"But you *were* almost a state champ, as a *junior*, the first time you ever ran track."

"As one of my mom's boyfriends used to say, '*Almost* only counts in horseshoes and hand grenades.'"

"You still had your senior year, right?"

Jon smirks and nods his head. "Yeah, I did. I was really tired of hearing the negativity. I didn't talk to anyone, except my mother and Heather. I didn't even talk to Chad, because he was talking shit about how I was overrated and injury-prone. All I did was train. I was determined to change everything. For a while, I did. Eight games into the season, we were undefeated, and I had scholarship offers from UVA and William & Mary. We just had to win one of the last two games to win our district and qualify for the play-offs. It hadn't been done here in fifteen years. Before the game, Heather and I had this huge fight. She was convinced I was seeing some other girl. Then during warm-ups, I see my mother making out with her new boyfriend in the stands. I had told her not to bring her boyfriends anymore. It was embarrassing, you know? She'd come to all my games, draped all over these dirt balls. Kids used to make fun of me. People thought my mother was a whore."

"It's a huge double standard," Morgan says. "When it's a man, he's a stud."

Jon nods.

"Did you ever ask her why she brought him, after you asked her not to?"

"No, … and I don't know if anything would have been different anyway. My head wasn't in it from the get-go. I dropped an easy touchdown pass that would have put us up. Then on the next drive, I dropped another pass, and I got drilled—a torn ACL and meniscus. I was carted off the field. The team lost that game and the next, missed the play-offs. My scholarship offers were withdrawn. I was forever branded as the tin man, with no heart. Shit, to this day, I won't go to any of the local bars because some drunk asshole is bound to say something stupid."

"What happened with Heather? I'm assuming she finally realized that it wasn't true about the other girl. She did marry you."

Jon frowns. "I don't think she ever believed me. We broke up for a while. She went out with a couple other guys from school, former friends of mine. I'm sure it was payback. A year later, we saw each other at the grocery store and got to talking, and one thing led to another. I shoulda never got back together with her, but I was lonely. I didn't have anyone except for my mom, and I felt like I was cramping her style a bit. She had her share of men coming around."

Jon stops at the security gate, leans over, punches the code, and drives through.

"It must have been really hard," Morgan says

"It doesn't matter. It's stupid high school bullshit. It's embarrassing that I'm even still bothered by it. Maybe if I'd gotten outta this town …"

They see a fit middle-aged blonde woman in short athletic

shorts and a sports bra. She's power walking and sweating in the late afternoon heat. Morgan rolls down her window as they pass her. The woman looks at the truck with her eyes wide and her brow furrowed.

"Stop the truck," Morgan says.

Jon puts on the brakes. Morgan hangs out the passenger window.

"Hey, Mrs. Walters," she says.

Mrs. Walters power walks to the passenger window. Sweat drips between her tan breasts crammed into a purple sports bra.

"I thought I saw you earlier this week," Mrs. Walters says. "Are your parents coming down? What about David?"

"My parents will be here for my sister's book party, but David has to work. I'm sure you'll get an invitation."

"I got it yesterday," she says with a smile, exposing crease lines, despite the Botox injections. She glances up at Jon with a smirk. "And who's your friend?"

"This is Jon," Morgan says, motioning. "He has a construction business here in town."

Jon waves with a stiff smile.

"Well, I should probably get back to it. Father Time is catching up with me."

Jon presses on the gas, leaving Mrs. Walters in the dust. Morgan looks at Jon. "Her husband's a lawyer in DC. His firm does some work for my dad. He stays in the city during the week and comes here on the weekends. Mrs. Walters stays here full time. I don't know how she doesn't get lonely in that house by herself."

"I could say the same thing about you," Jon says.

Morgan shrugs. "I'm here to get *away* from people."

Jon pulls into the paver driveway of the stone mansion, his truck idling.

"Thanks again," Jon says. "I don't know how, but you made that almost tolerable."

"Almost," Morgan says. "You want to come in for some ice?"

Jon hesitates.

"That's not code for sex," she says.

Jon laughs. "You mean, like *coffee* or *a nightcap*?"

"Do people still say nightcap?" Morgan grins.

"I figured your crowd might say that."

"My crowd?"

"You know, people who go to Georgetown, get engaged to lobbyists, and have family lake houses."

Morgan shakes her head with a smirk. "I have to stop telling you stuff." She hops out of the truck. Jon cuts the engine. "Do I need to come get you?"

"I'm coming." Jon gimps toward the front door. Morgan waits for him, letting him put his arm around her for support.

They walk inside. The ceilings are high. The kitchen is covered in granite and stainless steel appliances. Jon stops at the threshold, unlaces his work boots, and steps onto the floor in black socks. Morgan looks down at his feet.

"Why am I not surprised?" she says, laughing. "Seriously, Jon, do you own anything without holes?"

The living room is dominated by a stone fireplace and a panoramic view of the lake. A black leather sectional surrounds a big-screen television and a white fur rug.

"Why don't you sit down on the couch, and I'll get you some ice," she says.

"I'm pretty dirty. Would you mind if I took a shower?"

Morgan frowns. "Really, that's your move?"

Jon laughs. "No, really, I'm filthy. I didn't think you'd be invit-ing me in, and then I didn't think about my dirty body on the brand-new furniture. If I try anything, I'm pretty sure you can outrun me."

Morgan grins. "There are two showers down that hall," she says, pointing. "I'll go downstairs, so you don't have to climb the steps."

"One more thing."

"What?"

"Do you have anything I could wear that wouldn't turn me into a cross-dresser?"

"Why don't you pick a shower, and I'll get you something from downstairs. We usually have extra swimsuits."

Jon limps down the hall. Artwork and mirrors hang from the walls. He pushes open the first door and finds a modest guest bathroom. He flips on the lights above the mirror, leans on the marble sink, and stares at himself. He sees a small bruise already developing under his left eye. His hair is disheveled, and his stubble has grown back since he shaved for his "date" with Morgan. He pulls off his grass- and clay-stained T-shirt, then sits on the toilet lid with a groan, and pulls off his socks. Using his right leg, he stands and bends his left slowly, feeling the pain.

Morgan appears at the open door with a broad smile. She keeps her eyes up, but she sneaks a glance at his upper body. She holds a hand behind her back and the other out front.

"This is all I could find. I'm really sorry," she says, holding out a tiny piece of blue nylon.

Jon takes the Speedo with two hands, expressionless. He places it on the edge of the sink. Morgan breaks into a fit of laughter. When she settles down, she pulls a pair of board shorts and a white T-shirt from behind her back.

"I'm sorry, but that was so funny," she says, grinning. "You should have seen your face."

"That was just wrong." He shakes his head with a smirk.

"I made an ice pack for you and put it in the freezer. If you finish before me, just make yourself at home."

Jon showers and dries himself with a beach towel. He slips on the board shorts and the white T-shirt. He takes the towel from the rack, and hobbles down the hallway to the kitchen. He grabs the ice pack from the freezer and sits on the corner of the sectional. He props up his leg, spreads the ice over his knee, and wraps the towel around to hold it in place. Within minutes his knee is numb.

He hears Morgan climbing the steps. Her hair is damp and tucked behind her ears. She wears cotton sweatpants, flip-flops, and a Georgetown Track T-shirt.

"Clean now?" she asks, staring at Jon's chest.

"I feel much better. Thanks for the ice."

"You're welcome." She still stares.

Jon folds his arms over his chest, smiling. "Would you stop staring at my nipples? It's not my fault you gave me a shirt that might be rejected as too revealing for a wet T-shirt contest."

She laughs, putting her hand over her mouth. "I'm sorry. It was the only shirt I had that was big enough. I swear."

"I feel like Chad at the picnic."

"Only you look much better."

Jon's speechless.

She grins. "Are you blushing?"

Jon smiles, still blushing, and shakes his head.

"Do you wanna get drunk?" she asks.

"Do you?"

Morgan walks to the kitchen, and Jon follows her with his eyes. She opens and shuts cabinets and the refrigerator.

"There's some beer and white wine in the fridge. Which would you prefer?" she calls out from the kitchen.

"It doesn't matter to me. I'll just have whatever you're having."

She returns from the kitchen. "I couldn't find any wine glasses, and I have no idea how long this has been in there," she says, holding up the wine bottle in one hand, and the glasses with a cork screw in the other.

She screws into the cork.

"You might wanna stop screwing," he says.

She stops and looks at the corkscrew, piercing the bottom of the cork.

"Oops, I hope you don't mind a little cork with your wine."

She pulls out the cork with a pop. She pours the wine almost to the brim of each glass.

"Whoa," he says. "You really do wanna get drunk."

"You don't drink much, do you?"

"Not really."

"Me either," she says. "That's going to make this that much more fun."

+++

The ice on his knee is melted. The bottle of wine is empty. Jon feels no pain.

"We should get one more," she says.

Morgan hops up and falls backward on Jon's injured leg. He winces, but she didn't hurt anything crucial. She rolls away.

She puts her hand on her chest. "Oh, my God. Did I hurt you?"

"No, it's okay. I should probably put this ice pack in the sink though. It's getting the couch wet."

"I'll take it."

She unwraps the towel from his knee and puts the water-filled Ziploc bag in the towel. She rubs her warm hand over his cold skin. She slides the tip of her index finger along the four-inch scar.

"Does it hurt?"

He shakes his head, his gaze locked on hers.

She leans forward and kisses the scar. Her lips feel warm and soft. She skips to the kitchen with the towel and returns with another bottle of white wine.

"Maybe we should leave it at one bottle?" he says.

"Are you cold?" she asks, ignoring his question.

"A little."

She grins. "Let's get in the hot tub. We'll take the bottle."

They step outside on the deck. The sky is dark, the outlines of the forest visible from the bluff. The moonlight reflects off the lake. The night air is springtime cool. Morgan saunters toward the corner of the deck, where a hot tub is concealed by a lattice fence. She opens the gate, steps inside. She flips up one half of the cover and pulls it to the side. Steam rises from the clear, illuminated water. She smiles and tilts her head.

"Can you hold this?" she asks, handing him the wine bottle and the corkscrew.

Morgan takes off her T-shirt, revealing a white lacy bra and a toned stomach. Jon stops turning the corkscrew, his full attention on her. She slides down her sweatpants, revealing a matching white lace bikini underneath. She grins at Jon and presses a button on the side of the hot tub. The water erupts with bubbles, and she steps in. She sighs and leans her head back, as she places her body between the jets. Jon finishes opening the bottle and places it near the edge, next to Morgan.

"You coming?" she asks, eyeing him with a smirk.

He takes off his T-shirt and sits down at the water's edge. He holds his left leg out, and uses his arms and his good leg to pull himself into the water. She stares at his physique as he sits across from her.

"Come over here," she says. "This is the best spot. It'll be good for your leg."

Jon moves next to her. Morgan helps position him, where jets massage his knee.

"That feels good," he says.

She reaches over, and takes a swig from the wine bottle.

"Want some?" she asks.

Jon nods, takes a drink, and places it back on the edge.

"I know I might be drunk, but, another place and another time, we might have worked out."

He looks at Morgan. "I'm not drunk. Why not now, right here?"

"You wouldn't want me. … Trust me."

"How do you know that?"

"Maybe I'm a succubus too."

Jon shakes his head. "I doubt it."

"You going to tell me what happened with Heather?"

Jon shrugs.

"I probably won't remember tomorrow anyway."

"There's not much to tell. She said I worked too much, that I wasn't spontaneous. I gave shitty gifts. I didn't pay enough attention to her, and I was depressed. She probably said a hundred other things, but those are my big flaws." Jon bends forward at the torso and massages his knee along with the jets. "She said she wanted someone who was happier, someone who she thought wanted to be with her."

"And that was Chad?"

"I guess so."

"That guy will pay attention to just about anything with breasts."

Jon laughs. "Perceptive."

"I could see him giving good gifts though. He strikes me as the materialistic type. They're probably perfect for each other. You, my friend, deserve better."

"What about you? What do you deserve?"

"Purgatory."

Morgan pushes off the Jacuzzi wall and glides backwards through the water away from Jon. He slides his hurt leg off the bench seat, sitting up and facing her. She stands in the water, the level just above her hips. She gazes at him, barely out of reach. She steps forward. He places his hands on her hips and eases her toward him. She steps up on the bench seat and sits down, straddling him—her legs wrapped around his waist, her arms around his back, and her head on his shoulder. He squeezes tight. She fits, filling a void in all the hurt places. She kisses his neck, his cheek, his mouth. She holds tighter, their tongues touching, their mouths eager.

"Can you do something for me?" she whispers.

He nods.

"Pretend you love me and I love you. Pretend I had a bad day. Tell me it's going to be okay."

"It's gonna be okay," he says.

Chapter 5

Fear of Failure

Jon stands over the gas stove, pushing around scrambled eggs in a frying pan. Bacon crackles in a deep skillet. He alternates flipping bacon and tending to the eggs. He hears light steps made by bare feet on the wood floor behind him. He glances over his shoulder with a smile. Morgan's hair is wild. She wears the sweatpants and T-shirt from the night before, without a bra. She sits on the bar stool at the counter eating area. He removes the pans from the burners and turns off the flames, placing the food on the counter in front of her. Toast pops from the toaster.

"Hungry?" he says with a grin.

She rubs the sleep out of her eyes. "My head is pounding."

"We haven't eaten since the picnic yesterday."

He opens a couple cabinets. He grabs two glasses and fills them from the faucet.

"Do you have aspirin?" he asks, pushing a glass of water across the counter.

"The drawer next to the lazy Susan," she says.

He grabs the aspirin bottle from the drawer, glances at the instructions, pops a couple in his hand, and gives the pills to

Morgan. She places them on her tongue and washes them back with the water. She watches him limp around the kitchen, buttering toast, and placing the eggs and bacon on two plates. He pushes the breakfast dishes across the counter to Morgan.

He gimps around the counter and kisses her cheek; she flinches. He sits down next to her. She offers the hint of a smile, and looks away.

"Thank you," she says. "It smells good."

"I'm starving," he says. "I forgot last night that I didn't eat anything. I guess I was distracted."

She cringes. "About that. I'm a fucking disaster area, Jon. I am *not* making smart choices. I'm sorry. This is exactly what I told you that I can't do." She takes a small bite of her eggs.

Jon's body stiffens; his mouth turns down. "It wasn't a bad choice. I'm not oblivious. You needed someone last night, and so did I." He takes a sip of water.

"Someone? That's the thing, I did need someone, and you were there, but I have a fiancé. If I were home, he would have been there."

Jon exhales and shakes his head. "Like he was there to pick you up when you wrecked into my truck? I'm not some interchangeable piece. I know what I felt last night, and it wasn't one-sided."

"I needed a friend, not another guy trying to get into my pants. My life's already complicated enough."

Jon sets down his fork on his plate with a clang. He rubs his eyes and turns to Morgan. "If that's what you think this is, you don't know what the fuck you're talking about."

She crosses her arms. "Fine. Enlighten me then."

"Nothing happened. Actually something did happen, but not what you think. We talked. We held each other. We kissed."

"And then?"

"You don't remember?"

"I remember you taking me to my room. I remember being naked. I can fill in the blanks from there."

"You were about to pass out in the hot tub. I carried you to your room. You were pretty drunk."

She frowns.

"Your underwear was soaked. You took it off in front of me and climbed into bed."

Morgan crosses her arms. "So you saw me naked? You couldn't give me some privacy?"

Jon nods. "I am human."

She exhales. "Then what?"

"Then nothing. I went back to the hot tub and picked up your clothes and brought them to your room. I set them next to you and told you to put them on. I knew if you woke up naked—"

"I'd think we had sex?"

"Yes, but you wouldn't get dressed. You wanted me in bed with you."

Morgan closes her eyes and puts her head in her hands. "Did you get in?"

"No, and you were pissed about it. I really wanted to, but I wanted it to be real, not a drunken night you can barely remember."

She turns to Jon, her eyes wet. "I'm sorry. I've veered off course so far that I don't even know who I am anymore."

"Maybe you're just figuring it out."

"I like you. I really do, but we can't do this. I'm such an idiot. Will you please forgive me?" A tear slides down her cheek.

Jon turns his body toward Morgan. "I like being with you. I haven't felt like this around anyone for a long time. I realize that I barely know you, but, at the same time, I feel like we fit together, like we're the same. I know that might sound crazy." He looks away.

She puts her hand on top of his. He turns toward her. "It doesn't sound crazy," she says. "I just can't." Tears spill down her cheeks. "I came here to get myself together, to figure things out. It doesn't work so well if I start something."

"You gonna figure everything out all by yourself?"

She nods, her puffy eyes locked on his.

"Seems more like exile." He squeezes her hand. "And I may not know everything about you, but I do think that you need someone. It may not be me, but you need *someone*."

"I just can't. Believe it or not, I'm looking out for you. I'm toxic. If you knew, you wouldn't be here." She chuckles and says under her breath, "You'd probably call the cops."

"Try me."

"I can't. I can't have one more person look at me with that look of disgust and disappointment."

"We don't have to talk about anything you don't want to. I really do like you as a friend. Before last night, I was content just to spend time with you—no strings, like we said. So, let's be friends … really *be* friends. You help me. I help you. Like I said, I've got an opening for a friend in my life."

"Okay, but you can't cross that boundary. If we're going to do this, last night can't happen again."

"I'm not trying to split hairs here, but you were the instigator." Jon grins.

She smirks. "And I'm sure your Puritan sensibilities were so offended."

He laughs, then looks over his shoulder at the sunlight streaming through the panoramic windows. "It's beautiful today. You wanna go out on the lake?"

"I was going to run. You can come." She glances at his knee. "Oh, … I forgot. How does it feel today?"

"A little better. It'll be okay in a few weeks."

"Can you swim?"

"Probably not very far. I doubt I should kick much. I can paddle though. I saw you have a canoe."

+++

Jon sits in the back of the canoe, his left leg straight out in front of him, his right bent. He paddles steadily, two strokes on the left and two on the right. Morgan sits in front of him, paddling inconsistently. Her ponytail sticks out the back of her Georgetown baseball cap. Her bikini top is tied around her neck and concealed by a gray T-shirt. She paddles steady for a moment, then holds the paddle across her lap, looking at the water and the trees, lost in her own thoughts.

Sunlight glistens off the calm water. Birds chirp in the nearby trees. They paddle toward a secluded alcove, surrounded on three sides by fifty-foot walls of rock. The back corner has an outcropping of large rocks jutting from the water.

"Do you wanna stop?" he asks. "Morgan? Morgan?"

She turns around.

"Do you wanna stop for lunch?" He points to the outcropping of rocks. "That looks like a good spot."

She nods; her eyes are glazed over.

He paddles toward the rocks, guiding the canoe aground onto a gravelly shore shaded by the tree limbs dangling overhead. They step out and grab the nose of the canoe, dragging it from the water. He grabs the minicooler, and she carries the beach bag. They hike toward a large rock in the middle of the outcropping, where they sit, their feet dangling over the edge, only a foot above the rocks beneath.

"You all right?" he asks.

"Yeah. Why?"

"You seem out of it."

She shrugs. "I guess I'm still a bit hungover."

"Seems like more than that."

She looks out at the water. "When we were paddling—"

"You mean, when *I* was paddling." Jon grins.

Morgan smiles. "Right, when you were paddling Miss Daisy …" She shakes her head. "I was thinking about how calm everything is here. It's the polar opposite of my life in Arlington. Is that why you stayed?"

"I don't know why I stayed. Heather and I were married when we were twenty-two, right after I started the business. One year bled into the next, like I was along for the ride, going with the flow."

"Were you happy with her … in the beginning?"

"I'd like to think I was, and I guess I was in that first-love kinda way, but, if I'm honest with myself, I don't know if I ever really knew her."

She nods her head. "Swim with me," she says.

Morgan takes off her hat and T-shirt, and slides down her shorts. Her skin is creamy white, mixed with a hint of strawberry. She pulls a bottle of sunblock from the beach bag. She rubs the sunscreen on her arms, chest, stomach, and bends over to get her legs. She places her fingers under her bikini line.

Jon grins. "You're getting a bit personal there."

"It's the edges that get me. I have to practically bathe in this stuff or I get burnt. Can you do my back and shoulders?"

She hands the bottle of sunblock to Jon. He squirts lotion onto his palm, rubs it between his hands, then over her shoulders and back. Her skin is soft and radiant. Her shoulders slump in relaxation as Jon rubs his hands over her.

She dives into the water headfirst, her arms outstretched. Jon hobbles to the edge and pushes himself into the water. Morgan's head surfaces ten meters away. The spring water is comfortable because of the warm water discharge from the upstream nuclear power plant.

"Let's jump off the cliff," she says.

Morgan glides through the water to the cliff. She waits on a small rock, while Jon labors toward her, trying not to kick his left leg.

"You all right? I thought I was going to have to call the Coast Guard."

Jon smiles, shaking his head. "It may not be safe to jump here. I'm not sure how deep this is."

Morgan dives headfirst off the shallow rock, disappearing into the dark depths. Jon waits, watching the still water. After thirty seconds or so, his stomach is tied in knots. He feels frantic. He searches the water, looking for movement, a flash of white. *It has to be well over a minute.* Her head pops up, and she gasps for air.

"Shit, Morgan, don't do that!"

"I couldn't touch the bottom, so I'm pretty sure it'll be okay."

She pulls herself from the water onto the first rock. Jon joins her. She climbs rocks jutting out from the cliff face as a makeshift staircase. Jon struggles along, using one leg and his arms to climb. They stop on a small landing thirty feet up.

"This looks pretty high," Jon says.

Morgan grins. "Are you scared?"

"I'm not a huge fan of heights, but I'm pretty sure I can't climb down anyway."

"Let's see some good form then," she says, grabbing his hand and giving it a squeeze.

He inches out to the edge, putting most of his weight on his right leg. A few tiny stones slip down the cliff. He bends his good leg and pushes off away from the cliff. He holds his breath. His dive is awkward and off balance. The water rushes forward. His feet topple forward over his head. He knows it's gonna hurt. His back smacks the water with a splash. He can see the sun above him, as he pulls himself toward the light. He pokes his head out of the water. Morgan is doubled over laughing, still on the ledge.

"How was that?" he asks, smiling.

"Are you okay? I'm sorry for laughing."

"I'm fine. You gonna jump?"

She climbs higher, the cliff face more precarious as she ascends.

"This isn't a good idea," he says. "You should come down."

She climbs higher, her water shoes and her fingers fitting into tiny crevices as she scales the cliff face. She stands on the vegetated top.

"Morgan, come on. This is not a good idea," he calls out.

She waves at Jon, a broad grin on her face. She backs up a half-dozen paces. She runs forward and jumps off the edge. She tucks her chin and pulls her knees to her chest, rotating three times, and extending her hands just before the water impact. She enters the water with barely a splash. After a minute she surfaces, gasping. Jon claps.

"That was impressive," he says.

"I touched the bottom that time. I had a little momentum."

She swims to Jon. She sits next to him on a rock with just enough space for the couple. Their arms and legs touch.

"Lemme guess. You were a two-sport athlete at Georgetown?" he asks.

She nods, beaming.

"I'm impressed. That was pretty unbelievable."

They sit in silence, looking out over the still water, beads of water dripping down their bodies. She looks at Jon and purses her lips.

"Do you ever think about leaving?" she asks. "I don't mean like moving a town over but really leaving, far enough away that you never see anyone that you know ever again."

He nods. "I used to have this fantasy that I was gonna move to the Bahamas or Bermuda, some nice tropical vacation spot, and rent jet skis or something. Spend all day in paradise around people who are happy to be there, doing something that makes them a little happier."

"Why don't you do it?"

Jon laughs. "Because it's a dumb idea."

"Maybe … I think about it all the time. My fantasy is New Zealand, where I'm going to write books all day and spend all night with someone who loves me unconditionally."

"Unconditional love … I like that. I'll have to add that to my tropical fantasy."

She shrugs. "I'm not sure it really exists. If you think about it, everyone loves someone because of what they look like, how they act, what they do, or what they say, or a million other things all put together. So the idea that we just love without conditions is bullshit. If anything, it's the opposite. If we actually put the conditions in writing, it'd be about as long as *War and Peace*."

He smirks. "That's probably true. It'd be a funny book … dark humor maybe. You could prove the ridiculousness of unconditional love."

She frowns. "Nobody would ever read it. Trust me, I know."

"Do you write?"

"I do, but just for me … not seriously."

"I would love to read some of your writing. Are you working on anything now?"

"I don't normally show anyone. I don't like criticism."

"Who does? I doubt you'd get criticized by a high school dropout."

Morgan turns to Jon, her eyes narrowed. "Jesus, Jon, you never graduated?"

Jon shakes his head. "After everything that happened, I couldn't go back there."

"I'm surprised your mother didn't make you go."

He shrugs. "She didn't care. Once I was semihealed, I got a job with a local construction company. My mother was happy that I was bringing home a paycheck."

Morgan frowns.

"You seem disappointed."

"I'm sorry. I guess I'm sensitive, because I'm a teacher. If I was one of your teachers, I would have been at your house every day, until you agreed to come back. I can't imagine you had any trouble with the work. What were your grades like?"

"They were okay."

"Like you were an okay athlete? Tell me the truth."

"I was third in my class."

"Why do you do that?" Her face reddens; her eyes narrow.

"Do what?"

"Minimize everything, so you don't stand out. Like you're not supposed to ever feel good about yourself, like you don't deserve anything good in your life."

"I don't know." He looks down at the water. His chest feels tight.

"I think you do, but you're afraid."

He turns toward Morgan, his jaw set tight. "Afraid of what?"

"Failure, humiliation. If you don't stand out, nobody will notice if you fail."

"What about you? Your fantasy is to write, and you won't even show anyone your writing. It's not like someone took *your* picture and posted *you* in the newspaper with a caption that said, 'Worst Author in the History of the World.'"

They sit in silence, looking away from each other.

"I did show my older sister a novel I wrote."

Jon looks at Morgan. "What did she say?"

"She said she didn't care about the characters, and she couldn't get through it."

"So what? Maybe the story's not what she likes, or maybe she doesn't know what she's talking about."

"That's the thing. She does. She's a professional author. She's had a dozen novels published and sold all over the world. That's why I became an English teacher." She frowns. "Those who can't do, teach, right?"

"Even if she is right, big deal. You keep writing, and you'll get better."

"You don't understand. The main character was me and my search for love among the Georgetown elite. I thought it was funny and heartfelt, but she just shredded it. If I can't even write myself as a character, what does that say about me as a writer?"

"I bet it's good. I'd like to read it. You show me yours, I'll show you mine."

Chapter 6

Love, Sex, or Money: Choose One

Jon slows his truck and turns onto his gravel driveway, the headlights sweeping across the trees. He exhales and shakes his head.

"What the fuck?" he says to himself.

A Mercedes convertible with the top up sits in the middle of the driveway, blocking his typical parking space. He pulls up alongside, stopping the truck within inches of the driver's side door. He cuts the engine and hops out, his truck partly on the driveway, partly in some thickets. He tiptoes through the thickets, wearing his work boots and the board shorts Morgan gave him. He holds his dirty clothes and a neatly bound stack of papers. Apart from the running lights on the Mercedes, it's pitch black outside. He ignores his guest and hobbles toward the cabin.

Beep. Beeeep.

He continues toward the cabin.

Beeeeeeeeeeeeeeeeeeep!

He turns toward the Mercedes. Heather sticks her curly blond head out of the driver's side window.

"I can't open my door," she says.

"Go home, Heather."

"I need to talk to you. It's important."

Jon continues toward the side door of the cabin. She scrambles across the center console of her car and exits the passenger door. He can hear the gravel scatter beneath her feet, as she fast-walks behind him. She reaches the door at the same time he does.

"Can I come in and talk to you?"

"What do you want?"

"Please, just for a minute." She pushes out her lower lip. "*Pleeeease.*"

Jon turns on a floor lamp, limps to the kitchen, and sets the bound stack of papers on the counter facedown. He flicks on the hanging globe light over the metal kitchen table for two. She looks around the inside of the cabin with a frown, her eyes wide.

"Not up to your usual standards?" he asks.

"No, it's nice. Just a little drab. Could use a woman's touch … and some furniture … and some pictures … and a bathroom … and maybe a television."

She saunters close to Jon, inches from his face. He stands still. She leans in close, smelling his neck.

"You smell like the lake. Remember when we used to go to the lake?"

"I'm not interested in—"

She turns around and struts toward the single bed, her flip-flops clicking and her voluptuous hips swinging in a tight, short skirt. She sits on the edge of the bed, the floor lamp illuminating her heavy makeup that looks professionally done, like an airbrushed model in a magazine. She wears a pink tank top, two sizes too small, and a push-up bra that accentuates her tanned breasts. He hobbles toward her, standing, leaning on his good leg. She pats the bed next to her and looks up at him with a grin.

"Not interested in what?" she says. "Talking about old times, our summer trips to the lake? How we used to fuck in the water? How you would pull my bikini to the side and put yourself inside me?"

"Why are you here?" he says.

"I thought you'd be happier to see me. Don't I look nice?"

"Why are you here?"

"We used to be best friends. You were my first love. Don't you ever think about me? Don't you ever think about us?"

"I'm gonna ask you one more time. *Why* are you here?"

"Chad's cheating on me." She bites the corner of her lower lip.

Jon shakes his head with a smirk. "Why are you telling me this? Shouldn't you be working this out with him?"

She purses her lips. "I'd prefer to work it out with you."

He exhales and frowns.

"Don't you wanna get back at him? You can have me any way you want." She sucks her lips in and presses them out.

"You need to go home."

She stands and saunters to Jon. She kisses his neck. He feels her tongue. She kisses his earlobe and gently tugs with her teeth. She hikes her skirt, straddling his good leg, rubbing herself like a cat in heat. She feels hot and wet on his thigh. She places her hand on his crotch and squeezes. He pushes her. She stumbles back.

"Get out of my house."

She pulls down her skirt and crosses her arms. "Is it serious? You and little Miss Rich Bitch?"

"It's none of your business."

"I heard you stayed over at her house, and you two were on the lake together."

"Jesus, this town is small. Again it's none of your *fucking* business. And why do you care anyway? It's been three years since we separated. You've seen me with other girls."

She shrugs. "They were harmless. This one's different. I know girls like her. They come down here for vacation, have their little flings, then they go on back to their rich husbands. She's using you."

"Isn't that exactly what you're doing?"

She searches the floor. "I just don't wanna see you hurt."

Jon laughs. "You don't wanna see me hurt? That's the funniest fucking thing I've ever heard. You don't wanna see me *happy*."

She crosses her arms. "That's not true. That's all I ever wanted was for you to be happy. I couldn't stand seeing you depressed all the time."

"You wanted me happy, so I could focus on you. It had nothing to do with how I felt. It was an inconvenience for your shallow little life. Now it just kills you to see that maybe I can be happy with someone else."

Tears spill down her cheeks. She blots her eyes with a strap from her tank top. She wipes her nose with the back of her hand.

"That's bullshit, and you know it!" she says. "I stayed with you through *everything*. What do you think it was like for me, when I went out with my friends, and there would always be guys saying shit about you? I defended you, even to my friends. They said I was too good for you. I could have had any guy I wanted."

"So you deserve some sort of relationship medal because you defended me? Those guys were just trying to sleep with you. I was an easy target. And your dumbass friends? I wouldn't have friends like that."

She grins for a split second. "What about Chad?"

He tightens his jaw. "That piece of shit's not my friend anymore."

"You think you're so much better, but you're not. You act so high and mighty, but you guys are the same. You had an affair just like Chad."

"I told you then, and I'm telling you now. I *never* had a *fucking* affair."

"I know for a fact that you did, but I let it go, because I loved you, and because we were just kids."

He narrows his eyes. "What facts?"

"It came from a very credible source."

He shakes his head. "Bullshit, there is no way it's credible. Who? Tell me who."

"You won't believe me. And it's not right. I don't wanna cause you more problems. That's why I didn't tell you back then."

"Was it Chad? We both know what a lying sack of shit he is. He had his eyes on you back then."

"No. It wasn't Chad."

"Then who!"

Tears stream down her face.

"You really are fucking pathetic," Jon says. "Maybe Chad was right. He did do me a favor."

"Your mother, you fucking asshole! She told me."

He smirks, shaking his head. "You got three seconds to get the fuck out of my house."

She stands firm, a crooked grin on her face. "So now you're caught, and you don't know how to deal with it."

He hobbles forward, grabs the meaty part of her upper arm, and forces her toward the door.

"Let me go," she says.

He opens the side door with one hand, his other still gripping her arm. He shoves her through the door. She stumbles on the steps and regains her balance.

"If you're gonna turn this down, you must be a faggot," she says.

"Don't ever come back here again." He slams the door.

From outside he hears, "Faggot!"

He breathes a sigh of relief when he sees the headlights of her Mercedes backing down his driveway. He limps to the kitchen and picks up the bound stack of papers. He sits at the kitchen table and stares at the cover page with a smile.

Love, Sex, or Money: Choose One
A Novel By:
Morgan Anderson

+++

Jon leans out his window and punches the code on the keypad. The chain moves, and the gate slides open. The late afternoon sun sits low on the horizon, disappearing into the mountains. Jon parks in the street in front of the stone mansion. An unmarked police car sits in the driveway next to Morgan's Acura. Jon limps up the driveway to the front door, holding Morgan's manuscript. He's bleary-eyed; his hair is disheveled. His face is stubbly, and his shirt and pants are not altogether clean. When he knocks on the door, two detectives—one male and one female—exit.

"We'll be in touch," the female detective says to Morgan.

Morgan nods; her face looks pale. The detectives walk past Jon, staring at his red eyes.

"You okay?" Jon asks Morgan. "Did something happen?"

"I'm fine. It's a colleague from work," she says "I can't get into it."

"I'm sorry for just dropping by, but I wanted to talk to you about your novel." Jon grins. "Can I come in?"

"Yeah, sorry." She steps aside at the threshold. Jon limps in. "I would really prefer you called first."

"I did, but nobody picked up, and your answering machine is full. You should check your messages."

She shrugs.

"So your novel …"

"Couldn't get through it," she says.

"It was well written, witty, moving, sad, ironic—"

"Hold on a second. You read it already? I gave it to you yesterday."

"Yeah, I stayed up until three in the morning to finish it. Why do you think I look like I just fell out of a coffin?" Jon speaks faster. "I went to work on two hours sleep. I just couldn't put it down. I know I'm not a book critic, but I do read quite a bit, and I'm telling you that it's pretty great. I hope you don't mind, but I made a few notes of some things I liked, and I underlined some passages that were especially moving to me. You gotta get it published." Jon hands Morgan the manuscript.

She ignores the novel and wraps her arms around his lower back. Jon closes his arms around her, still holding her pages. She kisses him on the cheek.

"Thank you," she says in his ear.

"Thank you for trusting me with it."

She steps back with a smile. "Do you want to stay for dinner? I'd be lying if I didn't want to listen to my only fan rave about my novel."

"I would love to, but I have a standing Monday night dinner at my mother's."

She grins. "You're blowing me off? For your mother?"

He smirks. "She's been through a lot, and she lives alone. I think it's the highlight of her week."

She grabs his hand and squeezes. "It's nice that you do that."

"Maybe we can do dinner tomorrow? Then you can bask in the glow of my undying fanatical devotion to your literary genius."

She laughs. "I'd like that. Speaking of families, my sister's hosting a book launch party here next weekend. Would you be interested in attending an impossibly dull event surrounded by self-important, arrogant assholes?"

"Well, when you put it like that, … I'd love to."

+++

Jon parks behind his mother's Mercury sedan. He shakes his head when he sees a Harley-Davidson motorcycle parked adjacent. Jon takes the concrete steps to the vinyl-sided split level one at a time, using the handrail for support. He opens the door; familiar barking ensues. The black labs jump on Jon. He braces himself with his good leg and blocks them from doing any damage.

"Sorry I'm late, Mom," Jon calls out to the upstairs.

The dogs whip their tails back and forth, as Jon pets their heads. They follow him to the top of the stairs, where a baby gate blocks their entrance. Jon opens the gate just enough to slip through. The dogs whine as he resets the gate.

"I'm sorry guys," Jon says. "Special dinner tonight."

The smell of barbecue and Lysol mixed with sour milk, dog shit, and BO wafts through the air. He enters the kitchen. Ribs and corn fritters sit on the stove top. A Santa snow globe is on the counter. His mother is dressed in colossal blue jeans pulled over her pannus and a low-cut blouse with her gargantuan breasts front and center. A bear of a man has his hand on her ass. He gives it a squeeze and smirks at Jon. He wears a black vest, a black T-shirt, and a black bandanna, all sporting the Harley-Davidson logo. Jon wonders if the biker realizes that he's a walking billboard for a billion-dollar company the same way Japanese girls proudly display Hello Kitty paraphernalia.

She giggles at being groped and turns to Jon. "I almost forgot you were comin'. We was just gettin' started. You remember Dusty. You should see the snow globe he brought me." Betsy breaks from Dusty's clutches and grabs the globe, shaking it up. "So pretty."

Jon limps forward.

"Been a while," Dusty says.

Jon glares. "How long are you visiting for?"

Dusty grins. "As long as lil' Miss Betsy'll have me."

Betsy giggles. "You know I *always* keep the bed warm for my big ole Dusty Bear."

"I remembered how much your mama loves Christmas. It wasn't easy to find them globe things this time a year."

"That's my Dusty Bear. So sweet."

Dusty looks at Jon's leg. "I see you're still limpin' around."

"What happened, honey?" Betsy asks.

"It's nothing," Jon says. "I just tweaked my knee playing flag football."

His mother waddles over and gives him a kiss on the cheek. Jon pulls an envelope from his pocket and hands it to her. She stuffs it in the back pocket of her jeans.

"Thank you," she says in Jon's ear.

"Damn boy, you got hurt playin' *fag* football?" Dusty says. "Maybe we oughta wrap you up in bubble wrap."

Jon frowns. "I see you still haven't grown up."

"I'm just messin' with ya," Dusty says. "You always were so damn sensitive."

"Come on now, boys. Be nice," Betsy says.

Dusty puts up his hands. "I am bein' nice. Hell, just the other day some of the guys down at the club were callin' you a flash in the pan. I told 'em, 'It ain't your fault.'"

Jon exhales. "What's not my fault?"

"In my day it was just *different*. We'd rather die than come off the field. That was how we was raised. Goin' to the play-offs was expected. Shit, if we didn't go to state, we was mad as hell."

"So you old guys were really tough, but, my generation, we're soft?"

"I'm just sayin' what is. Times is different." Dusty brushes past Jon toward the dining room, his meaty shoulder pushing Jon aside with enough force to make a point but not enough to negate the "accident" defense.

Dusty sits at the head of the table. Betsy bustles about the kitchen, heaping food on his plate and opening a cold can of beer. Jon rolls his eyes, as she exits the kitchen.

"Here ya go, Dusty Bear," Betsy says in a singsong voice, as she places the food and drink in front of her man.

Jon makes a modest plate, and fills a glass of water from the tap. Betsy returns from the dining room. She grabs a beer from the fridge and piles food on her plate. She glances at Jon's dinner.

"That all you gonna eat? We got plenty."

"I know," Jon says.

"Suit yourself," she says, as she exits the kitchen.

Jon takes a deep breath before joining the happy couple. He sits at the foot of the table. Dusty and Betsy sit close, at the other end, making googly eyes. Dusty smacks his barbecue-colored lips, as he devours his ribs. Betsy's eating left-handed, her right hand hidden beneath the table. Her shoulder and upper arm move back and forth.

"Um, um, *ummm*," Dusty says with a barbecue grin. "I'll tell you what. Your mama knows how to take care of a man."

Jon eats quickly, despite his lack of appetite.

"I should probably get going," Jon says.

"You not gonna stay for cards?" Betsy says, glancing at Jon, then looking back to Dusty, her hand still at work under the table. "We was gonna play poker."

"Strip poker," Dusty says with a broad grin.

"I'll pass," Jon says. "Thanks for dinner."

"All right then. Lemme walk you out," Betsy says.

"You hurry back now." Dusty adjusts himself. "I got somethin' for ya."

Betsy giggles and waddles down the steps after Jon. She stands outside on the landing, not willing to venture down the steeper porch steps. Jon turns around at the bottom of the steps. His mother feels tall, like when he was a child.

"Couldn't you have at least waited until I left to be all over him?" Jon says.

Betsy scowls. "I was *not* all over him."

Jon shakes his head. "You didn't have your hand on him under the table?"

She crosses her arms over her plunging neckline. "On his leg, not that I have to be explainin'. You might wanna show your old mother some respect. I ain't gonna be around forever."

"Do you know how hard that was for me as a kid, watching you with your boyfriends? Some of them weren't so nice to me."

"You ain't no kid no more, Jon. It ain't fair that I should live alone. Maybe it's because I'm so fat. Is that why you don't like seein' me with a boyfriend? I know what I look like, but it don't mean I don't want what everyone else does."

Jon exhales. "You're right. I'm sorry. You should be happy with someone."

Betsy uncrosses her arms and softens her scowl. "See ya next week then?"

Jon looks down, then up at his mother. "I have something important to ask you."

"Okay," Betsy says.

"Do you remember when I had my knee injury senior year?"

"Like it was yesterday. If it weren't for bad luck, you wouldn't have no luck at all. Don't let them old-timers get to ya. I was around then, and you were better than every damn one of 'em. I just loved to watch you play. You made me so proud."

"Before that game, Heather was really mad at me. She was convinced that I was cheating on her. I wanted to know who told her that, but she wouldn't tell me."

Betsy stares blankly at Jon.

"Do you know who might have told her that?"

Betsy shrugs. "Don't know. Don't make no sense to me. You always been loyal. I know you'd never do that. I raised you better than that. I never did like that lil' hussy. And Chad, I know he was your friend, but I could tell by the way he looked at her then that he was up to no good."

"You think Chad might have told her that?"

"Could be. Would make sense after what they done. Why you wanna dredge all this up?"

"I just feel like I don't really know anyone."

"Well, you always got your mama, and I know you best."

Jon nods and takes a deep breath.

"Honey, I know life ain't always been kind, but dwellin' on the past ain't gonna make it better."

Chapter 7

No Future

Jon parks three houses down, because luxury automobiles occupy the driveway and street in front of the Stone Lake house. He strides to the front door, with a bottle of wine in his hand and a hitch in his step. Moths flutter about the porch lights. He gazes through the door window. He sees fancy people with fancy wine glasses. He thinks about ringing the doorbell, but decides to quietly find Morgan instead. He takes a deep breath, steps inside, and walks through the foyer. He stands next to a tray of dirty dishes, scanning the living room. Three-piece-suit-clad men and evening-gown-wearing women clutter the room, some sitting but most standing. *I should have bought a tie.* He cringes at the sight of Mrs. Walters marching toward him. Her blue gown clings tightly to her fit body. Her blond hair is pinned up, without a hair out of place, exposing a hint of dark roots. Her neck, fingers, and earlobes are adorned with platinum and diamonds.

"What are you doing here?" she says through clenched teeth.

"Morgan invited me," Jon replies.

"I know *that*. She's engaged. It's not appropriate."

"You're gonna lecture me on what's appropriate?"

"I won't have you ruin that poor girl's life. She's been through a lot. I've known her family since she was little. We used to summer here together. She's tends to pick up strays."

He exhales and shakes his head. He pulls a garage door opener from his pocket.

"I'm sorry I haven't been by in a while, but I think you should take this back," he says.

She stares down at the garage door opener, then looks up. Her eyes are red and glassy. "Keep it. You'll change your mind."

"I'm sorry, Sally. I need something real."

"It's not gonna be with *her.*"

"I know that, but she showed me what I'm missing. I don't wanna be somebody's plaything."

"I never thought that." She walks closer to Jon. He steps back against the wall. She leans toward his ear. "I love you."

She walks past. Jon catches a glimpse of tears glistening off her cheeks. She disappears down the hall toward the bathroom. Jon puts the garage door opener back in his pocket. He sees another woman stalk toward him. He feels like a Londoner during The Blitz.

"Do I know you from somewhere?" the woman asks.

She's wearing a long black evening gown that looks to be a couple sizes too small. Her hair is straight and blonde, but her eyebrows are brown. Her face is round and full but not unappealing. She looks like a chubby older blond version of Morgan.

"Are you Katherine?" Jon asks.

She smiles and puts her hand to her chest. "I am, and who might you be?"

"I'm Jon. I'm a friend of Morgan's."

She laughs. "I'm sorry. It's just so like her."

"This is for you," he says, handing her the bottle of wine.

She glances at the label and sets it on the tray next to the dirty dishes.

"So how do you know Morgan?"

"She hit my truck a couple weeks ago."

She smirks. "And now you're the best of friends two weeks later. That makes sense."

"Well, I don't know about best of friends, but I think we're friends."

She grins and purses her lips. "And if Morgan was a three-hundred-pound black woman instead of every guy's fantasy, would you be here tonight?"

"Do you talk to all your guests like this?"

"You do know that she has a fiancé?"

"I am aware."

She shakes her head. "You think she's gonna run away with you in your pickup truck and you guys are gonna live happily ever after in your double-wide?"

Jon laughs. "You almost got that right. I have a cabin with an outhouse, not a trailer, but I hear those double-wides are *real* nice."

Katherine glares at Jon. "If you were really her friend, you'd walk away."

"And miss all this fun? I never been to a *gen-u-ine* book party," he says in a thick hillbilly drawl.

"Well, enjoy it, because it's not going to last." She turns to walk away.

"I read Morgan's book."

She pivots around. "It *is* an easy read."

"What I don't understand is why you didn't like it?"

"Well, for one, I know good literary fiction, and, two, I'm not trying to sleep with her."

"I think you're afraid."

She scowls at Jon and places her hand over her chest. "I beg your pardon."

"I get it. She's athletic, pretty, and nice, but she can't be smart. She can't be a brilliant author like you. That's your domain."

"I think you should leave."

"I read your book too. I liked it. You're great at spinning flowery prose, but it felt like you were writing about something you learned in a book. Morgan's felt real, like something she lived."

"I said leave!"

The crowd quiets and directs their gaze toward Jon and Katherine. A pale balding man in a dark suit and a mustache marches over.

"Can I help you, sir?" the pale man says.

"Why do people say that," Jon says, "when they have no intention of helping me whatsoever?"

"I demand to know who invited you."

"You can demand all you want."

"He's Morgan's *friend*," Katherine says. "Don't encourage him."

Morgan slides up behind Jon. "I see you've met my friend Jon."

"Keep him away from the guests," Katherine says to her sister. "It's embarrassing enough having *you* here."

She walks away; the pale man follows.

"Glen, Katherine, nice to see you guys," Morgan says with a smile and a wave to their backs as they leave them. She turns to Jon. "I'm glad you made it."

"Your sister …" Jon shakes his head.

"I know. It's tragically predictable." She steps back and looks Jon over. "You look nice, a bit wrinkly, but nice."

"Sorry. I don't own an iron."

He looks at Morgan with a crooked grin, like he's trying to figure something out. She's barefoot with a knee-length floral sundress, her hair falling out of an updo.

"What? Why are you looking at me like that?" she asks.

"You look beautiful as usual, but you're even more out of place than me."

"Why should I dress up? I wasn't invited."

Jon cringes. "But you invited *me*."

"Yeah, because I knew it would piss off my sister."

"You coulda given me some warning. I thought she was gonna call security."

She laughs. "Good thing we don't have security."

She looks over at the lonely unopened wine bottle sitting among the soiled plates and empty glasses and picks it up.

"It's the same stuff we drank that night," Morgan says.

"I brought it for your sister. She didn't seem impressed."

"Oh, fuck her. It did the job pretty well, if I remember."

"Actually I don't think you do remember," Jon says with a grin.

She slips her arm around his. "Let's take this party outside."

They stroll through the party, arm in arm. Morgan swipes a corkscrew from the bar on the way out. Jon opens the back door to the deck. They wander down the steps headed for the boathouse and the dock. Lights built into the wood illuminate the steps. The air is humid, the temperature still in the seventies. Morgan sits crossed-legged on the built-in bench at the end of the dock. More lights attached to the dock posts brighten the pier in dim yellow circles. The occasional frog croaks and plops into the water.

"This is the farthest away I can be without leaving," she says. "I think that's what they want."

"Your sister?"

"And her stupid husband, Glen, and my parents."

"Are your parents here?"

She nods. "They're so fucking proud too. Can you open this?"

She hands Jon the wine bottle and corkscrew.

Jon sits down next to Morgan with the wine bottle between his legs. He works the corkscrew. Morgan looks over at Jon with a grin.

"I could say something crass, but it's just too easy," she says.

Jon smiles. The cork makes a pop. He hands her the bottle. She chugs a few gulps and passes it back. He takes a swig.

"You don't think your parents are proud of you?" Jon asks.

"Oh, God, no." Morgan frowns. "Especially these days. I had an official order to stay in my room during the party, like I'm fucking ten. So what did the power couple have to say to you?"

"Your sister wanted to make sure I knew you had a fiancé and that we wouldn't be driving off into the sunset in my truck to my double-wide."

Morgan laughs. "Did she really?" She takes a swig of wine and hands it back to Jon.

Jon smiles. "Yeah, … she did. She also said, if you were a three-hundred-pound black woman, I wouldn't be here."

"I think she might have a point."

"It was actually pretty brilliant. She was exposing me as a superficial racist in one sentence. From her point of view, it makes sense. I'm this redneck in the middle of small-town whiteyville. I'm a relatively young, unsophisticated guy, and men are interested in girls for youth and fertility the same way women are looking for men with money. It's all very shallow but also very biological."

"I think it's a good question though."

"I agree, but I think it says more about your sister than it says about me. I wouldn't even think to ask the question, but she just assumes that black is worse than white, and fat is worse than thin."

"That's what our society thinks."

"In general, maybe, but those things change. There were times throughout history when fat was more attractive than thin. As far as color goes, I do know that Oscar and Claudia get treated like second-class citizens in their *home* country because their skin is darker, and we're just talking about different *shades* of color."

"But you do have those loves that transcend cultural norms."

"All the time."

Jon takes a drink of wine and hands the bottle to Morgan. She sets the bottle next to her, looking off into the darkness, the lake and the outline of the mountains only visible through the moonlight. Her gaze reaches into the distance, reminiscent of the thousand-yard stare of a battle-hardened soldier. Her skin is like cream with a little chili powder mixed in. Her big blue eyes are normally bright and inquisitive, dominating her face, but now they look sad and regretful with a thin film of moisture. Her facial features are small and rounded, nothing blunt, only smooth lines urging forgiveness and understanding. She blinks and wipes her eyes with her thumb and index finger. She takes a drink and turns to Jon, the trance broken. She smiles and pats the top of his hand.

"Where did you go?" he asks.

She shrugs and shakes her head.

"There's something you're not telling me."

She smiles. "Well, of course. You've only known me for a few weeks. A girl has to maintain a certain bit of mystery."

"I'm here, if you need to talk about it."

"I know."

"Is there a bathroom in the boathouse?"

"No."

"I really have to pee. I'm gonna run up to the house real quick. I'll be right back."

"Just pee here."

"Where?" he asks, his brow furrowed.

"Right off the dock."

"You're joking, right?"

"What's the big deal?" she says. "I really don't want you to go up there without me."

"You could come with me. We could just get out of here. Go get some dinner or something."

She smirks. "Quit being a baby and pee already."

"You need to face the other way and be quiet. I can't pee with an audience."

She laughs. "Are you serious?"

He nods, his eyebrows raised.

"Fine." She holds up her hands and turns toward the house.

Jon moves to the corner of the dock, as far away from Morgan as possible. He unzips his zipper, hikes up one leg of his boxer briefs, and pulls out his penis. He stands for a moment, waiting.

"I thought you were gonna pee?" Morgan says.

"You're not helping by talking." He looks over his shoulder. She still faces the house.

She laughs. "I never knew you were so bashful."

"Morgan, seriously."

"All right, I'm shutting up."

He closes his eyes, and the flow starts. He feels immediate relief from the pressure. He opens his eyes and shakes out the last bit of urine. He sees Morgan from the corner of his eye, her mouth hanging open, her eyes fixated on his crotch.

"Jesus, Morgan, what are you doing?" he asks, shoving his penis back in his pants.

She grins. "I'm surprised Heather gave *that* up."

"I thought we were friends?"

"Hey, you saw *me* naked. It's only fair."

He shakes his head with a smirk. "Fine, whatever, you saw my penis."

She sits back down, with a grin plastered to her face. He sits next to her.

"So you can add me to the long illustrious list of girls who have seen your penis," she says.

"It's not that long and certainly not illustrious," he says.

"Heather's pretty hot."

"Ya think?"

She nods. "I bet she was the prettiest girl in school. The cheerleader who all the guys wanted."

"I guess."

"So me and Heather," she says. "How many others?"

"Are you asking me how many girls have seen my penis or how many I've slept with?"

She giggles. "Is there a big difference in the number? Are you running around town in a trench coat showing people your junk?"

He shakes his head with a smirk. "This is not exactly polite conversation."

"You show me yours. I'll show you mine. Remember?"

"Three."

"That's it? I'm surprised. I figured you for at least a baker's dozen."

Jon stares at Morgan with his eyes narrowed. "Are you making fun of me and my pathetic love life?"

She turns and kisses his cheek. "I'm sorry. That wasn't my intention."

"What about you?"

"Hold on a minute. You're moving too fast. We were still on you. So there was Heather and then who were the other two?"

"Amber. … We went to high school together. She was a couple

years behind me, really smart, went off to Duke, became a corporate attorney. She said she had a crush on me in high school. Her parents live in town, so she comes back for holidays."

"So you were her holiday fling? She could ring up the hottest guy from high school to service her whenever she's in town?" Morgan shakes her head with a smirk.

Jon looks away. "It sounds pretty sad when you put it like that."

"Sorry about that." Morgan puts her hand on Jon's knee. "When was the last time you saw her?"

"She stopped by on New Year's to tell me that she was getting married. She said she'd call it off if I would move down to Raleigh with her and really make a go of it."

"I'm guessing you told her no."

Jon nods.

"How'd she take it?"

"Not well, but my business is here. My mother's here. I couldn't just pick up and leave."

"I call bullshit on that. You could have left, if you *really* wanted to."

Jon exhales. "Maybe, but that was a big part of it." He shrugs. "She was attractive. She was smart, nice, but there was something about the relationship that made me uneasy. She was kind of a dork in high school, which I thought was endearing, but I wasn't sure if she loved me or if I was like this prize that she coveted. And when she finally got me, would she really want me, and would I want her?"

"What about the other one?"

Jon stares down at the dock. "You're gonna think I'm a piece of shit."

"It's not possible." She moves her hand to his thigh and gives it a reassuring squeeze. "We're friends, remember? We're supposed to help each other."

"It is *entirely* possible you'll think I'm a piece of shit." He takes a deep breath and lets it out slowly. "It was one of my clients."

"Okay?" She puts her hands out as if to say, *What's the problem?*

"Sally Walters."

Morgan stands and steps back with her arms crossed. "Jesus Christ, Jon! She's almost my mother's age."

"Is this about age?" he asks, knowing it isn't.

"We're not together. Who am I to judge?" She glares at Jon.

Jon looks away. "I feel like you're judging."

"I'm sorry. I guess it hit a little too close to home. I knew she seemed weird the other day, when we saw her walking." She sits back down next to Jon.

"I know it's fucked-up. I know she's married, but I just felt so lost. It was like we were a regular couple during the week, like we both separated it from reality."

"I really don't need to know the details."

"I understand."

She pulls her legs to her chest, making herself small. "Is it still going on?" she asks, looking out at the black water.

"No, I told her it was over tonight, and I haven't seen her since we met."

"Because of me?"

"Yes."

She shakes her head. "I don't want you to do that. It's not right. We don't have a future. I think you know that. If she makes you happy, you should continue."

"I got that. Everyone has made it abundantly clear that we have no future together. But you showed me what I want. You showed me the possibility of meeting someone like you. You showed me that I deserve better, even if it's not with you."

She puts her hand on top of his. "You do deserve better."

"So do you."

She leans over, her head on his shoulder, with her legs pulled up in a fetal position. He puts his arm around her, and she nuzzles into his chest.

"So what about you?" he asks.

"You already know everything," she says.

"Your book …"

She nods and crawls up into his lap like a child. She buries her head in his neck. He puts both arms around her, one hand stroking her hair. She sobs, convulsing, her cries muffled by his body, his chest wet from tears. He holds her in silence.

Chapter 8

What the Fuck!

"You cold?" Jon asks, looking at the goose bumps on her arms.

Morgan nods. "The temperature's dropping."

She pushes out of his lap; he unwraps his arms.

"I'd offer my suit jacket but—"

"You don't own one." She smiles small. "I should probably go to bed. Thank you for being here with me."

He nods, grabs her hand, and squeezes. He looks up at the lake house. "It looks like the party's over."

She looks up at the wall of glass, only the living room still lit.

"I'm off tomorrow," he says. "Maybe we can do something?"

"I'd like that. Can you walk up with me?"

He stands with a groan, bending and straightening his knee. He offers his hand, and he helps her off the bench. He grabs the empty wine bottle. They walk arm in arm up the steps. He opens the door from the deck to the living room. Morgan flashes a grin and steps inside. She stops, rigid, just inside the door. Jon's stomach plummets at the sight of five serious figures, sitting on the couch, their eyes trained on Morgan like some kind of intervention. They stand and approach. Jon moves closer to Morgan. The group eyes him, as if he were a disease that Morgan contracted. He recognizes Katherine and her husband, Glen, from earlier. He guesses the older couple are Morgan's parents, and the thirtysomething man with a paunch. *He must be a family friend.*

Morgan's dad is bald, with a short half-moon of white hair on the sides and back of his head. His complexion is light with age spots on his face. He's average height, but he has a commanding presence. Her mother looks younger, with a face that's been nipped and tucked. Her hair is blond, undoubtedly dyed. Her figure is thin, like someone who eats very little, not someone who exercises regularly.

"Morgan, we've all had about enough of your behavior," her dad says, as if he's scientifically measured everyone's threshold for *enough.*

Morgan searches the floor, avoiding eye contact, like a child being scolded.

"I thought it was a good idea for you to put some distance from your problems," her dad says, "but now you're simply creating new ones while running away from your old ones. David's here to take you home."

David's tall and bookish, with lanky thin limbs, and the aforementioned paunch. His face is forgettable but not unappealing. He has dark hair, retreating from the hairline. He looks fifteen years Morgan's senior, not just in his face and body, but in the serious way he moves.

David steps toward Morgan, eyeing Jon

"Morgan, let's not make a scene. Go pack your stuff, and we'll go home," David says, like he's talking to an unruly child who might burst into a temper tantrum at any moment.

Morgan glares at David. "I'm not leaving," she says.

"I told you," Katherine says with her hands on her hips.

"I'm going to stay," Morgan says.

"No, you're not," her dad says. "I'm not going to allow you to hide here anymore. It looks incriminating, and it's not healthy. You need to start taking responsibility for your behavior."

"Fine." Morgan looks at Jon. "Can I stay at your place for a while?"

Jon nods.

"Morgan, please don't do this," David says. "I'm not gonna pick up the pieces this time."

"Is that what you did?" Morgan asks. "More like hide the pieces in a dark room, never to see the light of day."

David turns to Jon. "This is a family matter. You shouldn't be here. Morgan is troubled, and you're just making it worse. I would appreciate it if you left."

"No!"

Everyone turns to Morgan.

"He's my friend, and we're leaving together."

"Son, I don't know what your relationship is to my daughter, but I need you to do the decent thing and walk away," her dad says.

"Sir, I can appreciate that this is a tense situation that I don't fully understand, but, as long as Morgan wants my help, I'm going to give it to her," Jon says.

"I bet that's not all you want to give her," Katherine says.

David cringes.

"Katherine, enough," her mom says.

Morgan looks down at her bare feet. "You know what? Fuck my stuff," Morgan says. She turns to Jon. "Can you get me out of here *now*?"

Jon nods, eyeing her family eyeing him. Morgan grabs Jon's hand. David grabs Morgan's arm.

She looks at David's hand as if it were a noose around her neck. "Let go!" she says.

She tries to wriggle from his grip. Her dad grabs her by the shoulders, his fingers pressing into her skin.

"You stop this, right now!" he says, shaking her.

Jon lets go. Morgan stares blank-faced at the floor, tears spilling down her cheeks.

"Take your hands off her. Both of you," Jon says.

Her dad stops shaking her. He loosens his grip and releases her. David holds firm, pulling her away from Jon. Morgan stumbles along like a marionette. Jon steps in front.

"I said, let go," Jon says.

David swings, but Jon dips his head before impact. David's fist connects with the top of Jon's head.

"God damn it!" David says, holding his hand from the pain of striking the hardest part of the human body.

Jon places his hand under Morgan's chin, lifts her head, and looks into her eyes. "Do you want to stay or do you want to go?" he asks.

"Take me away from here," she says.

"Morgan, honey, please don't do this," her mom says. "We love you."

"Let her go, Mom," Katherine says.

Jon and Morgan march out the front door to Jon's truck, hand in hand. He glances back over his shoulder at her dad standing at the front door with his arms crossed. Jon opens his truck door for Morgan and helps her inside. He hurries around to the driver's side, half expecting cops to show up on the scene.

Morgan is silent during the ride up the mountain to Jon's cabin. Her head is leaning on the passenger side window, her eyes glazed over, staring out the glass. Jon pulls into his gravel driveway and parks the truck. He cuts the engine and headlights. The cabin is dark, only its outlines visible with the naked eye. He hustles to the passenger door and taps on the glass.

"Morgan, I'm gonna open the door. Why don't you sit up." he says.

She pulls her head off the glass, like a zombie rising from the dead. Jon opens the door and reaches for her. She takes his hands, and he helps her to the edge of the seat, her feet dangling outside.

"I'm gonna pick you up," he says. "This gravel would not feel good on your feet."

He reaches one hand behind her back and the other under her legs. He heaves her up, she wraps her arms around his neck, holding tight. He kicks the truck door shut and treads to the cabin, ignoring the throbbing in his knee. He turns the door knob, still holding her, and pushes inside. He lets her down, her toes touching the wood floor. Jon flicks on the floor lamp.

"This is it," Jon says. "It's a bit rustic. The bed is over there." Jon points. "I'll let you have it. Help yourself to any of the books along the wall. The kitchen is over there obviously. I use the wood stove for cooking and heat. I use the sink for brushing my teeth and kitchen stuff. The bathroom is outside."

Morgan scans the room, her eyes still blank.

"Would you like something to eat or drink?" he asks. "Do you wanna sit down?"

She stands silent for a moment. "Could I use the bathroom?"

"Of course. Right this way." Jon walks to the back door, grabbing a flashlight from the kitchen table on the way. "Why don't you step into these?"

Morgan pushes her feet into his Adidas sandals. Jon flicks on the flashlight and guides her to the outhouse. Morgan stops and pushes her feet farther into the oversize sandals to prevent them from falling off. The outhouse door is open. Jon hands her the flashlight.

"If you have to do more than pee, there's some lime and a scooper on the floor. One scoop is usually good. Paper goes down the hole. Nothing special to do for urine. No need to use lime for that."

She nods and points the flashlight inside the outhouse. She sets the light on the bench next to the toilet seat, facing up. She shuts the door. After a minute she steps out, and he guides her back to the cabin.

"If you wanna wash your hands, I have hand soap next to the kitchen sink," he says.

She steps out of his sandals and trudges to the sink, each step like her feet are attached to cinder blocks.

"Do you wanna talk about what happened back there?" he asks, handing her a dish towel.

She shakes her head. "I just want to sleep." Her voice is barely audible.

"Why don't you sit, while I get you some clothes to sleep in."

She sits on the bed, her feet on the floor, only the outside of her soles touching. Jon catches a glimpse of the darkness she accumulated over the evening. He walks back to the kitchen and picks up the towel. He adds soap and runs water over it. He grabs a dry towel from the drawer.

"Your feet are really dirty," he says.

"I'm dirty," she says under her breath.

He kneels in front of her on one knee, his good one, and takes a foot in his hands. For each, he wipes off the dirt with the damp towel and dries with the dry. He throws the towels in a milk crate against the wall. He opens and closes the drawers of the metal filing cabinet, pulling out a pair of boxer shorts and a T-shirt.

"Why don't you put these on?" he says, handing her the clothes.

She nods. He turns around. He hears the swish of her sundress being pulled over her head, then her bra clasp click against the wooden bed frame as she hangs it there. He hears the touch of one foot on the ground, then the other, as she steps out of her panties into nakedness. He hears her step into the boxers, and the rustle of the T-shirt as she pulls it over her head and sticks her arms through. When he hears his comforter being pulled back, he glances over his shoulder. Her head is on the pillow, her eyes closed, and the comforter wrapped tight around her, like a cocoon. He approaches her. Her dress and lacy underwear are draped over the headboard. He steps to the bed. He bends down inches from her face, his mouth near her ear.

"Good night," he says.

She turns toward his voice, her eyes sealed shut, her lips lightly brushing his cheek. Her face is flushed, her lips swollen. He brushes an errant strand of hair from her face and presses his lips to hers.

+++

Jon awakes with a sharp pain in the hip that supported much of his weight during the night. Dim light filters into the cabin, the sun still low in the sky. He sits up from the floor and glances at Morgan still wrapped in her cocoon. He can hear her slow, rhythmic breaths, the comforter rising and falling with her diaphragm. He pulls off the two jackets he used as blankets, and he picks up the sweatshirt that doubled as a pillow. He stands with the speed of an octogenarian, wincing at the stiffness of his joints. He pulls on a pair of khaki canvas pants and a T-shirt. He sits down and slides a pair of dark athletic socks over his bare feet, then the

Adidas sandals, and heads to the outhouse. When he returns, Morgan sits cross-legged on his bed, staring at the back door, as if she were awaiting his arrival. She looks childlike in the over-size T-shirt and boxers. Her eyes, no longer despondent, have her familiar vibrancy.

Jon smiles at her. "You're up."

She nods. "I'm really sorry about last night. You must think I'm a freak."

He shakes his head. "Are you okay?"

"I feel 100 percent better." She smiles.

"Do you wanna talk about it? You know, what happened with your family?"

She shakes her head. "It wouldn't do any good anyway." She waves her hand, as if she's erasing a blackboard. "You know, I slept better last night than I have in, I don't know, for as long as I can remember."

"I'm here, if you change your mind."

"You don't have to keep telling me that."

"Okay, it's just I'm worried about you."

"You worry too much. Sometimes you gotta say, 'What the fuck and make your move.'"

Jon stares at her, blank-faced.

She laughs. "You know like in *Risky Business*? Didn't you ever see that?"

"A long time ago, maybe."

"Well, Booger gave Tom Cruise some good advice. From now on, we're gonna say, 'What the fuck.'"

Jon shakes his head with a smirk. "And what does 'What the fuck,' entail?"

She grins, her eyes bright. "Whatever the fuck we want it to."

"How about breakfast before anarchy?"

Jon lights the wood stove and cooks scrambled eggs.

"Can you go out and grab some strawberries?" Jon says.

"You want me to drive to the market?" Morgan asks.

Jon laughs. "No, I have a strawberry patch in the backyard."

Morgan's eyes widen. She skips to the back door and looks out the window at the garden. "This is unbelievable." She slides on Jon's sandals and opens the door.

"Hold on."

Morgan looks back at Jon with the door open.

"Take the basket." Jon points to the wire basket filled with old Cool Whip containers hanging on a hook next to the back door.

She flashes a grin and grabs the basket.

Jon butters the toast and splits the scrambled eggs on two plates before putting the dishes on the kitchen table and turning on the hanging globe light. He fills water glasses, and places metal forks and cloth napkins on the table. He sticks his head out the back door.

"Morgan, it's ready," he says.

She's reaching up, plucking ripe cherries off a branch. "I can't believe how much is out here," she says.

He shakes his head with a smile. "We can pick it later. Your eggs are getting cold."

She grabs the basket and treks inside. The Cool Whip containers are overflowing with strawberries and cherries.

"It's beautiful out there. The fruit is … I mean, it's really good, but it's more than that. It's like the strawberries taste like strawberries, but stronger, more *like* a strawberry."

Jon rinses off the produce and sets it on the table. They sit down and devour breakfast.

"I like it here," she says.

"Really?" he says, with raised eyebrows.

"It's quiet. It's beautiful, and it's simple."

"Simple?"

"Not in an easy-to-figure-out way. More like a devoid-of-ex-traneous-bullshit way. It reminds me of you. Humble and sweet."

Jon's face feels hot. "Maybe we could go for a hike today? There's a place I want to show you."

"I'd like that," she says. She looks away, her eyes downcast. "I don't have any shoes."

"Do you wanna go by and pick up some of your—"

"No!"

Jon stares at Morgan, wide-eyed, as if he stepped on a land mine.

"I'm sorry. I just can't go there today."

"There's a Target down the road. Probably not your style, but we could pick up a few things for you."

+++

Jon parks next to the shopping cart shelter, unconcerned about errant shopping carts denting his truck. Despite her lack of a hairbrush and makeup, Morgan looks beautiful in her knee-length sundress and Jon's oversize Adidas sandals. They walk arm in arm through the parking lot. Jon cringes at the sight of a black Range Rover.

"What's wrong?" she asks.

"Heather and Chad," he says, motioning toward the Range Rover.

"Sometimes you gotta say, 'What the fuck,' right?"

Jon nods. Morgan pulls him closer. The automatic metal doors whoosh open, and a blast of cool air blows in their faces. Jon grabs a red shopping cart, and they head toward women's clothing. She holds on to Jon's arm, as he pushes the cart down the aisle. She stops him, rises to her tiptoes, and kisses him on the cheek, lingering a bit too long for a friendly peck.

"Thank you," she says. "I'll pay you back."

Morgan looks through the racks of clothing, occasionally pulling out a shirt or a dress and holding it up to her body, asking Jon what he thinks, with him always responding that it looks nice.

"I can't believe I'm surprised that *you're* no help," Morgan says, with a wink.

"Neither can I," he says.

Morgan fills the cart with a couple cotton dresses, a pair of flip-flops, running shoes, a pair of running shorts, some cotton underwear, a sports bra, and a couple T-shirts. They wander over to health and beauty, with Morgan still leaning on Jon's arm.

On the way, they pass Heather and Chad in the electronics department. Chad is measuring a big-screen plasma television with a tape measure. He wears plaid shorts, a tight polo shirt, sunglasses on top of his head, and Teva sandals. His legs are caveman hairy. Even the tops of his feet sprout hair. Heather's curly blond hair is pulled back into a ponytail, making her features seem sharper. Her legs are tanned and smooth, exposed almost to her crotch in her short jean shorts.

Jon pushes faster, hoping to pass them undetected.

"Jon, is that you?" Heather says, wandering out of the electronics department into the main aisle.

Jon stops the cart. Morgan looks at him with a grin. They turn around. Heather is sauntering toward them, with Chad behind her.

"What are you two doin' here?" Heather asks with a toothy smile.

Heather looks Morgan up and down, smirking at her footwear.

"We're here for the magic show, David Copperfield," Jon says.

Morgan covers her mouth to stop the laugh from spilling out.

Heather smiles. "Well, I didn't know they had that here. Maybe Chad and I can check that out."

"What's that, honey?" Chad says, as he walks up to the group.

"Did you know they have a magic show here?"

"If it's here, it probably sucks. I wanna get the plasma hung today. My guys are comin' to install it at four."

Jon glares at Chad. "I didn't realize you owned the employees that work for *our* company."

"Damn, Jon, it's just an expression. You don't have to get your panties in a bunch."

"Who's paying for their hours?"

"We'll just add it to payroll. It's only a couple hours."

"Where does it end?"

Chad shakes his head and narrows his eyes at Jon. "We've been through this, dude. You know you can have the guys do whatever you want at your house."

"I live in a cabin, not a palace. It doesn't need a lot of work."

Chad shrugs. "I don't wanna embarrass you in front of your girlfriend, so maybe you should just let it go."

"She's not my girlfriend, so go right ahead, embarrass away."

Morgan grabs Jon's arm.

"There's nothing you can do about it," Chad says. "I can do whatever the fuck I want. If I wanna take a vacation, if I wanna use company resources, I can do that, and there's not a damn thing you can do about it. I'm the majority owner. That's just the way it is. Get over it. Quit actin' like you're still the boss. It's annoying."

Jon nods. "You've got that right. It is annoying."

"Come on, guys," Heather says, changing the subject. "It's Sunday. Let's not get caught up in work junk."

"He's the one," Chad says.

"So, Maria—" Heather says.

"It's Morgan," Morgan says.

"I thought you were engaged." Heather eyes Morgan, who's intertwined with Jon's arm.

Morgan looks into Jon's eyes. She turns his chin, rises to her tiptoes and kisses him open-mouthed, her hands grabbing his ass, and her tongue exploring his mouth. She smacks him on the butt and turns around. Jon can't contain his smile. Chad is slack-jawed, and Heather frowns with her arms crossed.

"It's his cock really," Morgan says. "I know you know. Right, sister? I just can't get enough of it."

Heather scrunches up her face, like she just bit into a lemon. "You're gross."

"I finally figured out why you let such a beautiful cock go. He was your first. You thought they all were gonna be like that. How much of a disappointment was it when Chad pulled down his pants for the first time?"

"Let's go," Chad says to Heather. "He's never gonna change." Chad looks at Jon, who's trying to contain his laughter. "You got a real classy girl there."

Chad grabs Heather's hand and yanks her along as they march away. Jon and Morgan double over in hysterics. A few shoppers glower at the couple, now on the floor laughing.

Chapter 9

Predetermined

Jon and Morgan enter his cabin, still laughing, each holding a Target bag.

"I can't believe you did that," he says. "Did you see their faces?"

"'You got a real classy girl,'" Morgan says in a spot-on imitation of Chad. "I was so sick of listening to his arrogant ass."

Jon's smile fades. "Was it real?"

She shrugs with a grin. "Did it feel real?"

Jon steps closer to Morgan. She looks up at him and drops her bag. He looks down and drops his. Reaching out, he puts his hands on her hips and pulls her closer, their bodies touching. He presses his lips to hers. Their mouths part, and tongues touch. She slides her hands under his shirt, to his upper back, pressing her fingertips into his flesh. She steps back blushing, biting the corner of her lower lip. Jon watches, captivated.

She slips her dress over her head and tosses it on the bed. She stands in her white lace bikini and matching bra. He drops his gaze to her inner thighs, the V between her legs, the shape of her hips. She slides her panties down and steps out, slow, one foot at a time. His heart beats faster, his body paralyzed. She reaches behind her back, unclasps her bra, and draws it down her arms. She turns and tosses it on the bed. He studies her body, mesmerized by her subtle curves, virgin skin, and her raw beauty.

"Can you grab that sports bra and some underwear from the bag for me?" she asks with a grin.

Jon's unresponsive.

She laughs. "You okay over there?"

He blinks. "Yeah, … sorry." He bends down and retrieves a pair of cotton underwear and the sports bra from the Target bags. He steps toward her and extends his fist full of undergarments. He pulls his hand back.

He narrows his eyes and grins. "I'm not sure I should give you these."

She reaches forward and snatches the underwear from his hand. "I thought you had something to show me," she says as she dresses.

"I think you've got that backward."

+++

They tread up the overgrown rocky path, as sunlight filters through the forest canopy. Jon picks his way, trying to keep his bad leg on flat ground. Morgan walks ahead and stops, watching him with a grin, while he catches up. She's like a mirage that moves farther away the moment he thinks he's closing in. They reach the crest of the mountain; the grade levels. Walking becomes comfortable. An impenetrable wall of stone, twenty feet high, stands in front of them, pushing up from the forest floor. Morgan stops with her hands on her hips, admiring the geological formation. Jon taps her on the elbow, as he passes by.

"This way," he says.

Using his good leg, Jon steps on rocks jutting out from the formation like a haphazard staircase. Halfway up, he sees sky between the boulders. He takes off his backpack, holds it out in front of him, and slips between the rocks. He turns his body sideways to fit.

"Are you serious?" Morgan says.

"If I can fit, you can fit."

They shimmy sideways between the stones. Jon steps out of the crevice onto a flat rocky ledge. He feels warm sunlight on his face and sees the tree-covered mountains standing majestic in the distance. Below the mountains, the lake is light blue, with the sun reflecting tiny starlike bursts of light. The valley surrounding the lake is covered in lush green vegetation. Morgan stands transfixed, her eyes absorbing the view. Jon sits on a rock the size of a small bench, ten feet from the edge.

"You okay over there?" he asks.

"It's beautiful," she says. "I'm not even sure *beautiful* is enough of a superlative."

He smiles at Morgan. "The best part is nobody knows about it."

"I can't believe this is so close to your cabin. How did you find this place? I mean, that trail was hardly a trail."

"The old guy who sold me the cabin made me a map. He was real secretive about it too. He actually made me promise not to show anyone, unless they were someone I really cared about. He used the cabin as a romantic getaway for him and his wife. He said this was their secret spot. I don't know if that's true or not, but I've never seen anyone else up here."

"What happened to his wife?"

"Don't know. I assumed she died, but I didn't ask about it. It took me every weekend for a month to find this spot even *with* the map. I started to think that maybe the old guy was crazy. I was sure I was gonna get stuck between the boulders the first time I squeezed through."

Morgan turns to Jon, her gaze locked on his. "Thank you for taking me here."

"You're welcome. Are you hungry?"

Morgan sits next to Jon on the small boulder. They share fruit and vegetables from the garden and a granola bar. After lunch, Morgan stands up and inches toward the edge.

"Careful," Jon says.

"I just wanna look."

Jon inches next to her. They peer over the edge of the vertical cliff face into the abyss. Jagged rocks line the bottom, like gnarled teeth.

"That's a long way down," she says.

Jon inches back. "Can we sit back down? I'm not a huge fan of heights."

"But you come here?"

Morgan still stands on the edge, her toes hanging over, her head looking down.

"I'm okay, if I stay away from the edge," he says. "You're really making me nervous. Would you please back away?"

Morgan steps back and turns to Jon. "Do you ever think about how fragile life is? How one false step in front of a bus or a cliff—or one yank of your steering wheel into oncoming traffic or off a bridge—could end it all?"

Jon looks at Morgan, wide-eyed.

"I'm not suicidal, if that's what you're thinking."

"That's not what I was thinking. What you said put something in perspective for me. Life *is* fragile, like you said. It's a miracle that you and I are here right now in this spot that very few people have ever seen. What if I would have left a little earlier that night you hit my truck or you left a little later or someone else was driving slow in front of you or you forgot something and had to turn around. And then for us to have this … connection … I mean, what are the chances? One in a million? One in a billion? It makes me think that my regrets and failures are so small in the grand scheme of things, that maybe it helps to take a step back and see the big picture."

Morgan grabs Jon's hand, looking out at the cloudless blue sky. "This is definitely a big-picture type of place."

Jon watches Morgan gazing off into the distance. She turns to Jon and purses her lips.

"In your novel, Roger is actually David, isn't he?" Jon asks.

She nods and pulls away her hand. She sits on the bench-size rock. Jon joins her.

"Does he know that?" he asks.

"I don't know. He never asked."

"That doesn't make sense. How could he *not* figure it out?"

"People see what they want to see."

"Did he actually read it?"

"He said he did, but he took it to work, and he never discussed any details with me, other than to say he liked it."

"And your sister's the only other person who's read it?"

She nods. "I did disguise the characters pretty well. You would have to know me really well to know that it's autobiographical. I don't think my sister or my fiancé know me. Like I said, people believe what they want to believe."

"Kate ends up marrying Roger, despite the fact that it was going to be a marriage of convenience, a marriage that makes everyone but Kate happy. Is that what you're gonna do?"

"It's inevitable. I'm on a train that I can't get off."

Jon frowns. "I don't buy that for a second. You could just say no and walk away from the engagement."

Morgan shrugs and stares off into the distance.

"Morgan, look at me."

She turns to Jon.

"I'm so sorry that you had to go through that."

Her eyes are glassy. She shrugs and shakes her head.

"Listen to me," he says. "I'm so sorry."

Tears stream down her cheeks. He leans forward, his arms around her, pulling her to his chest. She holds her arms in tight, letting him wrap her in his embrace. She dries her eyes with his T-shirt and sits up. He lets go.

"It doesn't have to be inevitable," he says.

She grabs his hand and kisses it, her lips lingering. "What about you? You don't think you're stuck?" she says. "You don't think that everything good in your life will be taken away?"

He looks down. "Unfortunately that seems to be the pattern."

"Was Chad telling the truth? Did the company used to be yours?"

"I saved some money for a few years after I dropped out of high school. I bought a used excavator, and I hired myself out. Chad came on a year after that. The business was really growing. We were both working long hours. He wanted to be a partner. He said, if the roles were reversed, he would do it, because I was his best friend."

She raises her eyebrows. "So you gave him the partnership?"

"I gave him 40 percent of the ownership."

Morgan shakes her head. "Did he even buy in?"

"No."

"Then the divorce."

Jon nods. "The court gave Heather half my share, so together Heather and Chad now own 70 percent of the company. I make 30 percent of what they do, but it's probably a lot less when you count the company resources they use for their household projects."

She frowns and shakes her head. "Then why do you work so hard? Why don't you just walk away?"

"If I do that, the whole company suffers. It's not fair to the employees."

"So you're just going to be taken advantage of forever? Continue to work your ass off so Chad can put flat screens in front of his gold-plated toilets?"

"It's not gonna be forever."

"One thing I don't understand," Morgan says. "You make one-third of what they do, but, from what I've seen, you spend about 1 percent of what they do. I mean, seriously, Jon. I know that truck probably has sentimental value, but it's twenty years old, and I love your cabin, but I can't imagine it costs you much to live there. Your dresser is an old filing cabinet, for fuck's sake. All your clothes are for work. A lot of your food comes from the garden. You have no television, no computer, no furniture. Shit, Jon, you don't even have indoor plumbing. What is going on? Where does your money go? Or do you just feel like you're not worth it?"

"Heather emptied our accounts before she filed for divorce, so three years ago I was broke. The old guy that I bought the cabin from let me make payments to him for two years to pay off the place. And then I have my mother's house and all her bills, and I'm trying to save. I'm just getting out from under it all."

"Doesn't your mother have a job?"

Jon smirks and shakes his head. "She's on disability, but it doesn't cover all her bills. It's not her fault."

They sit in silence. "Jesus, Jon, I'm sorry. Maybe we *are* heading straight to the inevitable. We can veer off course, but eventually we get pulled back on the track. We still end up in the same place."

Jon frowns. "I hope not. That's awfully depressing."

Morgan smiles and smacks Jon on the thigh. "It doesn't have to be. The other side is that you can do whatever you want in the meantime. Sometimes you gotta say, 'What the fuck.'"

"Like what you said to Chad and Heather earlier?"

Morgan nods. "And like what you said to my family last night. You stuck up for me. Nobody's ever done that."

Morgan stares at Jon, her eyes unblinking. He blushes and smiles.

"Do you wanna get going?" he asks. "We're gonna go back a slightly different way. I have one more place to show you."

He stands, grabs his backpack, and turns toward the stone wall. Morgan takes his hand; he turns around. She stands, looking up at him, biting the corner of her lower lip. His heart beats faster, his stomach tied in knots. He moves within inches of her. She presses her lips tightly to his, her mouth slightly open, their tongues touching. Her lips are soft, her mouth warm and wet. He drops the backpack; she pushes against his body.

She unbuckles his belt, unbuttons his pants, and slides down his zipper. She plunges her hand under his boxer briefs and grabs him. Jon shudders and grasps her hips. She pushes his boxer briefs down enough to pull him out, while he tugs at her running shorts and cotton underwear. She slides them to the ground and steps out, her lower body naked, except for her running shoes. He places his hand under her knee and lifts, her thigh against his hip. She stands against him with one foot on the ground, his penis against her stomach

"We should stop," he says, his breathing elevated. "I don't have anything."

"No, keep going. I'm on the pill," she whispers in his ear.

He bends his knees, positions the head of his erection against her vagina. He looks her in the eye, as he pushes inside her. She moans as he enters, wrapping her arms around his neck and both legs around his lower back. He turns around and presses her against the stone wall, her thick T-shirt preventing scrapes. He pushes deeper inside. Her fingertips dig into his back; she moans louder. They find a rhythm, their bodies fitting tight together.

"Keep going," she says. "Please, don't stop."

She holds him closer, her breathing heavier, and her hip movements stronger. He moves deeper, with more force, her moans synced with each thrust. He turns around and places her on her back on the bench-size rock. He remains standing but bends his knees enough to stay inside her. She holds her legs tight around his waist. He leans over, hovering just above her, his hands on the rock supporting his weight. She reaches up, cupping his face.

"Keep going," she says. "Please."

He moves inside her. She releases his face, and allows her arms and her head to dangle over the edge of the rock. From her viewpoint, she must see endless blue skies. Her moans intensify, as he moves deeper and harder. She's dripping wet. He feels her body contract, shudder, and release, inside and out, like an eruption. She moans quick and loud as her body convulses, then longer and softer with her release. He exhales heavy and groans as her climax forces his. She lifts her head and looks up at him, her blue eyes moist. She places her hands on his face, pulling him to her lips. She lets go. He pulls out, his penis glistening. Her face is red; she's grinning, with a thin layer of perspiration. He's still hard, his boxer briefs pulled beneath his erection. His pants and zipper are wide open, and barely clinging to his hips and ass. Her legs are still open. He grabs a cloth napkin from his backpack. He cleans her up, then himself.

"I really needed you," she says.

He smiles, bends over, and kisses her. He pushes his penis back into his boxer briefs and pulls up his zipper and buckles his belt. He retrieves her clothes, and she stands up to take them with a smirk. She steps back into her underwear and shorts, and slides them up her thighs.

"You want to get going?" she asks.

"I don't want this to be temporary," he says.

"Nothing's forever."

They shimmy through the boulders and stroll hand in hand. They branch off course near a creek. Their feet rustle in the leaves as they follow the creek bed down the mountain. Jon leads now, as they pick their way around trees, shrubs, and briars, the sound of flowing water getting louder. Jon stops at the edge where the creek plunges twenty feet into a blue pool below. The falling water drowns out the typical forest sounds.

Morgan smiles. "Can we get down there?"

Jon nods. "This way."

They scale down boulders, avoiding the wet ones, occasionally using trees and each other to hold on to. They stand just beyond the pool; the sound of the water crashing is thunderous. Morgan bends down and puts her hand in the water.

"It's cool," she says. "Does anybody come down here?"

"Sometimes during tourist season."

She bends down and unlaces her running shoes. She puts her socks in her shoes and looks up at Jon with a crooked grin.

"It's gonna be cold," he says.

"What the fuck. Remember?"

She removes her clothes and places them on top of her shoes. Jon stands behind her with a grin. She turns to him with her bottom lip pushed out.

"Come on," she says. "Don't be such a baby."

She steps into the water, her arms held out for balance. Jon takes in the curve of her hips, the small of her back, the brightness of her skin, and her toned yet feminine legs. Her girlish giggles reverberate off the rocks, barely audible over the water crashing. She's strong yet weak, beautiful yet broken, feral yet caged, and carefree yet burdened. She carries a weight no one should ever carry alone. She walks in, hip-deep, and dives into the pool, swimming to the middle.

She turns to Jon grinning. "Get in!"

Jon undresses, placing his clothes on top of his boots in a pile next to hers.

"Look at that!" she says.

Jon shakes his head, blushing as he steps into the pool. He feels exposed, with Morgan staring at his full frontal. He dives in, the cool water nearly taking his breath away. He swims to Morgan, the spray from the waterfall spitting at them. She swims toward Jon, putting her arms around his neck and her legs around his back. He puts his feet down, realizing he can touch and keep his head just out of the water. She puts her chin on his shoulder, her mouth near his ear.

She whispers, the water drowning out the sound beyond that short distance from her mouth to his ear, as if she wants to tell him everything but needs to retain plausible deniability. She whispers the parts she left out of the novel, the circumstances too humiliating and hurtful to write, as if they might haunt her forever should she immortalize them in print.

She whispers that it happened a year ago. She was drunk. She was having second thoughts about David. She went out with someone she was attracted to behind David's back. Who knows? She might have slept with the new guy after they got to know each other, but she never had the chance to consent. She was ashamed, humiliated, angry, and she wanted to press charges. Her parents begged her not to. They said they were concerned about the family's reputation, that these things were difficult to prove anyway. They couldn't even say the word. They referred to it only as "these things," or "this situation." It wasn't all about her, they'd said.

David was the cold, calculating lawyer, asking her the hard questions that she would undoubtedly face in court, breaking her with such ease. He said he did it for her own good, to save her the humiliation in open court. Her family praised David for being so understanding about the situation. Morgan was, after all, seeing someone behind his back.

Chapter 10

Vacation

Jon's eyes flutter. Her head rests on his bare chest, with her arms and legs wrapped around him. He feels the weight and warmth of her naked body, the smoothness of her skin, the rhythm of her breathing, and the softness of her hair. He glances at the clock, but he can tell from the light streaming in the cabin that he's already late. He kisses her on the forehead. He tries to move out from under her without disturbing her. She holds tight, a smile forming.

"Stay here," she says.

"I'm late for work."

She rubs her eyes and shifts her body farther on Jon.

"Doesn't that feel nice?" she says, her chest directly on his.

"It does."

He feels the warmth between her legs and the softness of her breasts pressed against him. Her smell is sweet, like ripe pears mixed with vanilla.

"Don't go. I want you." She purses her lips.

He smiles. "I'll try to leave as early as I can, then I'm all yours for the rest of the day. I've got three appointments today, a couple jobs going on. Mondays are really bad for me. I'm sorry."

"When was the last time you took a vacation?"

He laughs. "My honeymoon was the only one … eight years ago."

"How many vacations have Chad and Heather taken in the last year?"

"I have no idea, but it's been quite a few."

"Chad said he can go on vacation whenever he wants, and there's nothing you can do about it."

Jon frowns. "Yeah, I remember. He's a dick."

"So can you."

"What? … Be a dick?"

She smiles. "Don't be a smart-ass. You know what I mean. I'd like to take you to the beach for the week. My parents have a place in the Outer Banks that they never go to, and it's never rented in the off-season."

"It sounds great. Maybe I can cancel my appointments on Thursday and Friday, and we can take a long weekend."

She pushes up with her arms, so Jon has a good view of her front. "I thought we were gonna say, 'What the fuck.' Remember? I don't want to jinx it, but I think it might be the best idea I've ever had."

He smiles, his eyes wide. "Lemme get my phone." He slides out from under her and walks to the kitchen.

"Nice ass," she says.

He looks over his shoulder with a smirk. He pulls his phone from the charger and moves back to the bed. Morgan is propped up on her side, soaking up the view. He climbs into the warmth of her embrace, his phone in hand. He flips it open, dials, and puts it to his ear.

"Yeah," Chad says.

"You asleep?" Jon says.

"Why you callin' so early?"

"Because you need to get up and get to work."

"What are you talkin' about?" Chad's voice is clearer.

"I'm taking a vacation, so you have two jobs going on today and three appointments. Monday's are busy, so you better get moving."

Morgan covers her mouth to stop the giggles from spilling out.

"You can't do this. You have to put in for vacation time."

"I'm putting in for this week right now, and there's not a damn thing you can do about it."

"I'm not gonna do your job for you. You need to come in and take care of your stuff today and reschedule your appointments. You can take the rest of the week, if you need to."

"Here's the thing, Chad. Do it or don't do it. I really don't give a fuck. I'm not the one who needs the money to maintain a lifestyle. So take care of the appointments and my jobs or not. If you don't, I'll take next week off too."

"I'll fuckin' fire you then."

"Go right ahead. I still get 30 percent of the profits, and I don't have to work. Maybe I'll just quit, save you the trouble. Good luck finding someone to do my job."

The line goes silent.

"Fine, you don't have to be such a prick," Chad says. "If you had just given me some notice … Can you at least keep your radio on, so I can reach you with questions?"

"Umm, … no."

Jon flips the phone shut, turns it off, and skims it across the floor toward the kitchen. Morgan climbs on top, straddling him. She grins and sweeps the strands of dark hair from her face, revealing sparkling blue eyes in the early morning light.

"This is a bit better than work, don't you think?" she says.

+++

Jon moves clothes from the filing cabinet to an empty backpack. He places his toiletries in a Ziploc bag. A cooler half filled with produce sits open on the table. Morgan enters with a willow basket full of raspberries, strawberries, cherries, lettuce, and sugar snap peas.

"There's more out there," she says, as she heaves the basket on the kitchen table.

"There's always more than I can use. I'll call Oscar and Claudia, and let them know. They like to come by and pick."

Jon carries the cooler; Morgan carries the backpack and a sleeping bag. They put most of their gear behind the truck seat.

"We have two stops," Jon says, as he starts the truck. "We have to get your things from the lake house, and I need to stop by my mother's. We should probably do the lake house first. My mother doesn't get up early."

Jon pulls into the circular driveway of the stone mansion. A trash can sits by the curb, filled to the brim. They breathe a sigh of relief that Morgan's Acura is the only car in the driveway. They stride up to the front door. She grabs the handle and looks at Jon with her brow furrowed.

"It's locked," she says.

"Let's check the back."

They walk around the side, down the steep embankment, to the steps. They climb over the railing and ascend the steps to the deck. They try the handles of the glass back doors. Morgan tries pushing up a few windows.

"Shit," she says. "My keys are in there, not to mention my purse, and all my non-Target clothes."

"Is there an alarm?"

Morgan shakes her head. "Why?"

"We could break one of those glass squares next to the door handle and unlock it. The repair wouldn't be that expensive. I know a glass guy. I could call him to fix it."

"Fuck that. Leave it broken. Let them be reminded that bad things can happen, even in their fantasy world."

Jon grabs the skimmer from the hot tub. He lines up the metal handle and jabs the glass square. Jagged pieces of glass fall just inside the door. A few pieces stick to the frame. He knocks off those pieces and reaches through, unlocking the door.

"I should have worn gloves," Jon says. "What if your parents see the door and call the cops? If they dust for prints, they'll find mine. We should really fix it."

She frowns. "You worry too much. If anyone says anything, I'll tell them the truth. I needed my stuff."

They walk to her room. Jon sits on the bed, while she moves her clothing from the dresser and the closet to her suitcase.

"Is there anything I can do?" he asks.

"Can you check the kitchen? See if there's any food we can take?"

Jon looks at her with his eyebrows raised.

"It's gonna go bad if we don't take it."

Jon finds an empty wine box with handles cut into the sides. He removes the cardboard separators and fills the box with bread, cheese, peanut butter, jelly, a bottle of wine, two water bottles, a couple boxes of crackers, and some chocolate. He can hear the roll of the suitcase wheels on the wood floor as Morgan approaches, packed and ready, as if she's on a world tour. She wears a light blue cotton dress, with a skinny red belt cinched around her waist and sunglasses on top of her head.

"You look nice," he says.

She frowns and looks inside the wine box. "You found chocolate," she says with a grin.

She opens a couple drawers in the kitchen. She rifles through one with keys, reading the tags.

"Ha," she says, "here it is."

"Why would your parents keep keys to a vacation house at a vacation house?"

"They wanted to be able to go straight from the lake to the beach, if they wanted to."

Jon chuckles. "Yeah, I hate having to stop off at my mansion on the way from my lake house to my beach house."

She grins. "Rich-people problems. What can I say?"

They pass Morgan's Acura with the food and her suitcase.

"I don't have air conditioning in my truck," Jon says. "You might be more comfortable in your car. I can still drive, if you wanna relax."

She looks at her car. "It's been acting funny. I need to take it back in. I'm afraid it won't make it. Besides, it's beautiful out."

Jon dials his mom's cell phone.

"She's not answering," he says. "Sometimes she forgets to turn it on."

+++

They park in the driveway of the vinyl-sided split level, behind the Mercury.

"Before you meet my mom, I have to tell you something."

Morgan turns to Jon. "Okay?"

"She's pretty heavy, and the house smells. I just don't want you to be surprised. She has two black labs that don't always get let out, and there's some body smells."

Morgan scrunches up her nose. "Body smells?"

"I don't wanna get graphic, but I doubt she gets all the crevices. I just wanted to prepare you, so you would be more comfortable, and then she'd be less self-conscious."

"It's not a big deal. I teach high school kids. I've had a few who smell pretty bad."

Jon rings the doorbell. The dogs bark and ram against the door.

He turns to Morgan. "I don't wanna just walk in with company."

They stand on the stoop in awkward silence, watching the door shake from the dogs. The door cracks open, and a blob of a round face peeks around the corner.

"What are you doin' here so early?" Betsy asks.

It is lunchtime, Jon thinks.

"I tried to call, but you must have your phone off. I just wanted to let you know that I'm not gonna make our dinner tonight, and I'll be gone this week."

"Well, come on in then, and tell your old mom what's goin' on."

She opens the door and trudges up the steps, her heavy breathing audible from the front door. Jon and Morgan step inside, the smell of shit, grease, and armpits smacking them in the face after breathing in the sweet smells of spring on the ride over. Morgan winces. The dogs freak at the sight of an unfamiliar face. They try to jump on her, their tails wagging. Morgan catches one by the paws, holding him up on his hind legs, like they're dancing.

"Who's a good boy?" she says.

Jon grins at the dance partners.

The black lab's tail smacks back and forth. She puts him down, and pets them both on the head and neck. The dogs calm, and Jon and Morgan make their way upstairs to the living room.

Betsy sits on the sectional, her familiar spot sunken in. Her light green frock of a nightgown covers everything except her feet. Her toenails are yellow from the fungus growing underneath, and even from a distance emit a corn chip smell. A dog with a wreath around his neck is paused on the television.

"I'm gonna leave this on the table," Jon says to Betsy, holding up an envelope.

Morgan stands behind Jon, trying not to touch anything as they approach the living room.

"So who's your pretty young friend?" Betsy says.

"This is Morgan," Jon says, stepping aside, so his mother can see Morgan.

"Well, hi there, Morgan. Ain't you just the prettiest little thing? I used to look like you. Can you believe that?"

"It's nice to meet you, Mrs. Porter."

Betsy laughs. "I never was a Mrs. Porter—Ms. Porter but not Mrs. You can call me Betsy."

"We should get going," Jon says. "I just wanted to drop that off before we left."

"Why don't y'all sit for a minute, since it'll be the last time I see anyone this week."

"No Dusty?" Jon asks.

Betsy waves her hand across her face like a windshield wiper. "He ain't good at stayin'."

Morgan glances around the living room, looking for a place to sit that's not soiled. Jon grabs a small wooden chair from the kitchen table for Morgan. He sits on the edge of the recliner.

"So, missy, how long you two been datin'?" Betsy says.

"We're just friends," Morgan says.

Jon winces.

"That right?" Betsy asks. "You gotta lot a male friends?"

"Just Jon," she replies.

"So, how'd you two meet?"

"I hit his truck with my car. Jon gave me a ride home. We just clicked. I really enjoy spending time with your son."

"Uh-huh." Betsy nods her head, narrowing her eyes at Morgan, as if she's a cockroach to be squished. "You don't seem much like a local girl. You live around here?"

"I'm just here on vacation. I live in northern Virginia … Arlington."

Betsy frowns. "I seen your kind around here, ever since I was little. Rich folks around DC come down here and slum it. I seen guys and gals do it. Then the vacation's over. They leave nothing but a trail a tears. A lot a marriages ruined that way. Rich folks don't care neither."

"You can stop now, Mom," Jon says, standing, his jaw set tight. "I really don't appreciate what you're insinuating. I'm not gonna listen to you insult my friend. Besides, I'm not married. Remember?"

"I bet she got a man," Betsy says. "Don't ya, honey?"

Morgan blushes.

"I thought so. Just friends, … my big white ass."

"We're leaving," Jon says, holding his hand out for Morgan. "I hope you can be polite next week."

"It was nice to meet you," Morgan says, eyeing the door.

"He's got a big heart, missy, but it's easy to break."

"She's a good person," Jon says.

Jon and Morgan step down the stairs, out the front door, the fresh air bringing relief. They climb into the truck and head for the interstate.

"That was a disaster," Morgan says with a frown.

"Don't worry about her."

"Maybe she's right."

"About what?" Jon glances over, then back to the road.

Morgan gazes out the window. "That I'm gonna break your heart."

"I thought we were just friends," Jon says with a smirk.

She looks at Jon. "We have an expiration date, and it's going to hurt like hell. She's right. You do have a big heart, and I don't want to hurt you."

"Listen, I know that this may not work out. You may end up going back to David, back to your life in Arlington. I get that." Jon looks at Morgan. "But not right now. Right now, I feel like you wanna be with me." He puts his focus back on the road. "Right now, there's nowhere I'd rather be than in this truck with you. Why don't we enjoy the time we have, while we have it? Nothing's forever, right?"

Morgan nods, with a smile. "You're right."

She takes off her flip-flops and scooches across the bench seat, next to Jon. She puts on the middle seat belt and leans her head on his shoulder.

"This seat is huge," she says. "I don't like sitting so far away from you."

+++

Jon stands at a diesel pump just inside the North Carolina border. Morgan skips over with a bagful of snacks and drinks. A couple local middle-aged men drool. She kisses Jon on the cheek.

"I procured three different beverages—"

Jon raises his eyebrows. "*Procured*?"

Morgan grins. "To obtain, to acquire, to secure."

Jon chuckles. "I know what it means. It just seemed an odd choice of words."

"I don't let my students use the word *got*, so *procure* is one of the substitutes I give them."

"I'm sure I use it—"

"You do."

Jon laughs. "You didn't have to think about that. So what do you *got* there?" Jon eyes the snacks.

She smirks. "We should have tropical drinks on the way to the beach. I have one with real coconut, one with mango that's probably not real, and strawberry-kiwi. And I *procured* some barbecue chips and a Caramello bar."

Jon resets the gas pump and tightens his gas cap. He glances over her shoulder. "I think you picked up a few fans."

Morgan turns around and blows the men a kiss. One looks down, and the other pretends he's peering off into the distance, past her ass, not really at her ass at all.

"Salt or sugar first?" she asks, as they pull away from the gas station.

They munch on barbecue potato chips and sip on tropical drinks, before graduating to squares of caramel and chocolate.

"Want the last one?" she says.

"You can have it."

She shoves the last square in his mouth, letting her finger rest on his lower lip. She puts the trash in the plastic bag and resumes leaning on Jon. They pass a minivan with seven stick figures on the back window, a roof rack on top, and a bike rack holding bicycles with their tires spinning in the wind.

"Did you and Heather ever talk about having kids?"

He takes a deep breath. "I wanted to wait a little bit after we got married, so we could be more stable financially, and then, when we were, she wasn't interested in kids … or me."

"I think you'd be a good dad."

Jon chuckles. "It's not like I had a father figure."

"Did you ever know your dad?"

He shakes his head. "Nope. ... As far as I know, my mother doesn't either."

Morgan sits up, looking at Jon, her eyes wide. He glances over, then back to the road.

"Was your mother ... raped?"

Jon shakes his head. "I know it's hard to see in her current condition, but my mother had quite a few boyfriends in her day. And I use the term *boyfriend* very loosely."

"That must have been really hard on you." She puts her hand on his thigh.

"It wasn't great. If I got in a fight every time someone said something about my mother's promiscuity, I wouldn't have got through a single day of school. I don't blame her though. She's got some pretty bad self-esteem issues. She had it bad as a kid, way worse than I did. Her parents were strict Catholic, rode her pretty hard. They kicked her out when she was sixteen, when she got pregnant." He glances at Morgan with a smirk. "That was four 'gots,' I think."

She smiles a small grin. "Was it you, the baby?"

Jon shakes his head. "She said she had a miscarriage. Said she had dozens of them. I guess I was the only one dumb enough to stick." He smirks. "I think that's why she's overprotective of me. That's why she was giving you a hard time earlier."

+++

Morgan cracks the window and lets the cool salt air into the cab. Waves crash in the distance. They pass house after house built on stilts. They see sand dunes in the distance, but the water is simply black, bleeding into the night sky. They stop in front of a lonely house, just beyond the protected wetlands. A Toyota SUV sits in the driveway, the lights still on in the beach house.

"Shit, someone's here," Morgan says.

"Maybe tonight's their last night?"

"It's probably their first night. Who the hell leaves on a Tuesday?"

"I don't think so," Jon says, eyeing the overflowing trash can. "I bet they've been here a week. Why don't we knock on the door and find out?"

"I don't want my dad to know I'm here. He kicked me out of the lake house, remember? I doubt that meant it's okay for me to stay at the beach house."

"We can tell the people that we have it rented starting today, see what they say. At the very least, they'll tell us how long they're gonna be here."

Jon and Morgan walk up the paver driveway. The lawn is more sand than grass. The house is on stilts, with room for one car underneath. The wooden siding is painted light blue. Loblolly pines shade the sandy yard, and bayberry shrubs hold the sand dune together in the backyard. They pass the Toyota with New York plates and trek up the steps to the front door. Jon glances at Morgan and knocks on the door. They hear hushed voices and scurrying. A bushy-haired man with a five-o'-clock shadow opens the door.

"Can I help you?" he asks. His posture is rigid; his hands are shaky.

"Yeah, we rented this place, starting today," Jon says.

"That's really strange, because we were supposed to leave tomorrow. I wonder if they messed up the dates."

Morgan narrows her eyes.

"Why don't I give the guy a call?" Jon pulls his cell phone from his pocket.

"That's really not necessary." He stares at the ground. "I'm really sorry, man. My wife and I paid for a week, but we wanted to stay longer. This house is never rented. It's so small, you know? Just give us some time to get our stuff together."

"It's late to be driving back to New York," Jon says. "Can you be out tomorrow by noon?"

"You gonna tell the rental agent?" he asks.

Jon shakes his head. "Don't worry about it."

Jon and Morgan tread down the steps.

"Problem solved," Jon says.

"We still have to find a place *tonight*."

They head back to the truck. Jon bends down and locks the hubs on his wheels.

"What are you doing?" Morgan asks.

"Putting the truck in four-wheel drive. I have the perfect place for us."

Jon drives around the dune at the edge of the wetland. His right-side tires start to sink in. He guides the wheel to the left, out of the muck, closer to the dune. They drive onto the beach, the sound of the waves crashing in front of them. He continues until the beach starts to slope down to the water. He puts the truck in Park and grabs the sleeping bag from behind the seat.

He holds it up. "What do you think?"

"Where are *you* gonna sleep?" Morgan says with a smirk.

Jon laughs

"We should have asked him to use the bathroom," Morgan says. "I need to pee and brush my teeth. I had way too much sugar."

"The beach is deserted. I'll dig you a little hole to pee in, and we still have water to brush our teeth."

They settle into the sleeping bag, lying lengthwise across the bench seat. Jon's on his back, with Morgan curled around him, her head on his chest, the sound of the waves in the background.

"We're gonna be sore tomorrow," she says with a grin.

"Still no place I'd rather be," he says.

"Me too."

He kisses the top of her head. "I … I love you, Morgan."

She grins. "I'm a sure thing. No need to turn on the charm."

Jon exhales and shakes his head. "That's not funny. I'm serious."

"I'm sorry. I really do care about you, Jon—more than you'll probably ever understand. Another time and another place, I'd want to marry you and have all your babies, but I need to leave *serious* at home for now. Can we just have fun, try not to label how we feel? I need to be with you right now, enjoy it for what it is. Can you give me that?"

Jon nods.

Chapter 11

Time Flies When You're Having Fun

The late-morning sun streams through the white curtains; heating up the bedspread and the inhabitants hiding inside. Morgan rolls off him and pulls the covers from her bare chest. Her breathing is still elevated. She flashes Jon a grin.

"You're on fire," she says.

"That good, huh?"

She wrinkles her nose. "Your temperature, you're burning up." She sits up on her knees and puts the back of her hand to his forehead.

"I feel fine," he says.

She yanks the covers off his naked body with a crooked smile. "I guess you just run hot." She lays back down, her head on his chest. "We should have some French toast and get back in bed."

He smiles. "I'm not gonna argue with that plan."

"Later do you want to check out the wetland trail? As many times as I've been here, I've never hiked it."

+++

They stroll along the elevated wooden pathway, like a boardwalk through the wetlands. Swamp tupelos, willows, and cedars rise at the water's edge. Gigantic grassy reeds, bulrushes, and cattails dominate the shallow water. Occasionally a plop in the water is heard, beckoning their gaze, but only ripples remain. Turtles are sunning on a piece of driftwood. The pathway is deserted and far enough away from the highway to feel isolated.

"This is nice," she says. "Are you okay?"

Jon nods and squeezes her hand.

"Are you getting bit?"

"Not after you doused us in DEET. I can't kiss you either. My tongue's still numb."

She smiles and kisses the air in his direction. "You can wash me later."

They stroll in silence, listening to the sounds of birdcalls and tiny splashes in the water.

"Are you having fun?" she asks.

"More than fun."

"Me too." She smiles. "The time is going by too fast."

Jon nods. "Time flies when you're having fun."

"When I was a kid, my weekends and holidays would fly by, but the school days just seemed endless."

"You didn't like school?"

Morgan shakes her head and stares at the boardwalk.

"I'm surprised, as smart and pretty as you are. What didn't you like about it?"

She glances at Jon with a forced smile. "I went to a prep school—all girls, you know?"

Jon nods.

"Anyway, I didn't get along well with the other girls. I was like a pariah."

"How old were you?"

"I started having trouble with the girls in middle school, but it went pretty much through graduation."

"They must have been jealous."

Morgan shakes her head. "There wasn't much to be jealous about. I was a pretty late bloomer, a tomboy. Anyway we had these cheesy middle school dances, and the boys from the neighboring prep school would come in. There was one boy, Craig, who this girl Debbie liked. Debbie was *the* Queen Bee. She was developed, smart, and she knew how to control the mob. The girls basically worshipped her, like she was royalty. So Craig asked me to dance. I normally danced with the regular boys, never the popular boys. Craig was definitely out of my league."

"He's probably got a beer gut, an adjustable rate mortgage, and a fanny pack now."

Morgan laughs and smacks Jon on the ass. "You made me lose my train of thought."

"Social hierarchy and the stud of the middle school, Craig. I bet he had a Trapper Keeper and a rattail."

Morgan giggles. "Stop it, seriously."

"All right, all right. … So he asked you to dance?"

"I said yes, and a slow song came on. They only played a couple of those for the whole dance. He had his hands around my waist, and I had my hands around his neck, and we were just kinda swaying. I saw Debbie over his shoulder, and she gave me this look of contempt that I've only seen a few times in my life."

Jon frowns. "I can see where this is going."

"It gets worse. While we were dancing, he whispered in my ear about sneaking out. I said yes, because, with the evil eye I was getting from Debbie, I wanted to get the hell out of there. So we went around the corner into the janitor's closet. I could tell he was nervous. I was petrified. We kissed. It was my first … probably not his. Someone must have told on us for leaving, because a teacher found us and dragged us back to her classroom, where we had to call our parents and tell them what we were doing."

Jon winces. "That must have been embarrassing. Your dad doesn't seem like an understanding guy."

"He isn't, but that wasn't the worst part. On Monday the head-master made an announcement about how heavy petting would not be tolerated at school dances. Who actually says *heavy petting* anyway? It didn't take long for the whole school to know it was me, and it didn't take too long after that for us kissing to morph into a blow job. Debbie used to sneak up behind me and act like she was giving oral sex to a hot dog or a banana. The cafeteria crowd would break out in hysterics. I just wanted to crawl into a ball and die."

Jon shakes his head. "Kids are cruel."

"I was forever branded as the school whore, even though I was a virgin when I graduated. Every guy who knew me tried to put the moves on me, figuring I was easy."

"Shit, Morgan, I'm really sorry. I wish I had known you then." Jon squeezes her hand and pulls her closer.

"Like you said before, 'It's stupid high school bullshit.'"

+++

Jon and Morgan stroll hand in hand on the white sandy beach, the late-day sun giving way to cool night winds. Morgan leans into Jon, a sweater covering the top of her cotton dress. Jon tugs her gently uphill to avoid the cool water of the rising tide reaching for their bare feet. Crabs slide into their hiding places as heavy human footsteps approach. Jon and Morgan watch sandpipers picking small invertebrates out of the mud each time the waves are sucked out to sea, then with frantic legs, running to avoid the crash of seawater as another wave rolls in.

Jon squeezes her hand to get her attention. She glances over. He flashes a smile. She squeezes back.

He thinks about the time they spent wrapped in the comforter of the queen-size bed. He thinks about how perfect her body fits into his. He thinks about her sweet smell of fresh pears and vanilla, the smoothness of her skin, the softness of her voice, and her beauty radiating from the inside out. He thinks about the raw happiness of being in the moment, being in love.

He thinks about sleeping in, staying up late, and the lazy days on the beach, lying on each other, engrossed in novels they would discuss at dinner. He thinks about the banter, the playful touching, and the intimate conversations shared over meals. He thinks about her nightmares that she never remembered—the nightmares that started midweek and worsened with each day.

He held her tight, told her it would be okay. He wonders if he was telling the truth.

"We should probably head back," Jon says. "We're gonna be on the road really late."

"I wish I could live in this week forever, just replaying it over and over again," Morgan says. "Let's not go back. Let's drive south to Mexico and never return. We could move to the Bahamas. I could write. You could build docks or rent jet skis or just … be with me."

"Sounds nice."

She looks beyond the waves through aviator glasses into the deep blue expanse of the Atlantic Ocean. Wind blows her hair into her face. Her skin is still a creamy white with a healthy bit of pink hues, because of her obsessive sunblocking. She stops, wraps her arms around his waist and buries the side of her face into his chest. He holds her in silence, swaying softly from side to side. She pulls her head from his chest and looks up, her blue eyes visible through the golden shades.

"I'm serious about leaving," she says. "I just want to be with you."

"So am I. If you're really serious, we need to do a lot of research, make preparations, get our finances in order, passports, tie up loose ends."

"We'll figure all that out when we get to Mexico."

"I don't have a passport. We don't even know where we wanna live. These are huge decisions."

Morgan lets go and steps back. "If you don't wanna go, just say so. Don't make excuses."

Jon's eyes widen, and he holds out his hands with his palms up. "Where's this coming from? There's nothing I would rather do than be with you. You know that. You were the one who wanted to keep this light. Now you wanna run away with me to another country?"

She crosses her arms and looks down. Tears slide under her sunglasses, just missing the corners of her mouth. "Fine, forget it."

"No, I won't forget it. I would love to move away with you. If you want to go to the fucking Arctic Circle, I would go with you, but we need a plan. Otherwise we might come crawling back one day with our tails between our legs, because we didn't figure out this shit before we left."

She turns away and pushes her sleeve under her sunglasses, wiping away her true feelings. "You're right. I did want to keep this light. I'm sorry. I wasn't thinking straight."

"What the fuck does that mean?"

"It means, I'm ready to go home now."

The enthusiasm, the anticipation, the possibilities, and the sheer excitement of being with Morgan on the way to the beach is the polar opposite of Morgan on the return trip. She's curled up in the fetal position against the passenger door. The long bench seat makes it feel like she's in a different time zone. Jon fiddles with the radio stations, keeping it low out of respect for her. He replays the sequence of events over and over in his head. No matter how he analyzes it, he can't make sense of it. It was the best week of his life. Why does it feel like a lifetime ago?

She stirs and lifts her head, rubbing her eyes.

"What time is it?" she asks, the first thing he's heard out of her mouth in six hours.

"It's a little after one," he says.

She scans the dark highway. "Where are we?"

"We're close, twenty-five minutes from the cabin."

"Can you drop me off at the lake house?"

His stomach turns. "Whatever you want," he says, as if he's her driver.

He stops in the circular driveway of the Stone Lake house. She opens the door before the truck is fully stopped, as if she can't wait to get away from him. She pulls the seat forward and yanks on her suitcase. Jon walks around.

"Can I get that for you?" he asks.

She frowns and steps back. He dislodges the suitcase and hands it to her. She turns and walks toward the house. Jon slams the passenger door.

"That's it?" he calls out.

She turns her head to the side, not looking directly at Jon. "Go home, Jon." She continues to the front door. She fiddles with her keys, her hands shaking. She turns the lock, opens the door, and disappears.

Jon stands in stunned silence, watching the house light up from within. He rubs his temples and walks around his truck to the driver's side. He pulls out of the driveway, his mind racing and his head pounding.

+++

Jon puts his truck in Park in front of the warehouse and office of Stone Lake Excavating. He staggers into the office, bleary-eyed and downtrodden after an eventful morning of racing between jobs and estimates. Karen glances up from her reception desk with a warm smile. Karen's a middle-aged empty nester who's in a constant battle with the scale.

"You're back," she says, grabbing a stack of phone messages.

"I'm afraid to look at those," Jon says.

She nods with a sympathetic frown. "There's about fifty, but some of them are the same person calling more than once. I put those together for you, so you wouldn't accidentally call them twice."

"Thanks, Karen." He takes the messages. "I'll be in my office."

"Are you okay? You look …"

"Like shit?"

Karen laughs. "I wasn't going to put it like it that."

"I'm okay. I just didn't get much sleep last night."

"Did you have fun?"

Jon smirks. "It was fun while it lasted."

He trudges across the dingy linoleum floor. He passes Chad's office, where Heather sits on his lap, and they giggle at the computer screen. It's an oasis filled with plush carpeting, faux potted trees, a mahogany desk, black leather chairs, and a framed motivational poster. The poster features a sailboat over crystal blue waters with the word SUCCESS in large block letters. Underneath, in smaller text, is the phrase *The difference between the doers and the dreamers.*

Jon opens his office door and sits down at his metal desk. He starts his computer and glances at the top message in the stack. He picks up the phone, presses a free line, and dials.

"May I speak with Mrs. Winslow please?"

"This is she."

"This is Jon with Stone Lake Excavating. I was returning your call."

"Melanie Healey referred me. She said I should talk to you about my project. I wanted to dig a pond on my farm, but I have no idea how to tell if it's even a good idea or where to put it or if there's any permitting required. Have you done this type of work before?"

"We have. The permitting can be a nightmare, but, if we keep the parameters under the requirements for DEP and the Army Corps of Engineers, it's not too bad. As far as whether or not it's a good idea, that really depends on the topography and the soil type. We typically have enough clay around here to make a good seal but not always. I would need to come out to take a look, and we can discuss pond sites, and I can give you an estimate. Would you like to set something up?"

"That would be great. We would love to have a filled pond by our Fourth of July party."

"I can't guarantee a time frame yet, but it's something we can talk about when I come out. If it's okay, I'm gonna transfer you to Karen. She schedules all the estimate appointments. I look forward to seeing you."

"Thanks, Jon. Me too."

"Hold please."

"Karen, could you schedule Mrs. Winslow for me? She's on line three."

Jon rubs his temples. *Forty-nine more to go.* He picks up the phone, starts to dial, sees Chad in his doorway, and replaces the handset.

"Got a minute?" Chad asks.

"Not really. I'm pretty swamped."

Chad's eyes narrow, his nostrils flare. "That was my whole week last week."

"That's been the past eight years for me."

"I'm not here to argue about who works more. I just wanted to let you know that I placed an ad for an estimator, to take some of the workload off your back. I would like for you to train whoever we get, since you know our systems better than anyone."

Jon laughs. "All the sudden you're concerned about me? How many employees have I seen come and go over the years?"

Chad shrugs. "I don't know."

"Enough to know when I'm training my replacement."

Chad shakes his head, his face beet red. "You're paranoid, dude. Why would I fire you? Like you said, you would still get 30 percent of the profits."

"If there are any profits. It's pretty easy to raise your salary and Heather's, do more shit at your house, charge your vacations on the company credit card, and justify it as a board meeting."

"I can't have you holdin' this company hostage with your shitty attitude. You pick up and leave for a week with *zero* notice, then threaten me into doing your job. It's not right, Jon, and you and everyone else here knows it. A lot of people depend on this company. It's not all about you."

Jon tightens his jaw. "I take one fucking vacation in eight years, and it's all about me? If it *was* all about me, I'd toss these messages in the trash and walk away." He holds up his stack of phone messages. "You and I both know I'd do better without carrying your dead weight."

Chad stares, blank-faced.

Jon stands. "You know what? At this point I really don't give a fuck what you do. Fire me, hire someone else, cook the books until the end of time so I never get a penny, I don't fucking care. Get out of my office, so I can do my job."

Chad crosses his arms and narrows his eyes. "You really are an asshole. You know that?"

Jon marches toward the door. Chad steps back. "You do realize I have nothing to lose?"

"Is that supposed to be some kinda threat?"

Jon shuts the door in Chad's face, and returns to his desk and his pile of messages.

+++

Jon flips through the last few messages, picks up the phone, and glances at the clock on his computer. *Nine, I probably shouldn't call this late.* He puts the phone back on the receiver, flips open his cell phone, and turns up the ringer.

"God damn it," he says, as he looks at the screen.

He punches in his voicemail code, 3-3-3-3.

"You have eleven messages," the phone voice says. "Press one—"

He pushes one with a paper and pen ready.

"Jon, you comin' to dinner tonight?" Betsy asks. "I have somethin' important to tell ya."

"Press seven to de—"

Jon presses seven, deleting his mother's message.

"Next message," the phone voice says.

"Oh, another thing," Betsy says, "I hope you're comin' alone. It ain't a good idea for your girlfriend to be here."

Jon presses seven.

"Next message."

"I'm worried. Call your mom."

Jon presses seven.

"I still haven't heard nuthin'. You need to call me. I got important news."

Jon presses seven. His phone starts to ring, the ringer setting louder than necessary. Jon glances at the number, exhales, and presses Talk.

"Yeah, Mom," he says.

"Where you at? I went to your house," she says, her voice urgent.

"I'm still at the office. I'm sorry I missed dinner. I got buried in returning phone calls."

"You get my messages?"

"I was just going through them. Can this wait until tomorrow? I really didn't sleep last night."

"It can't. I'm on my way."

Ten minutes later Jon hears the front door open to the deserted office, followed by heavy footsteps and heavy breathing. His mother appears at the doorway in an oversize jean jumper, holding a newspaper with a green sticker on the outside, indicating that it's from the local public library. Without a word, she slaps it on his desk. Jon's mouth hangs open, and his eyes widen at the grainy black-and-white mug shot. He reads the front-page headline: Disgraced Teacher Headed for Trial.

Chapter 12

The Court of Public Opinion

Former North Fairfax High School English Teacher, Morgan Anderson, 27, of Arlington, VA, was slated to have her trial begin on April 3, 2006. Officials at the Fairfax County Circuit Court stated that the trial has been pushed back to May 30, 2006.

Anderson was arrested in November 2005 amid allegations that she had sexual relationships with three students, ages seventeen, sixteen, and fourteen, while teaching English at North Fairfax High School.

Ms. Anderson resigned from her job, shortly after the arrest. She was released on bond.

"I knew she weren't no good, I just knew it, could feel it in my bones," Betsy says.

Jon sits in a daze; his eyes glaze over.

"I'm sorry to be the one bringing you this," Betsy says. "I know you liked her. If it weren't for bad luck, you'd have no luck."

Jon stands up. "I gotta go."

Jon squeezes by his mother's mass.

"Now just hold on a minute," Betsy says.

Jon ignores her.

"Don't you be goin' over there. She ain't no good!"

Jon stops at the front door and turns to his mother. "I appreciate your concern, but do me a favor and stay out of it. And I don't want you spreading this *shit* around town."

Betsy stands dumbfounded, her mouth open.

Jon runs to his truck and hops in the cab. He spins the rear wheels, kicking up gravel as he leaves the parking lot. He speeds to the lake house and breathes a sigh of relief at the sight of Morgan's Acura. The tires screech, as he slams on the brakes in the driveway. He runs to the house, bounding up the front steps. He tries the handle, but it's locked. He bangs on the door and rings the doorbell. He presses his face to the glass, looking in the dark house, but sees no sign of life. He sprints around the side, down the steep embankment to the steps. He hops over the railing, using his arms to help hurdle over. He runs up the steps to the deck. Jon grabs the handle on the glass door with the broken panel. It's locked. He reaches through, unlocks it, and lets himself in.

"Morgan! Morgan! Are you here?" he says.

He sees three bottles of wine on the kitchen counter, without corks. He slips down the hall to her room. He hears snoring through the bedroom door. He pushes open the door. She's wrapped in her comforter, in the fetal position. He approaches her bedside and can smell the alcohol on her breath.

"Morgan, it's me. We need to talk," he says.

She stirs and moans. "No, please don't take me. I don't wanna go."

Jon puts his hands on her shoulder. "Wake up. You're having a nightmare."

Her eyes open wide, her body tightens. She pulls back from his hands. "No, don't."

Jon moves closer and shakes her gently. "Morgan, wake up. Wake up."

She sits up. Her eyes and body relax in recognition of Jon's face. "Why … you … here?" Her speech is slurred.

"I was worried about you."

"I … so … tired."

She flops down on the bed and passes out. Jon moves a chair next to the bed. He sits, watching her for signs of distress.

+++

He feels hands on his upper arms, shaking him.

"Wake up. Wake up," he hears.

His eyes flutter, trying to adjust to the sunlight streaming through the open blinds. He can smell alcohol. He sees a form standing over him. The form comes into focus. Morgan's hair is disheveled, her mouth turned down, her eyes red, and her arms crossed.

"What the fuck are you doing here?"

Jon sits up, rubbing his eyes. "I was worried about you."

She glares. "You broke into my house. We fuck for a few weeks, and now you're a stalker?"

Jon shakes his head. "I know what you're doing. It's not gonna work. I'm not leaving you."

Morgan narrows her eyes. "Fine. I'll just call the police. I wonder how much you'll get for breaking and entering."

"That's not gonna make me leave."

She exhales. "I was having fun with you. It was a fling. I was using you as a vacation fuck buddy until I go back to David, which is today. I'm no different than Sally Walters."

His head sags, then he looks up. "That's bullshit, and you know it."

She shakes her head with a frown. "Jesus, Jon, most guys would love to have a woman fuck them for a few weeks with no strings. You're like a high school boy, falling in love with any girl who gives them attention."

He sits up straight and crosses his arms. "I know you're trying to push me away. It's not gonna work. You're not saving my feelings, and you're certainly not helping yourself. You need support, not isolation."

She puts her hands on her hips. "And, after three weeks, you know what I need? You don't know the first fucking thing about me."

"I know you didn't do what you're accused of."

She exhales. "Get out."

He tightens his jaw. "No."

"It's rape, Jon, and I'm guilty."

"I don't believe you."

"How stupid are you? They don't take you to trial if they don't have sufficient evidence to convict."

He uncrosses his arms. "There had to be mitigating circumstances."

"Jesus, you sound like my lawyer. You need to leave." She taps her bare foot on the floor.

He looks up at her, expressionless. "I told you, I'm not leaving you."

"Fine, I'm out of here in fifteen minutes anyway. Back to my *fiancé*."

"You're not gonna marry him. How long have you been engaged anyway?"

She looks down. "Two years."

"Do you even have a date for the wedding?"

She looks up and clenches her fists. "My future's not exactly certain."

"You were engaged for a year and half before you were arrested. Long engagements don't usually end in marriage."

Her jaw tightens. "What difference does it make? I'm not gonna be with you either."

"We'll figure it out."

Her face reddens. "You have no problem being with a child rapist?"

"Tell me what happened." Jon reaches for her hand; she snatches it away. "I know you, Morgan. You wouldn't do this."

She sits on the edge of the bed, opposite Jon in the chair. She puts her head in her hands. Tears leak onto her palms and down her forearms. She shudders, her sobs almost silent. Jon sits next to her, putting his arm around her. She squirms.

"No," she says.

He holds tight, ignoring her resistance. He pulls her to his chest; her sobbing intensifies. His body acts as a brace for her weight and a sponge for her sorrow. He kisses the top of her head.

"We're gonna work it out," he says, "together."

"I can't."

"Talk to me." His voice is steady and calm.

"I can't see that look of disappointment." Her voice cracks. "Not from you."

"You're gonna have to trust me."

She buries her head in his chest. "Please don't hate me."

He leans back and puts his hand under her chin, raising her eyes to meet his. Her eyes are red and puffy. Her cheeks are tear-streaked.

"I could never hate you," he says.

She drops her head.

He lifts her chin again, looking into her eyes. "Never."

She sits up, sniffling, and pulls herself from his lap. She looks at him, her blue eyes glassy, her face tired.

"It started over a year ago," she says.

He nods, listening, his eyes locked on hers.

"I had this honors English class for seniors. It was an incredibly bright group, but some of the boys were a bit socially awkward. I always tried to be kind to the kids who I knew probably had trouble fitting in."

"Because of what you went through."

She nods. "There was one kid, Paul, who was especially awkward. Very bright but socially he was a mess. He was actually a very good writer. Introverts often are. Throughout the year I went out of my way to be kind to him. You know, compliment him on his writing or if he wore a shirt or something that wasn't completely dorky. I was trying to boost his self-esteem, so he would have more confidence."

"Okay," he says. "It all sounds perfectly innocent."

She takes a deep breath. "Then, toward the end of the school year, I went out with that guy behind David's back. After …"

Jon raises his eyebrows.

"I was a mess. My family and David just wanted to bury it. I had nowhere to turn. Then Paul started asking to stay after school, for help with his writing. I let him, because I told myself I was helping him, but really I enjoyed his company, because I felt so alone. We talked a lot about his home life, which was awful. I really felt like I was helping him."

Jon nods.

"We never talked about what happened to me, but we did talk

about things with David, things I should have never shared with a seventeen-year-old. It was inappropriate and just … stupid." She shakes her head.

"And then what happened?"

"It was the last day of school. The kids had a half day, and most of the teachers and administrators left early too. He was helping me clean up my classroom before summer break. I remember it was hot, even in the morning. I had a knee-length skirt on and no panty hose."

Jon stares, wide-eyed with a frown.

"We should stop," she says.

"No. … I'm fine. Please keep going."

Morgan takes a deep breath. "He was cleaning my whiteboard. I told him how proud I was of him. I made a joke about the muscles in his arms. Again it was totally inappropriate, but I was …"

"You were being nice. You were trying to help his self-esteem."

Morgan shakes her head; her eyes are red. "No, it was beyond inappropriate. It was reprehensible. What if I was a male teacher who commented on a female student's ass or her breasts?"

"That's not exactly the same thing. You weren't commenting on his ass or his penis."

"It's still really bad. I don't know what the fuck was wrong with me. I should have seen it coming a mile away."

He squeezes her hand. "Did you get any counseling after … the rape?"

Morgan shakes her head. A couple tears slide down her cheek.

"I can't imagine it was easy to function at all," he says.

"I was dusting the windowsill, and I kind of stopped. I was in a daze, just looking outside. It was like I was there, but I couldn't move, like I was watching myself." She frowns. "I'm sure that defense is going to work really well." She exhales. "It all happened so fast. He came up behind me and started kissing my neck, and, for a moment, it felt good." She looks up at Jon, her mouth turned down. "I didn't stop him. I just froze. He yanked up my skirt and pulled out his penis. It all happened so fast. He rubbed it against me, and, almost immediately, he came, over the back of my thighs." She covers her face with her hands. "I'm so ashamed. You must think I'm sick."

Jon peels her hands off her face. "I'm still here. You haven't told me anything that changes how I feel about you."

"I froze. I didn't say no. I didn't stop it, and, when he first started kissing my neck, I'd be lying if I said it didn't feel good."

"Morgan, you have to understand. You were vulnerable, dazed. Your body was just reacting to the stimulus. Then, when you figured out what was happening, you froze. That's normal, especially for people who have been victims. You didn't do anything wrong. He assaulted you."

Morgan shakes her head. "I'm the adult. He's the child. I fucked up."

"He was seventeen, definitely old enough to know what he was doing."

"He was my student."

"Did you report it?"

Morgan shakes her head. "It was my fault. What was there to report? Unless I wanted to tell on myself. I was shell-shocked. I just tried to put it out of my mind and pretend it never happened."

"Did he go to the police?"

"No, but at the all-night graduation party, apparently he was bragging about it. Some of the boys called him a liar, but he had pictures."

Jon looks at Morgan with his brow furrowed. "He took pictures?"

"I was so out of it. I didn't notice that he lifted my skirt and took a picture with his phone of my underwear and the sperm on my legs."

He squeezes her hand. "I'm so sorry. I don't know what to say."

Morgan frowns. "There's not much to say." She takes a deep breath, pauses. "At the time I didn't even know this was happening, this rumor. The next school year, it took on a life of its own. Two other boys from my creative writing class were saying they slept with me too. A parent heard the rumor and went to the administration. That's when I was suspended, and the police started to investigate."

"The police should be able to break the other two boys, figure out they're lying."

"I don't know. My lawyer told me that they have expensive representation, and they only talk in the presence of their lawyers. I think they're too far deep into the lie to turn back now. I imagine they're pretty scared."

"It's all hearsay. There's no evidence."

Morgan exhales and purses her lips. "They have the picture."

"They don't know it's you."

"The birthmark on the back of my thigh says otherwise."

"That can't be enough to convict. They're just trying to get a confession."

"They have the clothes, from that day, … and some semen was on my underwear. It must have been a small amount, because I didn't notice it."

"Are you sure? It didn't come out in the wash?"

"I wiped the semen off my legs with tissues from my classroom, then I cleaned up a bit more in the teachers' bathroom. I felt so … gross after I got home. I was going to just throw away my entire outfit, so I never had to be reminded. I didn't want to put it in the trash, because David does the trash every Sunday night. It was a Wednesday, so I hid the clothes in the back of my closet. I had plans to sneak them into the trash after he went to work on Monday. The trash guys usually come around lunch."

"So what happened?"

She shrugs. "I don't know. I mean, I was depressed, and I hated myself. I still hate myself. I just didn't think about the clothes in the back of my closet. I left them there, and, when the police had a warrant for my black-and-white striped bikini underwear, they found them, and I was arrested."

Jon shakes his head, his jaw tight. "I am so sorry. This is so fucked-up."

"After I was arrested, my principal asked me to resign, or he would fire me. I could never go back to teaching anyway."

"Do your parents and David know?"

She takes a deep breath. "Just what's in the newspaper. I refused to talk about it. I was going to, when my dad bailed me out. On the way home he called me a whore, and I clammed up. It was like prep school all over again. My family and David think I'm this idiot who doesn't have any boundaries, someone who needs to be controlled and contained."

Jon squeezes her hand. "Please tell me that your lawyer knows the truth."

She nods with a frown.

"So he can get out the real story."

She sighs. "He thinks I'm guilty too. They offered a plea. He wanted me to take it, said it was our best chance."

"What was the offer?"

"I had to plead guilty to misdemeanor statutory rape. They would drop the felony charge, but they wanted me to serve the maximum jail time of one year, and my teaching license would be revoked."

"I don't understand how you can have felony charges and misdemeanor charges for the same crime."

"One of the boys in my creative writing class was a freshman. He was fourteen. Statutory rape with someone under fifteen is considered a felony. I could get ten years in prison. That's why my lawyer wanted me to take the deal. Even my parents said I should take it."

"And what about David?"

"He said, if I take the deal, he'd wait for me, and we'd work it out. I'm starting to believe I did it."

"Why didn't you take the plea? I mean, I wouldn't have either."

She shrugs and purses her lips. "Either way, my life's over. At least I can give them a big FU on the way out."

He wipes the corner of his eye with his index finger. "It doesn't have to be like that."

"I'm lucky you don't watch TV. Once the trial starts, I'll be a household name. I'll never be able to get a job of any type. It's over. I'll be like Debra Lafave."

"Who?"

"The teacher from a few years ago, who was arrested for sleeping with a fourteen-year-old."

"You're gonna get off. I know it."

Her jaw tightens; she pulls her hand from his and balls it into a fist. "You don't fucking get it. I'm ruined either way."

He cradles her hand, opening her fingers and interlacing his. "I do get it. You're terrified. You're alone. You feel like you've lost everything that you can never come back from this."

"Maybe I don't want to come back from this. There's nothing left for me."

"What about me? You can live with me at the cabin. It would be a great place for you to write."

A tear slips down the side of her nose. "And who's going to take a child molester serious as a writer?"

"It doesn't matter. Write for me. I love your writing. If I love it, I'm sure others will too. You could write under a pen name."

She shakes her head with a microsecond of a grin. "What now?"

"Trial starts the day after tomorrow, right?"

She nods.

"We call your piece-of-shit lawyer today and tell him that either he plans your defense around the truth or you're getting a new lawyer. And his firm needs to hire a private investigator or someone to get evidence that these boys are lying. Then we stay at my cabin tonight and book a hotel room close to the courthouse tomorrow. We'll stay together, and I'll be at the trial every day in your corner. Someone will be there who believes in you, who knows the truth."

She reaches out and puts her arms around his neck, pulling herself close. "Okay," she says in his ear.

Chapter 13

Into the Oblivion

Jon scrapes the plate of chicken and roasted vegetables into a Tupperware container and places it in the refrigerator. He washes their dishes and places them on the drying rack. Morgan sits at the table, staring out the window, into the dark.

"You didn't eat very much," Jon says.

She turns to Jon. "I'm sorry. I should help."

"It's fine. I'm almost done. Are you sure you don't want something else?"

"I'm really not hungry."

He walks to the table and rubs her back. "It's gonna work out."

She shrugs. "Maybe. My lawyer's worried they won't believe me, because I didn't say no. They'll say I kept the underwear as a trophy."

He pulls out a chair and sits next to her. "The truth will come out. You only need one of the jurors to believe you."

She stares into the darkness. "I guess."

"What time do you think we should leave tomorrow?"

She turns to Jon. "It doesn't really matter." She turns back to the dark window. "I was going to go for a run in the morning."

"I have a job starting tomorrow, so I was gonna get the guys started, then I'll swing by here and pick you up around lunch. Is that okay?"

She nods. "That's fine."

Jon wipes his hands on a towel and hangs it on the drying rack. "I should probably pack."

"Do you mind if I lay down? I feel really tired."

"Of course. Do you wanna book?"

"Could you read me something?"

"Any requests?"

"You pick."

Jon crouches down, scanning the paperbacks lined up in milk crates along the wall. Morgan steps toward the bed with a slight lean, like someone's supporting her. She undresses, leaving on her white T-shirt and cotton underwear, then pulls back the comforter and nestles underneath.

Jon removes a black-and-white composition notebook from a milk crate. He pulls off his canvas pants. Morgan wriggles over and lifts the comforter. He slips inside, the bed already warm. She places her head on his chest and wraps an arm and a leg around his body. Her weight feels familiar; it feels like home.

"Are you ready?" Jon asks, opening the notebook.

She nods, her head still on his chest.

> I flick on my headlights and reverse the truck into the street. I put the truck in Drive and press on the gas. The gravel backwoods road turns into asphalt, and hunting cabins give way to luxury homes, as I come down from the mountain. After a hairpin turn, I stop for a rafter of turkeys. Hundreds of turkeys make the late afternoon crossing to their

nesting site. Some run across the road; some waddle, and some fly, afraid of their feet touching the asphalt. I hear the screeching of tires, and the crunch of metal and plastic. My truck lunges forward a few feet, as turkeys squawk and fly haphazardly from the scene. I step on the parking brake, exit my truck, and march to the rear of my vehicle, shaking my head.

The front end of a black Acura Integra is connected to my hitch. A young woman sits stunned in the driver's seat. She has straight dark hair, cut just beneath her chin, flawless porcelain skin, and blue eyes. It wouldn't be hyperbole to call her beautiful.

Morgan lifts her head and gazes into Jon's eyes. She leans forward and presses her lips against his. He places the notebook facedown on the edge of the bed.

"I like this story," she says. "I didn't know that you were an author."

He shakes his head. "I'm not … at all. After we got back from the beach, I was having trouble sleeping, so I started writing. I just wanted to remember our time together. I thought it was over. I didn't wanna forget anything."

"I'm so sorry," she says, her eyes glassy. "I'm sorry for being so awful to you this morning and on the way home from the beach. I'm sorry for being such a fucking train wreck. You are the *only* good thing in my life. You deserve better."

"Please don't talk like that—"

"No, listen to me, Jon. I'm broken. You deserve better than a fixer-upper."

Jon laughs.

She furrows her brow and narrows her eyes.

"I'm sorry. I'm not laughing at you. It's just … have you looked around my house? How about my truck? It would seem that I love fixer-uppers."

She starts a smile that fades before it can blossom. "You almost make up for everything."

"Almost?"

She gazes at Jon, searching his eyes for answers. "No matter what happens, I want you to know that I love you. I always will."

Jon smiles and presses his lips against hers. "I love you too, but let's not get all apocalyptic. You're gonna get off. I know it."

"Listen to me. If things go bad, I want you to know that I'm so sorry, and I want you to move on and be happy. You deserve to be happy."

"Morgan, seriously, you're taking a trip to negative town. I mean, if you really wanna go there, the worst thing that could happen would be that you'd get ten years in prison. I'd visit you. We'd write." Jon grins. "Maybe we'd even have conjugal visits. But that's the worst-case scenario, and I'm telling you that it's not gonna happen. I looked up that Debra Lafave. She didn't even get jail time."

+++

Jon slips his hooded sweatshirt over his T-shirt. His eyes are bloodshot. He spent much of the night comforting Morgan after a series of nightmares. She's finally sleeping. She hugs his pillow, a poor substitute for his body. Her cheeks are sun-kissed and her lips full. He stares for a moment. He kisses her cheek and her forehead. She's unresponsive, except for the monotonous breathing.

He kisses her one last time.

He parks in front of the office and warehouse at Stone Lake Excavating. Oscar's truck is in front of the bay door. It's being loaded with pallets of stone by a fork lift. Oscar stands with a clipboard and a pen, marking off the materials list.

"I think you have my job today," Jon says, as he approaches.

"Good morning," Oscar says, smiling wide, showing bright white teeth. "How's Morgan doing?"

"She's fine. Thanks for asking."

"I like her. So does Claudia. I'm glad you two got away. How was the beach?"

"It was nice, … quiet." Jon shoves his hands in his pockets. "So what time do you think you'll get to the job site?"

"It'll take me until eight thirty to get all the equipment and materials."

"Then I'll meet you there at nine."

Chad parks his Range Rover in front of the office, earlier than usual. He stomps to the office door at the same time as Jon, a stainless steel coffee mug in hand. He glares.

"We need to talk," Chad says.

"I don't have much time today," Jon says.

"It won't take long."

Jon steps back, allowing Chad to open the front door and enter first. Jon follows him into his office. He sits opposite Chad, a dark mahogany desk separating the business partners. Chad leans forward in his massive leather swivel chair, his Success motivational poster on the wall above his head like a halo. He takes a sip of his coffee. He's clean shaven, with a Stone Lake Excavating polo shirt tight on his muscular upper body. He pushes a piece of paper across the desk.

"I need you to sign this."

Jon glances at the paper.

> *I, Jon Porter have had unexcused absences from work on two occasions, one of which was for an entire week. This is my second warning. Pursuant to the employee handbook of Stone Lake Excavating, I understand that, if I have another unexcused absence from work, I will be terminated without recourse.*

Jon laughs. "Are you fucking serious? You think I'm your employee. I *gave* you ownership in this company, you piece of shit."

Chad frowns and exhales. "This is about what's best for the company, not only what's best for you. I can't have you showing up and leaving whenever you want. We have to be able to count on you."

Jon clenches his fists. "*Best friends.* Remember that bullshit you told me when I gave you 40 percent of this company?"

"It was a small company then. It wasn't worth anything. I'm the one who grew this into a real business. Without me, it would still be three guys and an excavator."

Jon signs the paper and pushes it across the desk. "I'm leaving early today, and I'll be gone for the rest of the week and next week too."

Chad's face turns red. "Then you're fired. Give me your phone."

Jon stands up and pulls the cell phone from his pocket. He winds up and hurls the phone at the motivational poster. The phone bursts into a handful of plastic pieces, and the glass frame covering the poster shatters, littering the plush carpet. Chad stands up with his fists clenched and his nostrils flaring.

"What the *fuck* are you gonna do about it?" Jon asks.

"Give me your truck keys," Chad says.

"Fuck off, Chad. I bought my truck with my own cash, before this company was even founded."

"You put it in the company name."

Jon yanks open Chad's office door. Two dozen employees mill around Chad's office, eavesdropping. Jon marches toward the front door. He hears heavy footsteps behind him.

"It's a company truck," Chad says.

Chad grabs Jon by the shoulder. Jon whirls around, steps toward him, and throws an uppercut to his stomach. Chad collapses, gasping for air, the wind knocked out of him. The employees circle around, wide-eyed. Nobody tries to help him up.

Jon stands over him, looking down. "You want my truck? You're gonna have to take it."

Jon strides for the door; his former employees move aside.

"¿*Que pasa, el patron?*" Victor asks.

"*Lo siento,* Victor. *Yo no soy el patron,*" Jon says.

Jon yanks open the front door and marches toward his truck. He hears hurried footsteps behind him.

"Jon," Oscar says.

Jon stops and turns around.

"You okay?"

Jon nods. "I'm fine. I won't be working here anymore though."

"We heard."

"I figured."

"What are you going to do now?" Oscar asks.

"I'm gonna be with Morgan."

"What about your job?"

Jon shakes his head. "It doesn't matter."

Oscar frowns. "This is *your* company."

Jon's smile is stiff. "I'll call you next week. Don't call me. My phone's in pieces in Chad's office."

Jon pulls into the gravel driveway of his cabin, the morning sun streaming between the trees. He smiles at the thought of climbing back into bed with Morgan. *It's gonna be a beautiful day.*

He opens the side door of the cabin and tiptoes inside. He looks at the bed. … It's made. He exits the back door, eyeing the outhouse. He hears rustling on the overgrown trail beyond the garden fence. He sees Morgan running, two hundred yards away, moving up the mountain trail. A wave of relief washes over him. He strolls back inside, to the kitchen. A single envelope lies in the middle of the kitchen table. The front reads "Jon" in Morgan's loopy cursive.

Jon sits, his legs feeling weak. *This must be my Dear Jon letter, my regret-to-inform-you-that-I-don't-really-love-you letter.* His fingers tremble as he slides a digit under the flap, ripping the seal. He pulls a single piece of paper from the envelope. It's nearly filled with neat loopy cursive. He scans the first few lines.

He rises from the chair, like he was shot from a cannon. He jerks open the side door, and sprints past the garden and the outhouse, up the overgrown trail. His legs burn; they feel heavy with his steel-tipped boots. He races up the rocky mountainside, ignoring the pain in his legs, his knee, and his heavy breathing. He hears the pitter-patter of agile steps and the rustle of Morgan brushing against the plants on the overgrown path. He glances up the windy trail but sees no sign of her. Yet the sounds of her steps are getting closer. A surge of adrenaline pushes him faster.

"Morgan!" he says with a valuable breath.

He sees a flash of white fifty yards ahead. He runs faster; his legs are rubbery, and he starts to wheeze. He's closing in, thirty yards away. He can see the muscles in her calves flex as she pushes off the rocks. Her breathing is elevated but controlled. *It's not too late.* He tries to contain his wheezing, his lungs' desperate attempts for more air. He focuses on her legs. Despite his stiffness and pain, he's gaining ground. Twenty yards away, … ten yards away. His left boot catches on a tree root; his knee locks up, and searing pain incapacitates his leg. He drops, his hip and elbow banging against the rocks.

"Morgan!"

She stops and turns around, her chest moving up and down with each gulp of air, and her dark hair matted with sweat to the side of her head. Her cheeks are red, and her eyes are wet.

"Please don't," he says.

Tears spill out of her eyes. "I'm sorry. I can't."

She turns and continues her run up the path to oblivion.

"Stop, please!" he says, as he staggers to his feet.

He hobbles up the path, unable to put his full weight on his throbbing knee. He reaches the crest of the mountain, and the path levels. He hobbles faster, almost a jog, every other step sending shooting pain through his leg. The stone wall looms large. He limps to the wall and hobbles up the makeshift stone ladder to the skinny opening between the boulders. He turns his body sideways and shimmies between the massive stones. He yells for Morgan.

"Morgan, wait! Please just give me a minute. I'm almost there. Just hold on. Just hold on. I'm almost there."

Jon emerges from the crevice, onto the rocky ledge. Sunlight warms his face. It's quiet. Wind nudges the tree leaves, and birds sing in the distance. The sky is bright blue, cloudless. The tree-covered mountains are green and lush, reflected as a perfect replica in the lake.

Jon rushes to the edge, his heart pounding. He looks over, his toes resting on air. He closes his eyes, holding them tight. He opens his eyes, and tears drip over the edge into the oblivion. He's catatonic. His chest and throat tighten. He leans forward. *It would be so easy. One step. That's all it takes. Get it over with. Do it. Do it, you fucking coward! Do it!*

He staggers back and sits on the ground, leaning against the bench-size rock. He straightens his legs; his head sags, and tears drip on his dusty pants, creating tiny ponds in a sea of stone dust. His body trembles with each sob. The image, her image, is the only thing he can see when he shuts his eyes. Her lifeless body on the jagged rocks below, her leg contorted, as if her knee could rotate 360 degrees, her blue eyes wide open, and an expanding pool of blood around her head.

Chapter 14

Truth

J on sits at his kitchen table, his left leg held out straight. His head hangs, as he rubs his red eyes and massages his temples. He lifts his head, exhales, and reaches for the note. He stares at the loopy cursive, the last words she would ever write.

Jon,

If you already know what happened to me, keep reading. If you don't, you can find me at the bottom of the secret spot.

My biggest regret in life, and I have lots of regrets, is that I hurt you. That was never my intention. I wanted to keep my distance, but I was selfish. I wanted to spend my last days on earth with you. I thought about how cruel I was, by getting closer to you, but I was trying to live in the moment, a moment with no past and no future.

I had planned on ending it the night I crashed into your truck. I was looking for a good place to yank the wheel and end it in an instant: a bridge, a rock wall, or an oncoming dump truck. I was driving like a maniac. I slammed on my brakes when I saw you, because I knew it wouldn't be a fatal crash. With the corner, I was going too slow. Our little fender bender woke me from my suicidal trance. Later that night, when you took me home, I knew I should stay away, but you were so easy to talk to. It had been a long time since I had talked to someone without feeling their judgment and disappointment. You looked at me like I was good, like I was special. It was intoxicating.

I know you're probably wondering why I left, if things were so great. Well, Jon, things really weren't so great. They were great with you; the rest of my life was in shambles. I truly was a broken person, broken beyond repair. If I had stayed, I would have taken you down with me. I wouldn't have been able to keep up the facade. Eventually you would have seen what a depressed, angry, awful person I really was. I wanted to leave you with the good, shelter you from the bad. Selfishly I wanted to leave knowing someone loved me.

Please know that I am so sorry. Another place and another time, I would have taken you to New Zealand or Bermuda or Mexico or wherever we decided to go. Under different circumstances, we would have been happy. Please know that I love you; and, whatever you do, please understand that this was inevitable. There was absolutely nothing you could have done to stop it.

One final parting gift: You have a lot to offer. Don't settle. Don't settle for a town with bad memories. Don't settle for being some rich woman's plaything. Don't settle for women like Heather or friends like Chad. You

*can do so much better. This last bit, I say to you with
the utmost care and concern. A mother is supposed to
take care of her son. I get the sense that, for you, it has
always been the other way around.*

Love,
Morgan

Thump, thump, thump. Someone bangs on the door.

Jon folds the note, shoves it in his back pocket, and limps to the side door. Two plainclothes detectives, one male and one female, stand stiff. Beyond them a half-dozen uniformed police officers mill about the driveway and nose around the outside of the cabin.

"Mr. Porter?" the female detective says. She's stout, in her forties, with short dark curly hair, a paunch pressing on her pantsuit, and a badge hanging around her neck.

"Yes," Jon says, stepping away from the door. "Come in."

The detectives step in the cabin, observing their surroundings with each step. The male wears a dark suit. His brown hair is slicked back. He's burley, with a barrel chest and a gut to match. He scans the cabin.

Jon limps to the kitchen table. His movements are slow and deliberate, like an old man in a retirement home. He braces himself with his arms on the table, as he slides into the seat. A rumpled, dirt-stained map sits on the table.

"One of you can sit," Jon says, motioning to the chair in front of him. "Feel free to grab that wooden chair by the bed, if you both want to sit down."

The female detective sits; the male stands with his arms crossed, looking down at Jon like the judge, jury, and executioner.

"I'm Detective Schneider," the female says. "This is Detective

Morrison." She motions to her partner. She pulls out a small spiral notepad.

Jon nods; his eyes are puffy, his face haggard.

"You called 9-1-1 and said that a…" Detective Schneider glances at her notepad, "Morgan Anderson committed suicide by jumping off a cliff?"

"Yes," Jon says.

"And you called from 41 Mountain Lake Drive, but this is 39 Mountain Lake Drive."

"That's my neighbor's house. I don't have a phone."

Schneider purses her lips. "No phone, huh?"

Jon frowns. "That's what I just said."

"Can you show us where she jumped, where the body is?"

Jon slides the worn map across the table. "I don't think I'll be able to make the hike for a week. This map will get you there, but you'll need a helicopter. It took me a month to find the place on foot."

Schneider glances at the map. "Looks like a treasure map. Who made this?"

"The guy I bought this cabin from."

"What is this place?" she says, tapping the spot.

"It's a lookout over the valley."

"You don't appear to be doing too well," Detective Schneider says.

Jon exhales. "What do you expect?"

"I mean, your leg. You can barely walk, and your elbow is scraped pretty bad. What happened?"

Detective Morrison glares at Jon with his arms crossed. Detective Schneider's eyes are open wide. She leans in toward Jon.

"I don't have any meniscus in my left knee, and, if I twist it the wrong way, it hurts," Jon says.

"Is that what happened? She hurt you?" Schneider says.

Jon frowns. "I slipped and fell. She told me that she was going running. I got worried and ran after her. I slipped and fell on the way."

"You seem like an athletic guy," Morrison says. "You slip and fall a lot?"

"The surface is uneven, uphill, and rocky," Jon says, his voice monotone.

Detective Schneider purses her lips. "So, Jon, what made you worried? What made you run after her so fast that you fell and hurt yourself?"

"I assume you already know she was supposed to appear at trial tomorrow."

Morrison stands stiff.

"We know about her trial," Schneider says.

"I went to work this morning for just an hour, and I expected her to still be in bed when I got back, but she was gone. I looked outside, and I saw her running up the trail. I called for her, but she ignored me. I thought maybe she couldn't hear me, but I think she did. Then I started thinking about how she's been upset about the trial, so I went after her."

"How did you know she was going to commit suicide?" Schneider asks. "Did she leave a note?"

Jon shakes his head. "I didn't know, and she didn't leave a note."

"So why did you run after her?" Morrison asks.

Jon exhales. "Because I was worried."

"But you didn't know she was going to commit suicide?" Morrison asks.

"No."

"Then why were you worried?"

Jon glares at Detective Morrison. "Because she was upset. Were you not paying attention? Take this fucking map and get her body before the wildlife does."

Detective Morrison steps toward Jon. "You need to relax, *sir.*"

"I don't need to do shit."

"Let's get back on track," Detective Schneider says to Jon. "The sooner we get our questions answered, the sooner we can find Ms. Anderson."

Jon nods.

"What was the nature of your relationship with Ms. Anderson?"

"It was romantic."

Schneider glances up at Morrison. "Did you know that she was engaged?"

"Yes."

"And that didn't bother you?"

"I would have preferred she wasn't."

Detective Morrison shakes his head with a smirk.

Jon narrows his eyes at him. "You got something to say, say it, or get the fuck out of my house."

Morrison grins.

"Relax, Jon," Detective Schneider says. "Let's be calm, so we can find your girlfriend's body."

Jon takes a deep breath.

"How did you feel about the trial and her charges?" Schneider asks.

"She was innocent."

Morrison chuckles under his breath. Jon pushes up from the table with his good leg.

"Get this fucking clown out of my house," Jon says, glaring at Morrison. "If this piece of shit doesn't get out of my house in five seconds, I will be asking for an attorney."

Schneider looks up at Morrison and motions for the door with a nod of her chin. Morrison puts up his hands in mock surrender as he exits the cabin.

"That better, Jon?" Schneider says.

Jon nods.

"They don't take you to trial unless they have some pretty good evidence."

"I am aware of that." Jon tightens his jaw. "She didn't do it."

"How long were you two … together?"

"Three weeks."

Schneider winces. "And you think you knew her better than the prosecutors and detectives in Arlington who worked on her case for a year?"

"She didn't do it. What difference does it make what I think anyway?"

"Maybe, just maybe, you found out that she slept with those young boys, and it upset you. It would certainly upset me. Maybe you found out up on that cliff. Tell me about the accident, Jon. Tell me what happened up there."

Jon clenches his fists. "This is the last time I'm gonna tell you this. She didn't sleep with any of them. If you say that shit again, you can get out too. I certainly wasn't upset with her."

"Was there anyone else on the trail?"

"No."

"Is it okay if we look around the cabin?"

"Not without a warrant."

Detective Schneider purses her lips. "I gotta say, not letting us search is suspicious." She stands and strides to the side door. She opens the door and turns, standing on the threshold, with a hint of a smirk. "Let us know if you plan to leave town."

Jon pushes himself up from the kitchen table. He hobbles to the sink, fills up a glass of water, and chugs it in a few gulps. He refills it and downs another. He limps to the front window and watches the police cars back out of his driveway. He moves back to the table. He takes the letter from his pocket and sits. He unfolds the note, reading and rereading her last words, trying to make sense of it all. It's evidence; he knows that, but it's the only letter she ever wrote him. *I don't even have a picture of her.*

He folds the note and hobbles to his makeshift bookcase. He pulls an old travel book from a milk crate. Jon remembers when he bought the book at a secondhand book store. He was with Heather then. They were going to visit a different place every year. They chose fifty places, one for every year they'd be married. He flips the book to New Zealand, shoves the letter in, near the binding, and places the travelogue back in the milk crate. It was just a fantasy. They never made it to a single one.

He takes off his shirt and his pants, careful not to rub the brush and rock burns on his forearm, elbow, and knee. He tosses the clothes into his hamper, grabs a towel, and limps outside. He turns on the spigot, and cool water pushes through the superheated black pipe on the roof, exiting through a showerhead dangling from the roof overhang. He stands back from the initial burst of scalding water before settling under the warmth. Coagulated blood loosens and flows into a drain that routes the water to the garden. He stands naked, warm water flowing from his head to his toes. Tears slide down his face, lost in the flow of the water.

He trudges inside, a towel wrapped around his waist. He hangs his towel on a bedpost and slips on a pair of boxer briefs. He climbs into bed, pulling his comforter over his body. He can smell ripe pears and vanilla. Her scent floods his mind with vivid memories. The highlights brighten and dim like fireflies in July.

The stunned look on her face the first time they met that had nothing to do with the accident. Holding her in the hot tub and telling her it was going to be okay. *What a fucking lie.* Her triple axel that barely made a ripple in the water. Her giving Heather and Chad some of their own medicine. Her softness as they made love in his single bed. Her breathing, her body pressed against him, her lips, pink and full. Her smile, warm and mischievous, always pushing him to go further, to experience more, to love more. The same smile that greeted him when she ran out of the surf, into his lap, as he wrapped her up in his towel. Her sun-kissed cheeks and her straight hair blowing with the ocean breeze as they walked hand in hand.

Her toned calves as she pushed up the rocky trail. Her look of despair as she turned around and said she was sorry, but she just couldn't. Her body contorted and lifeless, the life spilling out of her in a sea of scarlet.

Jon tries to go back to the blissful memories, but he can't shake the image of her body at the bottom of the canyon. He tosses and turns, opens his eyes, and shuts them tight. He tries to reconnect to her *living* memories, but he sees only death. He thinks of Arlington and what she was afraid of. He thinks of the people who hurt her. *She's gone, and they're out there. They're living their lives, and she's never coming back.* He throws off the comforter, dresses in jeans and his button-down shirt, the sleeves already rolled up, his shirt untucked. He grabs his duffel bag, and shoves clothes and toiletries inside. He locks the cabin and pulls himself into his truck.

He drives across town to a dilapidated strip mall. In the middle is a Latino market, flanked by a sandwich shop, a Dollar Store, a liquor store, a check-cashing place, and a Radio Shack. He parks and enters the Radio Shack. A few minutes later he exits with a small plastic bag.

He drives to his mother's split level, parks next to her Mercury, and limps up the steps. He knocks a few times; the dogs bark, and he enters. The television blares with Christmas spirit. He pets the dogs on their heads and tries to avoid their tongues.

"We need to talk," Jon says, as he pulls himself up the stairs to the living room.

Betsy groans and presses Pause on the remote. She's still in her nightgown, a family-size bag of Doritos as her companion. A couple orange streaks stain the light green frock. She glances up at Jon and furrows her brow.

"You look upset," she says. "That rich girl go home? I told ya." She licks each orange fingertip.

"She's dead. … She killed herself this morning."

Betsy wiggles and pushes herself upright on the couch. Her mouth turns down, but her eyes light up. "I'm sorry, honey. … Did you see her?"

Jon nods.

"How'd she do it? My money's on pills."

Jon frowns. "I'm not here to talk about it. I just came by to let you know that I won't be at dinner tonight."

"You been missin' a lot a dinners lately."

"I won't be able to help you out for a little while either. I'm really sorry, but I got fired today."

She sits up straight with her eyes wide. "Fired? How the fuck can you be fired! It's your company."

"I'm still a minority owner, but Chad can fire me from my job as project manager. I still have ownership, but that only pays if there's profit."

"He can't just up and fire people. You could sue. They gotta have cause."

"I missed some days without notice, and, according to the employee handbook, I can be fired without recourse."

Betsy's mouth hangs open, her hand on her chest. "I knew that damn girl would get your head all turned around."

Jon clenches his fists. "Don't say a word about her. This was my fault, not hers."

"I'm just sayin'. I still think you gotta case. What about that leg of yours? That happened at the company picnic. Remember, I got that settlement when I twisted my ankle goin' to the mailbox, when I was a secretary. That was good money too. Kept us goin' for a couple years."

Jon shakes his head. "I'll get another job, but it might be a month or so. You'll have to cut back in the meantime."

"Cut back?" Tears squeeze out of the slits housing her eyeballs and slide down her rounded cheeks, past her triple chin. "Cut back to what? It's not like I'm livin' in the lap a luxury here!"

"I'm sorry, Mom. I can't help you."

"You just gonna let your mom die here in this house? I got no way to get food, no way to pay the light bill or the water bill or the mortgage. I'll be on the street in two months."

"That's not true. Your disability can cover the essentials. You just can't be eating out anymore or getting on the Home Shopping Network."

She crosses her meaty arms. "And what am I supposed to eat then?"

"Go to the grocery store. Buy more sensible food, no sodas and junk. When I get back, I can bring over some produce from my garden. It'll be good for you."

"You think I like bein' fat? You wanna know why I don't go nowhere? It's embarrassin'. People stare and whisper. Kids point and say dumb shit. It ain't my fault I got a bad met-a-bull-rate."

Jon exhales. "It's metabolism, and I'll go to the store for you."

"I'm still gettin' my oatmeal cream pies. The oatmeal's part a my breakfast."

Breakfast? You don't get up until noon.

Jon bites the inside of his cheek. "I gotta go. I'll be back in a few days."

"Where you goin'?" Betsy asks.

"Arlington."

+++

Jon parks in a parking spot, labeled Visitor. He sits in his truck. The final school bus billows black diesel fumes as it exits the lot. He glances up at the sprawling brick two-story campus. Dull silver lettering proclaims North Fairfax High School on the building above the main entrance. He approaches the row of metal doors in front. He grabs a metal handle and pulls. *Shit.* He tries them all, then he peers in the window. Two female students are walking toward him, one carrying a case for a trombone, the other a stack of textbooks. The girl with the books turns sideways and presses her forearm against the door. It opens a crack, and Jon grabs the handle, opening the door wider for the pair. The girls breeze through and thank Jon as they walk past.

He trudges inside, trying to disguise his limp. He hobbles past the main office, not making eye contact with the administrative staff through the office windows.

"May I help you?" he hears behind him.

Jon stops and turns around. A frumpy white-haired woman in a jean jumper stands in the hall with her eyes narrowed and her arms crossed. He moves toward her with a smile.

"Hi, I'm Jon from the reunion committee, class of '93. I was told I could find yearbooks from '91 and '92 in the library."

"Visitors need to sign in," she says. "Come with me."

Jon follows the woman into the main office. She hands him a

sign-in sheet.

"I'll need to make a copy of your license," she says.

Shit.

Jon hands over his license. He fills in his address, his name, and his old cell phone number on the sheet. He writes *yearbook research* under Reason for Visit, trying to avoid putting details in print. The woman returns his license.

"Do you remember how to get to the library?" she asks.

"It's been a while," Jon says with a smile. "Could you point me in the right direction?"

They walk out in the hall. Jon clips a Visitor badge to his lapel. She points down a long corridor.

"If you follow that hall," she says, "it's on the left. You can't miss it. The librarian, Mrs. Muir, should still be here."

Jon gimps down the long deserted hallway, past lockers and classroom doors. He stops at a set of propped-open double doors. Overhead is a sign that reads Media Room. He hobbles through the doorway into a cavernous room, two stories high. Above are walkways with railings and more classrooms. In front are bookshelves ordered in symmetrical rows, round tables set in the middle, and a row of computer desks off to the side. A long, prominent wooden desk sits behind the round tables, with two computers and a single middle-aged woman. She moves books from a bin to a cart. She glances up.

"May I help you?" she asks, eyeing his tag as he approaches.

Jon smiles. "I'm Jon Porter. I was looking for a yearbook." He holds out his hand.

She takes his hand. Her hands are bony and cold, her grip soft. He squeezes softly and makes eye contact. She squints, as if she's trying to remember him.

"Trisha Muir," she says. "You look so familiar."

Jon laughs. "You must have a pretty good memory then, with as many kids as you must see."

She smiles, showing her crow's feet and crease lines around her mouth. "What can I do for you, Mr. Porter?"

"I was looking for a yearbook … '91 and '92."

She frowns. "I can show them to you, but they can't leave here. What do you need them for?"

"That's fine. I was just looking for a couple classmates. I couldn't remember their last names."

She leads Jon to the back of the metal bookshelves.

"Right here is every year in order since 1953, when the school began."

"Thank you. I really appreciate it."

"Let me know if you need any help."

She strolls back to her desk. Jon slides his finger across the bindings. He pulls out a leather-bound maroon yearbook with Class of '04 in gold on the cover. He flips through the staged smiles, friends with locked arms, goofy faces, and neat rows of uniformed teenagers on various teams, usually with a ball of some sort front and center. He slows at the rows and columns of head shots, looking for Pauls. He scans with his finger and stops on Paul Cannon. Underneath his name, his activities are listed as baseball. His quote says, "Chicks dig my dingers." Toward the end of the yearbook, he finds Paul Skinner. His hair is dark and greasy, his face red under his eyes from rosacea. His eyeglasses are tinted, definitely not sunglasses cool. He doesn't smile. His quote is blank, and his only activity listed is Book Club. Jon slams the yearbook shut and slides it on the shelf.

He exits the school parking lot with Paul Skinner on his mind. He stops off at the corner gas station and picks up a map of Arlington, Virginia. He sits in his truck, flipping through the index, looking for the public library.

Jon drives the congested streets of Arlington before parking in a mostly empty asphalt parking lot. He hobbles into the entrance of the colossal brick structure, with two stories of tinted glass above the doors. Inside, the high ceilings feel churchlike. The middle of the structure is open, with the second floor wrapping around the outer edge. Bookshelves are arranged in a circular pattern. A young woman sits at a welcome desk, front and center. Jon asks where he can use a computer with Internet access. She directs him to the digital commons room on the second floor.

He takes the steps one at a time, lifting himself with his arms and his right leg. He sees the glass fishbowl room with desks and computers. He picks a computer in the corner, away from the handful of people surfing the Internet. He types "Paul Skinner, Arlington, VA" into the search engine. He clicks on the White Pages. He pulls a pen and a scrap piece of paper from his back pocket, and scribbles down the address.

Jon parks in a visitor's spot in front of the two-story redbrick apartment building. He limps to the glass door and pulls. It's locked. He presses the buzzer for 3B and waits. He presses again. … No answer. He hobbles back to his truck and watches the entryway. His stomach rumbles. *Morgan would have brought snacks.*

Jon slouches in the truck seat, as he stares at the door with heavy eyes in the twilight. The sound of an old muffler startles him. Jon sits up, eyeing the source of the racket. A worn Ford Fiesta parks in the empty spot up front. A young man with khakis, a blue polo shirt, and a yellow name tag exits the microcompact car. His hair is dark, like his glasses. He shuffles with his head down, as if the world is standing on his neck. Jon steps from his truck and hobbles toward him, closing in on him as he pulls his keys from his pocket.

"Paul Skinner?" Jon says.

The young man jumps back with his hand over his chest and his eyes wide.

"I'm sorry, Mr. Skinner. I didn't mean to startle you."

"Who are you? How do you know my name?"

"I'm a friend of Morgan Anderson."

He winces and cowers. "I can't talk right now." His hand trembles as he tries to fit his key in the lock.

"She's dead, Paul."

Paul drops his keys on the concrete stoop.

"She jumped off a cliff this morning."

Paul bends down and picks up his keys, his hands still shaky. "I really can't talk about this. My lawyer said so."

Jon moves closer, stepping into his personal space. Paul steps back against the door.

"How do you know what I wanna talk about?" Jon asks.

"I'm not supposed to talk about *her* … at all."

"Don't you give a shit about the one person at that high school who cared about you? She's gone. There's not gonna be a trial. You can talk now."

Paul turns around, trying to fold into himself. His hand vibrates as he tries to push the key into the lock. He turns the lock and opens the door. Jon follows behind him into the hall.

"You're not allowed in here," he says over his shoulder, as he fast-walks toward his apartment.

"You can't get away from this. If you don't talk to me, your life is going to be pretty humiliating. I know you know what it's like to be humiliated."

Paul stops at his apartment door. He turns and looks at Jon's feet. "You can't come in. I'm going to call the police."

"Go ahead. I think they'd like to hear what I have to say about you. Now *open the door*. You're really starting to piss me off."

Jon pushes inside behind Paul. A shabby brown couch, a wooden chair, and a television on top of a trunk, with a gaming system attached, sit in the front room. Beyond the living room is a small kitchen and a single bedroom.

"No roommate?" Jon asks.

Paul shakes his bowed head.

Jon puts his hand into his pocket for a moment then grabs Paul by the arm. Paul flinches. "Sit down," Jon says.

Paul sits on the couch, guided by Jon, his eyes still on the floor.

"Stop looking at the floor," Jon says. "Look at me."

Paul looks up; his eyes are glassy and red.

"If you bottle it up, the truth will eat you from the inside out."

Paul wipes his eyes on his collar. Jon picks up the wooden chair, places it across from him and sits down.

"Tell me about your relationship with Ms. Anderson," Jon says.

Paul purses his lips. "I was in her Book Club and her English class. She was nice. I liked her."

Jon narrows his eyes. "Then why did you accuse her of rape?"

"I didn't. I never said she raped me. I wanted it. It's not my fault. I was seventeen."

Jon shakes his head. "I'm sure you did want it. But did she?"

"She liked me. I stayed after school a lot. She told me about the problems she was having. She said I had nice muscles in my arms."

Jon frowns. "You're still a virgin, aren't you?"

He looks down. "I've been with lots of girls."

"How was high school for you?"

"It was okay."

"Look at me," Jon says.

Paul looks up.

"Really? I mean it's been a while since I was in high school, but

I can tell you right now that you wouldn't get through a single day in my old high school without being picked on. What was that like, being humiliated every day? It must have been hard."

Paul's head hangs down, hiding his face.

"Ms. Anderson told me all about you. She said she felt sorry for you, because you're such a loser. She said she complimented you to try to boost your self-esteem. Your self-esteem is so low that you can't even look me in the eye." Jon clenches his fists. "Look at me, Paul."

Paul raises his head, and tears slide down his cheeks. He sniffles and wipes his eyes with his collar.

"You're fucking weak. God *damn*, you make me sick. If any girl is ever dumb enough to end up in your bed, she's gonna fucking laugh in your face, just like Ms. Anderson did. She said you'd probably die a virgin."

"She wouldn't say that. She liked me. She wanted me." He wipes his runny nose with the back of his hand.

Jon shakes his head. "You think just because a woman talks to you and is nice to you that they wanna fuck you? See, this is how I know you're a virgin. Virgins are always so overeager, thinking that any girl who gives them attention wants them. It's really pathetic."

"She wanted it."

Jon tightens his jaw. "Did she kiss you back?"

Paul stares at the floor.

"Did she move her hips on you or did she freeze? If someone freezes, they're scared. You of all people should know about fear." Jon speaks faster and louder. "She was a good person, and *you* killed her. She jumped because *you* ruined her life. That's how much she didn't want you. She had to kill herself, just to get away from the memory of *you*!"

Paul looks up, his face tear-streaked. "I didn't mean for this to happen!"

"You have a choice. You can tell me what happened, or I will tell the real story to everyone you know. Then it'll be like high school all over again. I bet you've got your eyes on a couple girls at Best Buy. They're gonna be pretty disgusted when they find out."

"I didn't do anything wrong. She was the adult. She wanted it, so I gave it to her."

Jon shakes his head and cracks his knuckles. "What exactly did you give her, Paul?"

"My … you know."

"No, I don't know. Please tell me, because I'm confused."

"My penis, okay?"

Jon narrows his eyes. "That's not exactly true, is it? No, you gave her a fucking semen deposit on her legs, because you're a premature ejaculator. And then you went around bragging that you had consensual sex with her, after you assaulted her. What kind of piece of *shit* does something like that?"

"Okay, fine. You're just gonna say whatever anyway."

Jon leans forward and grabs the scruff of Paul's collar and pulls him close. "No, I'm gonna tell the *truth* to anyone who will listen. So you have a choice. You can tell the truth and stop being a lying sack of shit, or I'll do it for you." Jon lets go and sits back in the chair. "Do you know why politicians come out and admit shit? I mean, why wouldn't they just continue to lie?"

Paul shrugs.

"It's because they look a lot less like a douche bag when they're admitting the truth, as opposed to getting caught in a lie."

"She *did* let me stay after school. She *did* compliment me. I'm not lying about that." Paul puts his face in his hands. "I didn't know. I didn't mean for it to happen like that."

"To happen like what? The truth doesn't involve leaving shit out."

Paul looks up, his eyes puffy. "She was standing by the window, and she was so beautiful, you know? I just wanted her so bad. She's all I ever thought about. She was the only good thing in my life, and I ruined it. I don't know what came over me. I was feeling good about what she said about my arms, and her smile was so nice. Nobody ever smiled at me like that. I thought she wanted it. I walked up behind her and kissed her neck. I expected her to pull away, to slap me, but she didn't. She didn't move at all. I thought she wanted more, so I lifted her skirt and pulled out my thing. I was so excited, because it was all I could think about. I'm really not a premature ejaculator."

"You were that day."

Paul nods.

"Can you repeat that, Paul?"

"Yes, okay, I prematurely ejaculated on her legs. How many times do I have to say it, jeez?"

"What happened after?"

Paul shrugs.

"The truth! She's fucking dead because of you, and you don't even have the balls to stand up and tell the truth."

"She was frozen there, and she was crying, okay? That's when I knew I did something wrong."

"Then why did you take a picture? And why did you go around saying that you had sex with her, if you *knew* you sexually assaulted her?"

He looks down, as if the answer were written in the carpet. "I knew it was wrong, but I wanted to have something to remember it. I didn't mean for anyone to ever see the picture." He looks up at Jon, his eyes wet. "Then I was at the all-night graduation party, and everyone was talking about who was a virgin, and then they were talking about who had the least experience. It was between me and the kid with Down's. Everyone was saying that the Down's kid got more play than I did. They said I probably never even kissed a girl. That's when it came out. I didn't mean for it to happen. I just wanted them to stop." Paul puts his head in his hands. "I can't go to jail. I'd be a prison bitch."

"If you go to the police before those other two boys, the police would probably be inclined to make a deal with you."

"I didn't have anything to do with those other boys. They're lying, but that wasn't my fault."

"Did you know them?"

Paul shakes his head.

Jon leans forward. "Then how do you know they're lying?"

"One of the kids I work with is a year behind me. He said some seniors figured it out, because they didn't even know what a breast felt like. Then they admitted it."

Jon raises his eyebrows. "Do you know these kids?"

"Not well. They play baseball. Tyler and George, I think."

Jon stands up and reaches into his pocket and pulls out a tape recorder. He presses Stop. Paul looks at the recorder with his eyes wide. Jon puts the device back in his pocket. Jon grabs him by his collar.

"Fucking stand up," Jon says. "What you did was unforgiveable. She cared about you. She genuinely wanted to help you. She's gone, and your sorry ass is still here. This was the point where I had planned to beat the shit out of you, but she wouldn't have wanted that. What she would have wanted is for you to confess the truth, learn from it, and be a better person. So you have a choice. Tomorrow you can go to the police with this information, or I will. For once in your life, don't be a coward."

Chapter 15

The Lies That Bind

Jon slides the key card into the door. A green light flashes; he turns the handle and pushes inside. He enters a short corridor; the bathroom is on his right. Beyond the hall, a single queen-size bed dominates the room. The bed faces a dresser and a flat-screen television. The motel room is dimly lit by a single lamp and smells like lemon Pledge.

He tosses his duffel bag on the bed, grabs the remote, and turns on the television. He flips through the channels, until he finds the local news. His eyes widen as he sees footage of the cliff face. *The secret spot's not so secret anymore.* He feels short of breath. He sits on the edge of the bed, his eyes glued to the image of a police helicopter lifting a covered body from the bottom of the canyon. A female voice speaks over the images.

"Former North Fairfax High School teacher, Morgan Anderson, was found dead today at the bottom of this ravine in Stone Lake, Virginia. The disgraced educator was due to appear at court this morning, where she was facing charges of one count of felony statutory rape and two counts of misdemeanor statutory rape. District Attorney Alan Mosely made the following statement earlier today."

A lanky white-haired man with a face younger than his hair would advertise appears on the screen behind a podium.

"What happened today is a tragedy, but let's not forget the real victims who were robbed of justice. We were prepared to give them the justice they deserved. The victims can take solace in the fact that she will never touch a child again. I hope this sends a clear message to any and all child molesters, male or female. My office will continue to pursue the maximum penalties allowable for the most heinous of crimes against the most precious and vulnerable among us, our children. Thank you."

+++

Early morning sun streams into Jon's truck as he drives around the two-story apartment complex. He backs into a space, partially concealed by an SUV, but with a good view of Paul's Ford Fiesta.

Two hours later Jon sits up straight, as he sees Paul shuffling toward the tiny car in his khaki pants and blue polo shirt. Jon cranks his diesel truck and follows Paul's Ford Fiesta to the apartment entrance and onto the main road. Paul turns into a shopping center, parking near the Best Buy building. Jon parks in the back of the lot. He watches Paul walk inside.

Jon steps out of his truck, slams the door, and marches to the store with a hitch in his step. The metal-and-glass doors slide open, and Jon moves through. Apart from young men and women in blue polo shirts, the store is empty. Paul stands by a register, his hand on the counter, talking to a short blonde, with large breasts pressing on her polo shirt. She looks around, picking at her fingernails, as he talks to her chest.

Jon saunters up to the register. The girl notices him first. She breaks from her trance and smiles.

"May I help you, sir?" she asks.

Paul looks at Jon, slack-jawed, with his eyes wide open.

"I should get to my department," Paul says to the girl.

Jon smiles wide. "You're not gonna introduce me?"

"I can help you … with what you're looking for," Paul says, looking down.

Jon glances at the girl's name tag. "Hi, Megan. My name's Jon. My friend here is not very polite."

"It's nice to meet you," Megan says with a giggle.

Jon turns to Paul. "So this is the Megan you've been going on and on about?" He turns to Megan. "He talks about you all the time. I keep telling him to ask you out, but he's a bit shy."

She frowns. "I have a boyfriend, so … you know."

Jon smirks. "Before you, he used to be obsessed with my friend Morgan. She was nice, like you, but, also like you, not interested. Then he sexually assaulted her."

Megan recoils and scrunches up her face, as if she ate something rotten. "Eww, gross."

Paul gasps and fast-walks toward the computers. Jon follows, limping to keep up. He walks within a few paces of Paul.

"You can't ignore this," Jon says.

Paul stops in the relative privacy of the laptop display row.

"I won't do it," Paul says.

Jon shakes his head. "Did you think I was just gonna take your word for it?"

"I have to work today."

Jon glares at Paul. "It's more important than clearing an innocent woman's name?"

"I'm scared, okay?"

"Do you think Ms. Anderson was scared when she jumped off that cliff? Do you think she was scared when she lost her career?

Do you think she was scared when her friends and family thought she was a child molester? How about when she was arrested?"

Paul looks at Jon's feet.

"Look at me, Paul, because this is your last chance. We can go to the station right now, together, or I will make it my life's mission to tell everyone you come into contact with what you did. Shit, I'll post the recording on the Internet, start a website. What's it gonna be?"

Paul looks down, silent.

"You really are a fucking coward. You'll be seeing me *a lot*." Jon starts to walk away.

"Wait."

+++

Paul braces himself on the railing, as he ascends the steps to the glass-and-steel high-rise. Jon opens the glass doors embossed in white lettering that reads Arlington Police Department. Paul shuffles inside. A young male police officer sits at a desk. Chairs line the walls of the waiting area.

The police officer narrows his eyes at the pair. "Can I help you?" he asks.

"We have information regarding Morgan Anderson. We'd like to talk to the detective assigned to her case," Jon says.

"Sign in here." The officer pushes the clipboard toward them. "And I need to see IDs."

Jon and Paul write their names, addresses, add their signatures, and show their licenses to the officer.

"Have a seat. I'll call upstairs."

Jon and Paul sit facing the desk, within earshot. The young officer puts down the phone.

"Detective Grimes will be down in a minute," the officer says.

The shiny elevator doors open. A short man exits, with a skinny blond mustache, a paunch, and a crew cut. Behind him is a bald man, tall, black, in his forties, who moves with the grace of a dancer. The detectives approach. Jon and Paul stand up.

"Paul Skinner?" the white man asks.

"Yes, sir," Paul says with his head down.

"Jon Porter?"

Jon nods.

"I'm Detective Grimes. This is Detective Jones." He motions toward the tall man at his side. "We're going to take you upstairs separately to take your statements. Mr. Skinner, Detective Jones will take you upstairs now."

Paul shuffles forward, his movements shaky. Jones leads him to the elevator.

"Mr. Porter, right this way," Detective Grimes says.

Paul and Jones step into the first elevator. Jon and Grimes wait for the next one in silence. They step into the elevator; Grimes presses 5. The detective leads Jon into a windowless room with a camera on a tripod, a metal desk, one chair on one side and two on the other.

"Have a seat, Mr. Porter," Grimes says, motioning toward the chair facing the camera.

Jon glances at the camera.

"You don't mind if we film this, do you?" Grimes grins. "Unless you have something to hide."

Jon shakes his head and sits down.

Detective Grimes sits across from him. "Why don't you tell me why you're here today?"

"I brought Paul Skinner in because he sexually assaulted Morgan Anderson. She did not rape him, nor did she rape those other two boys."

"Hold on a second, Mr. Porter. One thing at a time. How do you know he assaulted Ms. Anderson?"

"He admitted it to me. He came here to confess."

"He's a pretty docile young man, don't you think? The type of boy who will tell you what you wanna hear. Did you coerce or intimidate that boy to confess?"

"No."

Detective Grimes smirks. "I find that hard to believe. I've been doin' this a long time, and I've gotten a lot of confessions. I doubt one of them came out without any duress."

Jon frowns. "What's your point?"

"The point is that I'm a professional. I know how to apply stress without getting false confessions. The other issue I have is your motivation in all this."

"My motivation?"

"I spoke to Detective Schneider from Stone Lake. They're really concerned that you picked up and left, given what happened yesterday. Especially after she explicitly told you to let them know if you were going anywhere."

Jon crosses his arms. "I wasn't under arrest. I don't have to tell them anything."

"You *were* the last person to see Ms. Anderson alive. Now you're getting involved in our police investigation. From my perspective, you look suspicious."

"I didn't touch her."

"Detective Schneider said you had a romantic relationship with her."

"That doesn't mean I hurt her."

"First you said you didn't touch her. Now you didn't hurt her. Which is it?"

"This is bullshit. You have no interest in clearing her name."

"She's clear as far as we're concerned. You, on the other hand, are a person of interest."

"If she's cleared, are you gonna tell the press that you fucked up? Are you gonna arrest the kids who lied?"

"When I say she's clear, I mean to say, we're not gonna be prosecuting her anymore."

"No shit, she's dead!" Jon slams his fists on the table.

Grimes narrows his eyes, and his face reddens. "You calm down, or I will put you in cuffs."

Jon stands up. "I'm leaving."

Grimes stands up. "Sit down!"

"I don't think so." Jon walks to the door; Grimes moves in front. "Arrest me or get the fuck out of my way."

Grimes steps aside. Jon yanks open the door. Detective Jones stands by the elevator, watching the doors shut on Paul. Jon stalks toward the elevator, with Grimes on his heels.

"Why is he leaving? You're not gonna arrest him?" Jon says to Detective Jones.

"It's confidential police business," Jones says.

Jon shakes his head. "The whole high school knows those kids were lying. She'd be alive right now, if it wasn't for your incompetence."

"I suggest you leave before we find a *reason* to arrest you," Grimes says.

Jon grabs the door to the stairs. He hobbles down, using his arms on the railing to speed his descent. He fast-walks across the lobby to the outdoors. He sees Paul scurrying down the sidewalk away from the parking garage. Jon gives chase, jogging with a limp. Paul glances over his shoulder to see Jon within ten yards. He starts to run, his arms and leg flailing. Jon grimaces and pushes off on his good leg into a ragged, limping gallop of a sprint. Despite the hitch in his gait, Jon catches up. Paul's neck snaps forward as Jon grabs his collar and yanks him off his feet. Jon stands over him.

"What are you running for?" Jon says.

Paul looks up through bloodshot eyes and tear streaks. "I did what you said. Leave me alone."

"Stand up." Jon pulls him up by his upper arm. "What did they say?"

"They just thanked me for coming in."

Jon clenches his fists. "That's it?"

"I asked them if I was going to jail, and they said, since she didn't say no, and there isn't a live complaining witness, they wouldn't press charges."

Jon takes a deep breath. "Morgan was a good person. You took advantage of her kindness. Now you have a second chance. There are no second chances for her anymore." Jon shakes his head. "I don't know how you can live with yourself, but here you are. Don't fucking waste it. Be the person she wanted you to be." Jon turns and limps toward the parking garage.

+++

Jon sits in his truck, watching the North Fairfax High School varsity baseball team take batting practice. After practice, the coach addresses the team in the dugout. The coach dismisses them, and players straggle out to the parking lot. Jon exits his truck and approaches a thin young man sporting a maroon hat with an intertwined *N* and *F*.

"Excuse me, could you tell me where I can find George and Tyler?"

The boy points to two tall teens walking across the lot to a black Toyota pickup truck. Jon thanks him and limps along, intercepting the two.

"Tyler, George?" Jon says.

The teens narrow their eyes. They both have long, lanky bodies, one with dark hair and olive skin, the other blond with red skin. The blond carries a baseball mitt, the other a long leather bag over his shoulder.

"Yeah?" the blond says.

The swarthy one pulls off his hat, revealing a handsome face. He curves the brim of his hat and places it back on his head.

"I'm Jon Porter. I'm a friend of Morgan Anderson's."

The blond raises his almost white eyebrows. "I'm Tyler," he says.

Jon glances at the darker teen. "George ... I'm George."

Jon shakes their hands. "Did you two know Ms. Anderson?"

George nods his head. "I had her for Advanced English Comp last year. I was so bad at it, but she helped get me through the class. If she hadn't, I woulda been ineligible for baseball."

Jon nods toward Tyler. "Did you know her?"

"Everybody did. I just knew her from the hall," Tyler says. "My locker was next to her room. She would stand outside her door and say hello to just about every kid who walked by between classes. I never had her for class. I'm not in the advanced classes, but everyone says she was the best teacher at this school."

"Did you two hear what happened to her?"

Tyler nods with a frown.

"It was on the news last night," George says. "It's all over the school now."

"It's fucked-up too. ... Sorry, I mean, it's messed up," Tyler says. "Everybody knows she didn't do anything. Those kids were lying. Are you her boyfriend or fiancé or whatever?"

"We were close friends," Jon says. "I'd like to clear her name. I heard you two found out those kids were lying."

George smirks. "I knew they were lying from jump."

"How'd you figure it out?"

George shrugs. "It was really easy. I used to have parties over at my house sometimes, and those two clowns tried to get in. I let 'em in because I heard what they were saying about Ms. Anderson, and she was gone from school, you know? Anyway, I knew they were making that shit up, so I let 'em in, so we could have some fun with 'em. So I started grilling 'em in front of everyone."

"They knew some stuff," Tyler says. "Probably from watching porn, but they didn't know basic stuff, like even how to kiss a girl. That's how we knew they were lying."

"Do you remember what you asked them?" Jon says.

George grins. "Shit, we got better than that. We videoed it."

"Do the cops know?" Jon asks.

George frowns. "Yeah, I showed my parents, and we took it to the police station. They took it and asked if I had any other copies. I told them no, but I have a copy on a thumb drive. It's messed up because my parents were so pissed that I was having parties, so I got in big trouble, then the cops didn't do shit anyway. I thought we'd be heroes or some shit, get on TV."

"I'm not surprised," Tyler says. "Cops never do shit when you need 'em to."

"Could I get a copy for her family?" Jon asks.

"As long as you don't say where it came from," George says.

Jon follows the black Toyota pickup through the affluent suburbs of Arlington, consisting of brick and stone-faced houses with vinyl on the sides and back, and asphalt roofs that barely last two decades. Throw-away houses for a throw-away society.

Houses built for the short term but worth a fortune because of their proximity to DC. Jon thinks he'd rather have his cabin, his garden, and his mountain.

The Toyota pulls up along the curb in front of a redbrick-faced colonial with black shutters and a three-car garage. Jon parks across the street. The boys wait for Jon at the driveway apron.

"I appreciate you two helping me," Jon says, as they walk up the driveway.

"It's cool," Tyler says.

Inside, the grand foyer is open, three stories tall, with a slate floor. Jon follows the boys, taking in his surroundings as they walk toward the kitchen filled with stainless steel appliances and granite countertops. George opens a door on his right before reaching the kitchen. They descend stairs covered in white carpet.

"My room's in the basement," George says.

Downstairs, a black leather sectional is arranged around a fifty-inch plasma television. A gaming console sits inside an entertainment center. Wireless controllers and DVDs are strewn about a cherry coffee table. They walk through open double doors to a cherry bar, with mirrors and placards hanging as a backdrop, celebrating various alcoholic beverages. An open door in the corner reveals the white tile of a bathroom. They walk through a doorway on the opposite wall to a sprawling bedroom with a round king-size bed in the middle, illuminated only by the sunlight filtering through a few small windows near the ceiling along one wall. Tyler flicks on the overhead light. The far wall has a cherry desk with a laptop and a printer. George sits at the desk and powers up the computer. Tyler grabs a wooden chair from the corner and hauls it to the desk. He sets it next to Jon.

"You can sit, if you want," Tyler says.

"Thanks," Jon says, sitting, his eyes glued to the screen as icons appear out of the black.

Tyler rolls over a blue stability ball and sits down, bouncing slightly.

George opens the desk drawer as wide as possible. He moves papers to the side and fishes out a tiny black thumb drive from the back corner of the drawer. He places it into the USB port.

"Do you wanna watch it, or do you just want a copy?" George asks.

"I'd like to see it," Jon says.

George opens the contents of the thumb drive and presses Play on the video. The picture is shaky.

"It gets better," Tyler says. "I was trying to get situated."

The video steadies. Two scared boys sit on bar stools. The boy on the left looks young, like he still belongs in middle school. His face is smooth; he's small but chubby, and his hair is straight and blond like a little Dutch boy. The boy on the right looks older, but not by much. He's lanky, average height, with brown curly hair, and his face is bumpy with acne. He grows patchy lip hair that should really be shaved. By comparison the teens in the background and George standing next to them in the foreground are more physically mature and less awkward. The crowd is raucous. George says something to the two kids, but it's inaudible on the tape because of the background noise. He tells the crowd to shut up, and they do.

George presses Pause and glances at Jon. "Bret's the older one, the skinny kid on the right. Damian's the little fat kid."

Jon nods. George presses Play; the video comes to life.

"Come on now. We want details," George says to Bret. "I've been hearing this rumor at school but no details."

The crowd starts to chant, "Details! Details! Details!"

"Shut the fuck up!" George says to the crowd.

The crowd quiets. Bret looks at the ground. "We had sex with her," he says, "but I don't wanna get her in trouble."

"It's too late for that. Don't be a punk. Nobody's gonna tell," George says. "So what position were you in?"

"Just … on top," Bret says.

"Who was on top?"

"Um, … I was."

"Little man here said you were double teaming her. How did that work?"

Damian bites the corner of his lip and fidgets with his hands.

"Damian just got a blow job while I was doing her," Bret says, his eyes downcast.

"Is that what happened?" George looks at Damian. "You get your little noodle sucked?"

Damian's face turns red. "It's not little."

"You know you're still a virgin, little man. Blow jobs don't count. There's gotta be penetration."

"I did it a different day, … when Bret wasn't there."

Bret flashes a desperate look at Damian that says, *Shut up*. The crowd laughs. Damian smiles at their perceived approval.

"Did you grab her titties?" George asks.

"Hell, yeah," Damian says with a grin. "She had some nice ones too."

"What did they feel like?"

"They were nice, hard and muscular."

Bret puts his face in his hands, shaking his head. The crowd laughs, and George cracks a smile.

"Were they big?" George asks.

"Yeah, they were pretty big."

"Is that true, Bret? Did she have big, hard, muscular tits?"

"He's confused," Bret says.

"Confused? I can't imagine any boy who ever touched a tit being confused about it. I remember my first like it was yesterday. Unless you're with a bodybuilder, tits are soft, not muscular and hard. I think little man's lying, like a little *bitch*."

Damian's face turns red, and his smile disappears.

"This is why I don't let punk-ass bitches in my parties. It's disrespectful to the ladies." George walks closer to Damian. "Did you kiss her? I mean, I would assume you did, if you had sex with her."

Damian nods, looking at the floor.

George looks around the crowd. "Hey, Hannah, come over here."

A well-endowed brunette in a tight black skirt and a tank top saunters in front of the camera. She kisses George open-mouthed. He steps back with a smile.

"So, Hannah, am I a good kisser?"

She blushes. "I've had better." The crowd laughs.

George smiles and puts his hand over his heart. "You really know how to hurt a guy. Can you at least tell that I've had *some* experience with the ladies?"

She licks her lips. "Yes."

"What if I had never kissed a girl? Would that be obvious?"

She nods. "Very obvious."

"My man Damian is a pimp. Would you mind kissing him?"

Damian looks up, his eyes wide, his face frozen. Hannah moves closer. She leans in; he leans back, turning his head. Hannah steps back. The crowd boos.

"That's a first," she says.

George puts his hand on Damian's shoulder. "What happened, little man?"

He shrugs. "I don't know. … Didn't want to."

"I don't care that you're not getting any, but what I do care about is you coming to my house lying about Ms. Anderson. She helped me after school when I had her for English Comp. I would have been ineligible for baseball if it wasn't for her. We were alone, but she never gave *me* any special treatment. I'm not trying to be cocky, but I'm a pretty good-looking dude." George flashes a glistening white smile into the camera. "What do you fine young ladies think?" The crowd cheers in approval. "And what about these two? Would anyone here fuck either of these tools?" The crowd jeers. "I just find it difficult to believe that Ms. Anderson wanted you two dorks so bad that she was willing to risk her whole life." George moves into Damian's personal space, looking down at him. "Did you do anything sexual with Ms. Anderson? Tell the fucking truth."

"No," Damian says, his head down.

"That is so fucked-up," a girl from the crowd says.

"So it was a big fat lie then?"

Damian looks up, his face tear-streaked. "Yes, okay, just leave me alone."

"Someone get this kid out of my house."

A large teen grabs him by the upper arm and escorts him offscreen.

George turns to Bret. "So, what about you, Bret? Do you wanna tell the truth?"

"I never wanted her to get into trouble, but I'm not lying. I can't talk about it. My lawyer said so. … I should go." Bret starts to get off the bar stool.

George puts his hand on Bret's shoulder. "Hold on there. We're not quite finished with the cross-examination." George grins. "Damn, I should be on *Law & Order*." He turns around, scanning the crowd. "Hannah, come back here for a minute." The brunette wades through the crowd; a boy whistles at her. George takes her hand. "Hannah is my lie detector. Would you please kiss Bret here and see if he's telling the truth?"

Bret looks up at Hannah, wide-eyed. He wipes his mouth with the back of his hand. She leans in, closes her eyes, and presses her lips against his. His eyes are still wide open. She opens her mouth and slips her tongue in his. Bret pushes his tongue out, choking her, slobber dripping down her chin. She pulls back in revulsion, wiping her mouth. The crowd laughs. Bret blushes.

"Eww, he slobbered on me," she says. "His tongue was practically down my throat. Fucking gross. Definitely an amateur. I haven't had a kiss that bad since middle school."

George puts his hand on the small of Hannah's back. "I'm sorry to subject you to that. Justice is pretty gross and saliva-filled." He grins, looking directly into the camera. He turns and glares at Bret. "I think you're lying about having sex with Ms. Anderson."

"Whatever. I'm leaving," Bret says.

George stands in front of him. "Not until you tell the truth."

Bret looks for an exit, but the crowd closes in.

The crowd chants. "Tell the truth! Tell the truth! Tell the truth!"

"Did you have sex with Ms. Anderson?" George asks. "Answer the fucking question!"

Bret puts his head down and mumbles something inaudible.

"Shut the fuck up, everybody," George says to the crowd. He turns to Bret. "What did you say?"

"I said no."

George shakes his head. "Court adjourned. Get this douche out of my house."

George in real life presses Stop on the video and looks at Jon. "You don't look surprised," he says.

Jon shrugs. "I'm not. She told me the story, and I believed her before seeing this. But it will help to clear her name though. I appreciate you guys giving me a copy."

"You do know about the other kid, right? He's not on the video."

"I know. I have his confession on tape."

George pulls out the thumb drive and hands it to Jon. "You can take the original. I'm actually kind of freaked out having this, after what happened. Just please don't tell anyone I gave it to you."

Chapter 16

Death Favors the Living

Jon fights through bumper-to-bumper traffic to exit the Washington DC metropolitan area. He turns at the Stone Lake sign. He continues up the windy mountain road toward his cabin. He passes the sharp turn, where he met Morgan for the first time. He flashes back to all the signals he missed. He thought she was afraid for her life, but she was actually afraid of living. He thinks about it from every angle. *I could have done something different. I should have done something different.*

He breathes a sigh of relief, as he drops his duffel bag on to the floor of his cabin. He undresses, leaving his clothes in a pile next to the bed. He climbs into bed, rolls on his side, and presses his face into his pillow. Her scent has faded; just a hint is left. He tosses and turns all night, haunted by the senselessness and finality of it all. He falls into REM sleep just before dawn.

He jerks awake, a sturdy knock at his door. He sits up and places his feet on the wood floor. He rubs his eyes. Late-morning sunshine streams in through the back window. The knock is louder now, the door rattling from the force.

"Hold on!" Jon says.

He leans forward, and grabs his jeans and T-shirt off the floor. He stands with a groan, and pulls on his pants. He slips his T-shirt over his head. He runs his hand through his dark disheveled hair and hobbles toward the door. Someone knocks again, almost hard enough to take the hinges off.

"I said, *Hold on*!" Jon says.

"Police, open up," the voice says.

Jon yanks open the door. Detective Morrison and Detective Schneider stand firm.

"We need to talk," Detective Morrison says. He leans his arm on the door frame, giving a glimpse of his Glock and the sweat rings under his jacket.

Jon limps to the kitchen, leaving the door open behind him. The detectives follow. Jon fills up a glass with water from the sink. The detectives stand just outside the kitchen, blocked by the counter. Jon downs the water in a few gulps.

He turns to the detectives. "Want something to drink?"

"No thank you, Jon," Detective Schneider says. She's short and stout, carrying her weight around her hips and stomach. "What were you doing in Arlington?"

"Clearing her name," Jon says.

"Detective Grimes said you were pretty angry."

"Does that seem unreasonable to you, given the circumstances?"

"It is when you're interfering in police business," Detective Morrison says.

Jon exhales. "It's too damn early to listen to this blowhard." Jon looks at Morrison. "I would like for you to leave. You're not allowed in my cabin without a warrant."

Detective Morrison stands firm, looking at Jon with a smirk.

"Go on. Get out," Jon says.

Schneider nods at Morrison, and he walks out.

"I specifically told you to let us know if you were going out of town," Schneider says. "We needed to talk to you, and you don't even have a phone. It looks bad when you disappear like that."

"I'm here now. What did you wanna talk about?"

"Why did you break into the Anderson's lake house?"

"So Morgan could get in and get her stuff. Her family locked her out. I'm not sure if that was intentional, but Morgan didn't have her keys."

"When was this?"

"Not last Monday, but the Monday before."

Schneider flips open her notepad and jots something down. "Why didn't she have her keys?"

"She got into an argument with her family at her sister's book party, and she left with me in a hurry."

"Book party?" Schneider raises her eyebrows.

"Yeah, her sister's a pretty successful author, and she just put out a new book. They had a party at the lake house for her that night."

"What was the argument about?"

"At the time I didn't know exactly. Morgan's dad, her fiancé, and her sister mostly bitched about how Morgan needed to take responsibility for her actions."

"Was anyone else there?"

"Her sister's husband and her mother."

Schneider scribbles in her notepad. "What was Morgan's state of mind at the time?"

"She was almost comatose. She was like a child being scolded, like she was being beaten down."

"Was she being abused?"

"Not physically as far as I know, but, mentally, I think so."

"What makes you say that?"

"Morgan was date-raped a little over a year ago. Her family

wanted her to bury it to protect them from the embarrassment. I think they blamed her for what happened, because she was seeing the guy behind her fiancé's back. She also told me that her dad called her a whore when he was driving her home from bailing her out on the statutory charges. She was innocent, but her family didn't believe her. The cops were on a political witch hunt. Even her lawyer thought she was guilty."

"You don't think she was guilty?"

"She's innocent. I'm gonna prove it."

"And how do you know that?"

Jon shakes his head and laughs. "I don't trust you guys with the truth."

Schneider frowns. "You're not helping yourself, Jon."

"I'm not trying to help myself. Are we done?"

"For now."

Jon escorts Schneider out the door. He watches the unmarked Crown Victoria back out. A postal jeep pulls to the edge of his driveway to let the cops through. After the cops pass, the jeep motors up the gravel driveway, stopping behind Jon's truck. He hobbles outside toward the mailman.

"Jon Porter?" the mailman asks.

"Yeah."

"I have a certified letter for you."

Jon thanks the mailman, signs the form, and takes the letter. His stomach churns when he sees that it's from a lawyer's office. *Fucking Chad probably trying to take the truck*. He opens the letter and reads the text. He checks the date to appear in Arlington. One week from today.

+++

Jon punches the code, opening the gate to Lake Landing. He drives to the end of the cul-de-sac and turns around. The Anderson house is empty. He turns into a concrete driveway, five houses down. The driveway is empty. The two-story colonial is faced with a brick-and-stone combination. He stops his truck in the middle of the driveway, reaches over his bench seat, and opens the glove box. He pulls out a garage door opener and presses the right-hand button. The right-side garage door motors up, and he pulls into the empty space. Once he's safely inside, he presses the button again, shutting the door. He steps out of his truck, next to the BMW sedan. The door to the house opens, and Sally Walters stands on the threshold, smiling in spandex shorts and a light blue tank top, her tan breasts smashed together in a sports bra and her blond hair in a ponytail. Jon steps around the BMW and stands in front of her, expressionless.

"I knew you'd come back," she says. "I'm free the rest of the day ... and night." She grins and bites the bottom of her lip.

"I'm sorry," Jon says. "I didn't come here to start this again. I meant it when I said it was over."

Her grin fades; her shoulders slump. "What do you want then?"

"I really need to talk to you about Morgan."

"It's just awful what happened. Her family's devastated." She puts her hand to her chest. "Were you with her when she ..."

"Not exactly, but I found her body."

"Oh, my God, are you okay?"

Jon shakes his head. "Can we talk inside? I need to sit down."

He sits at the wooden kitchen table. Sally Walters fills up a glass of water, sets it in front of him, and sits down.

"Are you sure you're okay?" she asks. "You look a little ... out of it."

"I'm fine. I just haven't been sleeping much."

"I missed you."

Jon frowns. "Sally, I can't. I'm sorry."

She exhales and wipes her eyes with her index finger. "I know."

Jon takes a sip of water. "Do you know much about Morgan's past? You said you've been around the family since she was young."

Sally nods. "As tragic as this is, I wasn't entirely surprised. Morgan was a troubled young woman."

"Can you be more specific?"

"She spent most of her teen years depressed. Her sister always had friends with her over the summer, but Morgan was always by herself."

"You said you weren't surprised? Because of the depression?"

Sally shakes her head. "I wasn't surprised because she's tried this before."

Jon frowns. "To commit suicide?"

"Yes. … Twice that I'm aware of. She overdosed on her mother's sleeping pills when she was, I think, thirteen or maybe fourteen, and she rammed her brand new car into a telephone pole on her sixteenth birthday. They said it was an accident, but I didn't think so at the time."

"Why not?"

"Morgan had a rough time at that girls' school. Did she tell you about it?"

Jon nods. "She did, but I'm not sure I got the whole story."

"I guess some of the girls found out her family had the lake house, and they were being nice to her and convinced her to have her sixteenth birthday party here. Her parents were so happy that she had friends that they agreed to have the party catered. They even sent a stretch limo to bring the girls down. They scheduled her gift, the car, to be delivered during the party. None of the girls showed at the limo meeting place. The girls gave her a gift that

Friday at school and made her promise not to open it until her actual birthday.

"The Andersons had tons of food. The car was delivered. It should have been a dream birthday party for a sixteen-year-old. Her parents tried to take the blame for the girls not showing, saying that the limo got the meeting time wrong. Morgan knew better. She knew that the gift she got from them would tell the truth. That gift from those little bitches meant more to Morgan than her new car in the driveway. She opened the present, and it was a large black dildo. The card said something like 'Just the right size for a whore.' She didn't sob or wail or say anything at all. Tears were sliding down her face, but she didn't make a sound."

Sally sniffles as the tears come. "Looking back on it, I think she was used to suffering in silence. I remember she set the gift—if you can call it a gift—on the table next to her uncut cake and her car keys and walked to her room without a word. The Andersons tried to comfort her, but Morgan didn't want to talk about it. She took the car and crashed it that night."

Jon shakes his head. He wipes his eyes with the back of his hand. "Do you know anything about what happened with the statutory allegations?"

"Just what was in the paper. It's not exactly dinner-table conversation. I thought maybe Morgan was trying to relive her high school days, because they were so … stunted."

Jon bites the inside of his cheek. "She wasn't. The first boy sexually assaulted her, and the other two are lying." He looks at Sally with his eyes narrowed. "She's innocent."

Her eyes widen, and she puts her hand on her chest. "I didn't mean to suggest … I wasn't placing blame."

"I have evidence."

Sally's mouth hangs open. "Where? How?"

"I found the original kid, and, well, he told me the truth."

"You didn't …"

Jon smirks. "What? … Hurt him?"

Sally nods.

Jon shakes his head. "No."

Sally breathes a sigh of relief.

"I need a favor."

She raises her eyebrows. "How can I help?"

"I would like to give the evidence to the Andersons, but I doubt they trust me. The last time they saw me, I was taking Morgan away from them, and now she's gone. I mean, they probably think it's my fault." Jon looks down. "Sometimes *I* think it's my fault. I should have known. I should have never left her."

Sally takes a deep breath. "It could be a bit tricky. I really shouldn't be telling you this."

Jon looks up, his eyes glassy. "What?"

She frowns. "I spoke with Susan yesterday, and the Andersons hired a private investigator to look into your involvement with her death."

Jon rubs his temples. "So they probably don't want anything from me."

"Probably not. I would vouch for you, but then I would have to tell them why I know you'd never hurt anyone. That could be … problematic. Mr. Anderson is friends with my husband—"

"You don't have to explain." Jon stands up. "I should go."

Sally stands. "Stay."

"I can't." Jon limps toward the garage.

"The funeral," she says.

Jon turns around.

"It's the day after tomorrow at the Arlington First Christian Church. Maybe you could try to talk to them after the funeral."

"Thanks, Sally."

"Did you love her?"

"Yes."

"Did you ever love me?"

"I'm sorry."

+++

Jon pulls into a parking garage. He takes the ticket from the automatic dispenser, the arm raises, and he drives through. He squeezes his full-size truck into a tight space.

He exits the garage on foot, wearing a black suit, a black tie, and sunglasses. His suit is a magnet for the midday heat, and he welcomes the warmth of the sun's rays. His feet pinch a little in his new dress shoes as he hikes twelve blocks to Arlington First Christian Church.

A crowd of protestors blocks the church entrance. They hold up signs that read No Rest for Child Molesters and No Justice for the Children and Rot in Hell. The protestors are primarily white females, mothers still carrying baby weight, even though their babies are probably grown. Their faces are scrunched, with their eyes narrowed, brows furrowed, and nostrils flaring, resolute in the universally acceptable cause of bashing child molesters. Jon sees a well-dressed teen couple standing on the edge of the crowd, looking for an opening.

"You guys here for Ms. Anderson?" Jon asks.

"Yes," the girl says. "This is crazy."

"You guys can follow me. I'm gonna push through. Stay close together and keep your head down."

Jon pushes through the throng of women. The teens draw in a tight formation behind him. A few women thrust their signs in his face. He pushes past. One woman slips and falls.

"He pushed me!" she says.

"Do you condone raping children?" a female protestor asks.

Jon holds the door for the teens as the women yell obscenities at him. Inside, the cavernous church is mostly filled with young people in their late teens and early twenties. A shiny mahogany casket sits closed, covered in flowers. Pictures of Morgan are displayed in front of the casket. *I don't have a single picture of her. Will I forget what she looks like? Will I only remember her on those rocks?* Jon resists the urge to walk to the front and look at them, to see her once again. He finds an empty seat toward the back.

The service starts when a somber, wrinkled white-haired man leads the congregation in prayer. Jon sits silent, while most pray. The pastor speaks in generalities of a life taken too soon and the lives she touched.

"Richard Anderson, father of the deceased, will read the eulogy," the pastor says.

Mr. Anderson treads to the podium, his head down and his movements robotic. His hairless dome is pink and sun-spotted, except for the white crescent around the sides and back. He stands at the podium with his hands gripping the edges, as if he's holding on to a roller coaster. He takes a deep breath, his chest heaving up and down, visible from the cheap seats. His face is haggard, the skin around his eyes wrinkled and dark. He stares at the crowd.

"Morgan was a free spirit who lived life to the ragged edges," he says. "She experienced more life in her short time than I will in a hundred years. Sometimes I think she felt too much. It burned her out. When she was a child, we'd go to a different museum every weekend. The first time we went, she was five years old. We took the Metro downtown to the Mall. She was so inquisitive, so fearless. She spoke to the people on the train. She asked me so many questions. When we exited the train at our stop, she said good-bye to everyone and said she hoped she'd see them again." Mr. Anderson's voice cracks. He pulls a handkerchief from his pocket and dabs the corners of his eyes.

He continues. "She made these complete strangers happy. You could see it on their faces. We took the long escalator to the Mall, and, as soon as we exited, we were inundated with men trying to sell us a map to the museums. She asked me if we could buy one, but I told her I knew how to get to the Air and Space Museum. Still she begged me to buy one, so I did. The man smiled when he gave us the map. Morgan wasn't concerned about the map. She was happy that the man was happy. We bought a map from the same guy every weekend."

Mr. Anderson looks at his wife in the front row. She sobs quietly, bent over in her seat. Katherine massages her back.

He turns back to the audience. "On the way to the museum we passed a few homeless people sitting along the sidewalk, some with signs. Morgan stared as we walked by. I could almost see the wheels turning in her little head. A few asked for spare change. I ignored them. Morgan was always so bright. She could read pretty well, and she asked me if we could take them home with us, so they'd have a home.

I tried to explain that it wasn't safe, that some of the people had mental problems. She was so determined. She said that, if someone had a problem, you should help them solve it. I had to lie to her and tell her they had a home to go to at night, it was just the day that was a problem, and our house was too far away. She finally accepted that, while we were eating freeze-dried ice cream.

"Then she said we should feed them, because the signs also said they were hungry. To be honest, I just wanted to have a day with my daughter. I really didn't want to go anywhere near those people, but she was adamant, and I knew, if I refused, it would ruin the day. So after we finished lunch, we bought five extra lunches from the cafeteria, to go. We went outside with our boxed lunches, and she handed them all out.

"The men were so grateful. They smiled at her, thanked her and said, 'God bless you.' I don't think it was the food either. I think they smiled because someone looked at them like they were worth something, that they weren't a nuisance. Morgan had that genuineness about her." Mr. Anderson looks down for a moment, taking a deep breath. He looks back to the crowd, his eyes red and puffy.

"Every week we'd go back to the Mall and go to a different museum, and, after we'd seen them all, we'd just go to which-ever one Morgan wanted to visit. And every week we'd buy more lunches, and there would be more homeless people waiting for us. The last time we went, I think we had thirty lunches. One guy didn't get one, and he got upset and started to yell at Morgan. He said something really awful to her, before the other guys got on him. She was beside herself with grief for weeks after that.

"There are two sides of every coin. Morgan had such an open heart." Mr. Anderson stops and dabs his eyes with his handker-chief. "She had such an open heart that it allowed her to be the empathetic teacher who all these nice young people came here to remember, but it also left her vulnerable. She always felt so much." His eyes are glassy. "The world is a better place with Morgan in it. I miss her so much. I'm so sorry I didn't—" Tears stream down his face. He pivots and walks out the back door.

At the conclusion of the service, two men in dark suits push the closed casket on wheels down the aisle toward the waiting hearse. Mrs. Anderson sobs as soon as the men touch the casket. The Andersons in the front row follow behind Morgan's body.

Katherine supports her mother, who can barely stand up. They're followed by subsequent rows of mourners.

After the casket passes, and much of the crowd exits, Jon makes his way toward the front. He gazes at the collage of pictures behind the glass of the large wooden frame. He stares at the pictures, lost in her blue eyes, trying to see the sadness behind the smiles. He sees Morgan swimming at the lake as a child, diving in college, running in high school, and school pictures as a student and a teacher.

"Sir? Sir?" a soft voice says.

Jon turns to see a slender young woman in a black pantsuit.

"I'm sorry, but we need to take that."

Jon feels the urge to grab the frame and hold it tight to his chest. *I should have never let her out of my sight.* He squeezes the moisture from his eyes with his thumb and index finger. He looks up at the woman.

"I understand," he says.

She nods, with a tight smile, and picks up the frame from the stand. Jon follows the pictures with his red eyes.

She turns to Jon. "Would you like a picture? The family gave us tons of school pictures. I'm sure we could spare one."

"I would."

Jon follows her to a back office. She opens a manila file on the desk labeled Anderson, Morgan. She pulls out a cluster of recent head shots.

"Is this one okay?"

Jon manages a small smile. "That's perfect, thank you."

"Do you need directions to the burial?"

+++

Jon parks in the cemetery, along the curb, at the end of the giant procession. He takes long strides along the cars and headstones to the burial site. A crowd, roughly half the size from the church, circles the casket, with their heads bowed. The pastor says a prayer, while Jon stands on the edge. Birds sing in the trees, but the crowd is silent as the mahogany coffin is lowered into the ground. Mr. Anderson pushes the ceremonial shovel into a loose pile of soil and dumps a small shovelful on the casket. A handful of male relatives and friends follow suit in silence. The crowd disperses. Jon edges closer. Mr. Anderson glares, heading directly toward Jon on a collision course, with Katherine close behind.

"You've got a lot of nerve, coming here," Mr. Anderson says, his voice trembling.

"I'm sorry for your loss," Jon says, with his hand extended. Mr. Anderson's arms are frozen to his sides.

Katherine scowls at Jon. "It's inappropriate for you to be here. Haven't you done enough?"

"I would like to talk to you about her case," Jon says. "I have—"

"We told you to stay out of it," Mr. Anderson says, pointing a shaky finger at Jon. "You didn't listen, and now my little girl is *dead*. We don't need or want you dredging anything up, and, if you do, we will serve you with a lawsuit so fast it will make your head spin."

"I think we could—"

"Is that clear!"

Katherine puts her arm around her dad. "Come on, Dad. Let's go."

Jon watches the family walk toward their cars: Katherine with Mr. Anderson, and Glen and David with Mrs. Anderson. Mrs. Anderson looks limp, like she would fall over if not for her escorts. In death, history is skewed to protect the living. Enemies become friends; abusive parents become grief-stricken, worthy of sympathy. Family secrets are buried with the body.

Jon steps to the edge of the lonely hole. He peers over, into the oblivion. Loose brown earth litters the top of the casket. A small pile of lightweight soil sits next to the hole, with a shiny long-handled ceremonial shovel. A larger pile of red Virginia clay sits ten meters away, awaiting the backhoe. He picks up the shovel and presses it into the soil. He lifts the loam soil and dumps it in the hole. He digs out another shovelful, then another. He works faster, his tie and jacket flailing as he digs in, pivots, and dumps, over and over again, until the small pile is vanquished. He leans on the shovel, his breathing elevated, looking down at the casket covered in soil.

"It hurts so much," he says to Morgan's casket. He blinks; tears slip out and slide down his face. "I should have never left you that morning. I should have known. I should have been more convincing. We would have weathered all this. I know we would have." Jon takes a deep breath. "Our time together was the happiest of my life. You showed me what love is. Sometimes I wish we never met, because then I wouldn't know what I'm missing. I could go on thinking that Heather and I were once in love, or that my mother loves me or Sally, but they don't. It's a tough pill to swallow without you. I can't go back to my old life, and I can't have you. What am I supposed to do now?"

Chapter 17

Atonement

Jon grabs his keys, wallet, and the certified letter from the kitchen table and shoves them in the pockets of his jeans. He exits the side door and sees a Honda Civic creeping along his driveway. The Honda stops behind Jon's truck. Oscar steps from the driver's side in cowboy boots, a plaid shirt, and his black hair slicked back. He smiles wide, showing his bright white teeth.

Jon grins.

"You were supposed to call me," Oscar says.

"I know. I'm sorry. I've been dealing with some stuff."

His face turns serious. "I heard about Morgan. I'm really sorry. I've been by here five times looking for you, but your truck was gone, and you have no phone. Claudia and I were really worried."

"I'm sorry. I've been … I don't know." Jon shakes his head.

"It's not just us. All the guys have been asking about you. We about had a mutiny the other day. Everybody's pissed that you got fired."

Jon frowns. "Is that why you're not at work?"

Oscar shakes his head. "There's no work today."

Jon furrows his brow. "What do you mean, *there's no work*? It's the busy season."

"We had work through Wednesday, but nothing's scheduled for today or Friday."

"What about next week?"

"It looks like we have a short week again. You were selling most of the work, remember? Also I think some of your old clients dropped us, after they heard you were fired." Oscar purses his lips and looks down.

Jon frowns. "What is it?"

"Chad's been telling everyone that people are dropping us because they found out about Morgan and those kids."

Jon exhales and rubs his temples. "People are dropping us because Chad can't manage the sales workload. So phone calls don't get returned. Site visits never happen. Quality control visits never happen. Bids don't get done in a timely fashion."

Oscar nods his head and looks away.

"Do you think she did it?"

Oscar shrugs. "I don't know. It's really bad if she did. I think about Oscar Jr. and it's … I don't know. It's all over the news."

Jon crosses his arms. "She never did anything wrong. She was sexually assaulted by the first kid, and the other two are flat-out lying. I should go." Jon turns toward his truck.

"If work keeps going like this, we'll never make it through the winter."

Jon turns back to Oscar with a frown, his hazel eyes downcast. "I'm sorry. I didn't mean to let you guys down."

"It's not your fault." Oscar looks at his boots, then back to Jon. "I bet Chad would take you back if you asked."

Jon shakes his head. "I can't do it. … I can't."

"I know what Chad and Heather did to you was bad. I know that. Everybody knows that was wrong. But we depend on *you*.

We can't depend on Chad."

"I just can't carry that weight anymore. I'm sorry, but I really need to get going."

"Jon, please, this is gonna end badly for everyone, not just Chad and Heather."

Jon frowns. "I gotta go."

+++

Jon bypasses the elevator and opens the door to the stairs. He takes them two at a time to the fourth floor. He walks down a corridor and finds 4B. He sees the reception desk through the glass doors. He strides inside; the young woman at the desk smiles. Behind her, silver letters spell out Roth, Meyers, and Pittman.

"May I help you?" she asks.

"I'm Jon Porter. I'm here for—"

"Mr. Meyers is expecting you. I'll take you back."

She opens the door to a conference room with a dark varnished mahogany table and black leather chairs.

"Mr. Meyers, this is Jon Porter," the young woman says, before shutting the door behind him.

Five sets of eyes glare at Jon, as he stands at the foot of the table. Mr. Meyers sits at the head of the table, with a stack of papers in front of him. His face is full, wrinkled, with an orangey tan, and his hair is salt-and-pepper. Mr. and Mrs. Anderson sit on one side of the table, and Katherine and David sit on the other. The men are dressed in dark suits and power ties, Mrs. Anderson in a skirt suit and Katherine in a pantsuit. Jon sticks out like a sore thumb in his jeans, untucked button-down shirt, and dark tousled hair.

"This is highly unorthodox and inappropriate," Mr. Anderson says.

"I'm sorry, Dick," Mr. Meyers says. "She requested that he be here."

Mr. Anderson narrows his blue eyes at Jon. "His involvement with her is *highly* suspect."

"Her name is Morgan," Jon says.

"Shut up," Katherine says. "You barely knew her. It's sick that David has to be in the same room as you."

David blushes and looks away.

"Mr. Porter," Mr. Meyers says, "have a seat. We are about to begin." Jon sits in the only open chair at the foot of the table. "Before you came in, I was explaining to everyone that *Morgan* made changes to her will shortly before she passed."

Jon furrows his brow.

Mr. Meyers continues. "She requested that you all be here for the reading of the will. She has written a note to each of you that she requested to be read aloud in front of everyone, as well as the matter of distributing her estate. You are, of course, not bound by law to be here. You do so of your own free will. Does anybody have any questions?"

Katherine shakes her head.

"Please begin, Eric," Mr. Anderson says.

"Mrs. Anderson, I am going to read Morgan's words exactly," Mr. Meyers says. "Do you understand?"

"I do," she says.

"Mom, I hope my demise hasn't pushed you to drink more or eat less. I would be lying if I told you that your alcoholism and lifelong battle to eat as little as possible didn't have an effect on me. Mostly it made me sad for you. I wish you could have been the kind of mom who baked cookies and had only one glass of cheap wine on special occasions, but you're not, just like you probably wish I wasn't depressed and suicidal. Despite our problems,

I loved you right up until the moment my brain splattered over those rocks."

Mrs. Anderson's eyes water, and her mascara runs over her caked foundation. From a distance she looks like a blonde thirtysomething, but, up close, bits of age creep out from under her heavy makeup, Botox, and plastic surgeries.

"Sorry for that. Is it too soon to joke about my suicide? What I would like is for you to stop pretending you're not an alcoholic and go to a rehab center. After that, start eating, for fuck's sake, and go outside. Get some fresh air.

"I am leaving you all my photo albums. Feel free to give pictures away if you want or hoard them, whatever. Also I am leaving you my clothing. Please don't keep the clothes, not that we have the same style anyway. I would like for you to give my clothes to the homeless. It made me happier to give things to people less fortunate. Maybe it will for you too. I really did love you, Mom."

Mr. Anderson hands his handkerchief to his wife. She nods in appreciation and dabs the corners of her eyes. She hands it back. Mr. Meyers turns to David.

"David, I really do appreciate you giving it the old college try, but let's be honest. We were headed on a one-way trip to marital misery. I never loved you, and you never loved me."

Katherine rolls her eyes. David frowns.

"I'm sure Katherine just gasped or scrunched up her face. I doubt David is at all surprised by what I'm saying. Are you, David? I do apologize for seeing someone behind your back. I was confused, and I was wrong for being dishonest. I suppose I received adequate punishment when I was raped. That's right everyone. I said 'rape.' I'm so sick to death, literally, of hearing the rape that I endured being referred to as *an attack* or *the incident* or *the assault* or *that horrible thing*. It was rape, pure and simple.

At the time I needed a friend, not an attorney, David. Were you really saving me from the shame of a lawyer's cross-examination or did you enjoy humiliating me?" David looks down at the table, his receding hairline glistening in the fluorescent light.

"Was it your way of getting revenge on the victim without the guilt? I'm not sure if that was the intent, but it was certainly the result. You made me feel small and weak and dirty, and yet my family praised you for standing by me. I hope you can let me go and move on. I don't think it's appropriate for you to hang around my family as some sort of surrogate son because of your relationship with me. I think it's best for everyone if you move on. For your troubles, I'm leaving you my equity in our house, all the furniture, appliances, and any other household items."

Mr. Meyers turns to Katherine. She narrows her eyes, showing her crow's feet. She tightens her jaw, as if she's ready to take a punch.

"Kathy, my big sister, what can I say? We haven't exactly had a Hallmark-card relationship, have we?"

Kathy smirks.

"I idolized you as a kid. You were so beautiful and smart and popular. You were everything that I wanted to be. Do you remember that summer at the lake when you drove down with three of your friends? You were seventeen. I was eleven. I tried so hard to hang out with you and your friends, and I know I was too young, but I wanted to know what it was like to be around the popular girls.

"And I did learn what it was like to be around the popular girls. To you, I was someone to use. I was your waitress, your faithful servant, your jester, the butt of your jokes, and another worshiper at The Temple of Kathy. With you, I didn't have my own identity, my own self-worth. I was the ugly duckling, until I wasn't. You preferred that I stay in my ugly box where I belong. I was never talented and brilliant, like you. You made sure I was put in my place with my amateurish writing. I couldn't possibly be attractive *and* smart. Those who can't do, teach, right?

"You were always the one who had it all, and you weren't going to give up the crown without a fight. I never understood competition among siblings. I always bragged about your success. Your success made me happy. Your success made me feel hopeful, like maybe I could do it too. My success, what little I had, made you angry. I had a part to play in the book of your life. I was the incompetent sister. I was the character in your life who your readers wouldn't care about, the character who could jump off a cliff and they'd shrug."

Katherine stares, blank-faced.

"Would you like me to continue?" Mr. Meyers says. She nods, her eyes red.

"Despite my brash behavior over the last few years, I was still that girl who was in awe of her big sister. You *are* the literary genius that I aspired to be. I wish we could have lifted each other up. Who knows? Maybe time and maturity would have healed our relationship. By the way, I'm sorry about how I acted at your wedding, and, yes, the coughing fit that was timed perfectly to coincide with the pause after the pastor said, 'Does anyone object to this union, speak now or forever hold your peace,' *was* on purpose. I do still think Glen's a dick. You can do better.

"I *bequeath*—I always wanted to use that word. How's that for literary genius? To you, I bequeath my jewelry, because Mom already has too much, and my Acura. It was in a slight fender bender, but it's been fixed, and it's cooler than that old-lady car you drive.

"I almost forgot. There is one more thing. I have an emerging young author working on a project for me. He's talented but raw. I would like for you to help him develop his talent. Maybe, with him, you can be the supportive big sister I always wanted."

Mr. Meyers stops and scans the table. "Does anyone need a break?"

David stands up, his long, lanky body hunched. "I should go." He exits the conference room. Nobody tries to stop him.

"Does everyone else want to continue?" Mr. Meyers asks.

Jon and Katherine nod.

"Please continue," Mr. Anderson says.

Mr. Meyers turns to Mr. Anderson. "Dad, I wonder if you told the museum story at my funeral. Probably not a dry eye in the house, if you did. We were so close then, before the world chewed me up and spat me out. I loved you so much. All I ever wanted was for you to be proud of me. Everything changed after I took Mom's pills. I remember that look of shame you gave me, when I was recovering from having my stomach pumped. That shameful, dismissive look, like I was no longer a competent young woman but a damaged child. Over the years that dismissive look turned into disappointment, and eventually disappointment turned into disdain."

Mr. Anderson wipes his eyes with his handkerchief.

"Should I continue, Dick?"

Mr. Anderson nods.

"I know it must have been hard for you to have a daughter involved in controversy, given your position in politics. I know your business was at risk. I know the argument for burying the rape. I could have stomached letting it go for the sake of your business and the family reputation, but the argument was based on how I was weak, how they would break me down with questions about my promiscuous past or questions about my mental state.

Everyone just assumed I had a promiscuous past. Why? Because Kathy heard rumors?"

Kathy looks toward the exit, then down at the table.

"Because I'm a free spirit? Because I went out on a lot of dates? Were you worried they'd bring up the famous middle school blow job or the time I did three guys at the same time? Someone supposedly had a video of that. The sad truth is my rapist was the second guy I had ever been with. David was the first, although I never told him that. The twisted thing is that nobody ever asked. Everyone just assumed the worst. I was the awful movie cliché, the depressed, suicidal girl who fucks every guy with a pulse."

Mrs. Anderson sobs softly. Mr. Anderson again offers his handkerchief. She buries her face in it.

"Despite everything that happened with the rape, I was getting over it. I was moving on. Then I was arrested. It was going to be just like middle school and high school, except, this time, I'd be hated everywhere. I remember thinking for a brief moment, when you bailed me out, that you believed I was innocent. I thought that maybe I could get through it, but when we were in the car and you said what you said, I knew it was over. You had already convicted me. As usual you never even asked what happened. You just assumed I was the dirty whore who received a big dildo for her sixteenth birthday. I bet you thought I must have done something awful to be the target of such venom."

Mr. Anderson swallows hard, choking back tears of regret.

"I wish you could have believed in me, given me the benefit of the doubt. The boy who started the statutory rape allegations had an awful home life. His dad was in and out, coming and going like the wind. His mother brought home boyfriend after boyfriend to their trailer. He told me how he couldn't sleep through the noises they made. I could go on and on about the neglect and abuse he suffered. He never blamed his mother. It was never her fault. Despite everything, he loved her. As a teacher, there's something universally sad and sweet in a child. Children will love their parents to the bitter end, even when they don't deserve it. I wonder if on some level parents take full advantage of that fact. I suppose I'm no different. I love you, Dad, right to the bitter end."

Mr. Anderson's head sags. He wipes at his eyes with his palms.

Mr. Meyers looks at Jon. "Jon, I really hope you're here right now. Truth be told, when I wrote this, I wasn't sure whether or not you'd show. Of all the things I've done that I regret, leaving you was my biggest. You believed in me when nobody else would. You loved me like nobody ever has."

Jon wipes the corner of his eye with the side of his index finger. Katherine frowns. Mrs. Anderson gazes at Jon.

"You were supposed to be a fling, just someone to have a few final laughs with. I tried my best to keep it that way, but I couldn't. I fell in love with you—something I've never experienced before. A big part of me wanted to cancel my plans, but, if I'd stuck around, I would have eventually ruined everything. Why not end it on a high note? Why not quit while I'm ahead? You have to know when to fold 'em, right? I do understand the pain I've caused you. For that I can never be sorry enough. Had we met before, we would have been great together."

Mr. Meyers looks up from the stack of papers in front of him, then back to the page he is reading.

"Jon, my dear, I would like for you to have my manuscript. I know Katherine doesn't think it's worth the paper it's printed on, but maybe you can update the story. Also, Katherine, I would like for you to be Jon's editor for the project."

Katherine scowls at Jon.

"Jon, I would like for you to have my trust fund. I've only spent a small fraction of it. There should be about four million dollars left. I know that you will put the money to good use. I do have a few requests. These requests are not legally binding, but I know you are the type of person who will honor a girl's final wishes.

"Please take care of yourself. Get indoor plumbing and some new T-shirts and underwear that don't have holes in them. Do not, under any circumstances, give any of this money to your mother. You and I both know why. Most of all, I want you to move on and meet someone wonderful. You have a lot to offer. After that, I trust that you'll know what to do. I love you more than you'll ever know. Morgan."

Mr. Meyers looks up from the stack of papers. Katherine and Mr. Anderson glare at Jon. Mrs. Anderson stares at her hands.

"This concludes the reading of Morgan Anderson's Last Will and Testament," Mr. Meyers says.

Mr. Anderson turns to Mr. Meyers and whispers, "Can she do that, legally? I mean, come on, Eric. The trust fund is my money."

"I'm sorry, Dick. It came from you, but it was hers to give," Mr. Meyers whispers.

Jon stands up.

"I hope you're happy now," Mr. Anderson says to Jon. "You're a rich man."

Jon frowns and shakes his head. His eyes are bloodshot. "Do I look happy?" He pauses.

Mr. Anderson looks down.

"Look at me! I said, … 'Do I look happy?'"

Mr. Anderson lifts his head

"I would burn it all," Jon says, "for just one more minute with Morgan."

Katherine glares at Jon. "That's bullshit, and you know it. If you're so fucking noble, then give it back."

Jon turns toward Katherine and bites the inside of his cheek.

"I thought so," she says.

Jon pulls a tiny tape, a thumb drive, and a folded piece of paper from the front pocket of his shirt. He unfolds the piece of paper and places all three items on the table.

He picks up the tape. "This is a taped confession from Paul Skinner."

Mr. Anderson raises his eyebrows.

"He's the first boy who accused Morgan of statutory rape. In the confession, he states that he sexually assaulted Morgan." Jon replaces the tape on the table and holds up the thumb drive. "This is video evidence of the other two boys admitting that they lied about having sex with Morgan."

Mrs. Anderson gapes at Jon with a tiny smile. Katherine's mouth hangs open. Mr. Anderson looks away.

Jon replaces the thumb drive on the table and picks up the piece of paper, typewritten on both sides. "This page has all the information you would need to find these people and verify my sources. Addresses, phone numbers, everything."

Mr. Anderson turns to Jon. "I question the authenticity."

"Why? Because that would mean you really fucked up, right?"

Mr. Anderson looks down. Mrs. Anderson glowers at her husband.

"You still don't fucking get it, do you?" Jon says, looking around the room. "Morgan was the victim, and you all victimized her worse than those boys."

Mr. Anderson stares at Jon, blank-faced.

Jon shakes his head, his jaw set tight. "She jumped off that cliff to send you a message."

Katherine furrows her brow. "What message?"

"That she'd rather die than live in a world where her family thinks she's a child rapist."

Mr. Anderson's eyes are glassy. "Now hold on. Nobody ever said that."

"You hired a private investigator to look into my life, but you couldn't hire one to prove your daughter's innocence?" Jon motions toward the paper, tape, and thumb drive in front of him. "It took me two days to find this evidence. You didn't have her lawyer push for a plea deal to keep everything out of the papers? You didn't call her a whore after you bailed her out?"

Tears spill down Mr. Anderson's cheeks.

Mrs. Anderson stands and points a bony finger at her husband. "You fucking bastard!" she says and stomps from the conference room.

"Dad?" Katherine says.

Mr. Anderson hangs his head while he sobs.

"I don't know if you can atone for what you did to Morgan," Jon says to Mr. Anderson, "but, if I were you, I would spend the rest of my life trying." Jon looks at the attorney. "Mr. Meyers, I would like to give the trust fund back but with stipulations on what it can be used for. Can I do that?"

"We can write a contract for just about anything, but both parties need to sign for it to be binding," Mr. Meyers says.

"I would like for Mr. Anderson to have the trust fund in its entirety, but it can only be used to clear Morgan's name of the statutory rape charges. So he can hire lawyers, take out ads, whatever he needs to do to get the truth out there. I don't know how to do this. I don't have the right connections. Mr. Anderson does."

"Dick?"

Mr. Anderson looks at Mr. Meyers, his eyes wet, his mouth open. When he looks at Jon, his face softens.

"Atonement starts right now," Jon says.

Chapter 18

Fair's Fair

Jon hikes up the overgrown mountain trail, the sound of leaves crackling beneath his feet, a chill in the air. He carries a bucket, a brush, and a bottle of paint thinner. His breath condenses into a fog each time he exhales. He stops at the tree root, where he twisted his knee, the spot where he failed Morgan, six months ago.

He climbs the rock outcropping and shimmies between the massive boulders, holding his bucket out front. He hears giggling. He smells marijuana. He squeezes through to the rocky ledge. Two teenage girls dressed in all black, with black eyeshadow and nails, sit on the bench-size rock, smoking. They're watching a young man with chains dangling from his belt loop, peeing in the corner.

Jon sets down the bucket. The girls turn toward him, their eyes wide. Jon glances at the graffiti on the rock wall. Two signs in white spray paint say Look Out Below and Jumpers' Paradise. The young man turns around, stuffing his penis into his tight black jeans. He's tall and thin, with long greasy locks and patchwork facial hair.

"What the fuck are you lookin' at?" the man says.

"Your white finger," Jon says.

"What was that? My white dick?" He laughs. "You lookin' at my dick?"

The girls giggle.

Jon pounces with the quickness of a cat. Before the smirk is off the man's face, Jon has him pressed up against the rock wall with his hands around his throat. The young man's eyes bulge, his head tilted back as far away from Jon as possible.

"Do you know how easy it would be to throw you off this cliff?" Jon whispers.

Jon releases his choke hold, and the man gasps for air.

"What the fuck, man?" he says, his eyes glassy.

"Get the fuck out of here, all of you," Jon says.

The girls drop their joints and scurry between the boulders. The young man follows them, glancing back at Jon.

Jon dumps paint thinner into the bucket and dips his brush. He scours the spray-painted signs. They bleed white down the rock wall as he scrubs. He stops and sits on the bench-size rock, looking out over the valley. It's crisp and cool, but sunny and cloudless. The trees surrounding the lake are gray and mostly leafless, making the brilliance of the sunny blue water pop as if it were a black-and-white painting with only the lake painted in color. Wind whistles through the trees. He can feel the bite on his neck and the tip of his angular nose. His head and ears are warm under his knit hat.

He closes his eyes for a moment, trying to picture her, trying to remember her sitting right next to him, with their hands intertwined. He tries to picture the intricacies of her face. He closes his eyes tighter, trying to form the images. Everything's fuzzy; the details he could once conjure are now faded. He opens his eyes, and a few tears leak out. He stands and walks to the cliff edge. He looks over; the gray rock below is still stained brown. He closes his eyes, and he can see her contorted body lying there with blood spilling from her skull. The detail is stunning. His memories are like sand. The harder he tries to hold on to them, the faster they slip through his fingers. The more he tries to let go, the more every grain sits on his palm, just as vibrant as the day they were formed.

+++

Jon sets the bucket next to his back door and steps inside the cabin.

He strides to the kitchen table. A makeshift workstation with a laptop and a printer sit, with cords hanging over the edge. He moves the mouse to wake up the computer. He checks the time in the lower right corner of the screen.

"Shit," he says.

He grabs his keys and the typed pages sitting on the printer, and bounds out of the cabin. He drives down the mountain to Lake Landing. He punches in the key code and enters the gated community. He pulls into the paver driveway of the majestic stone mansion and parks behind Morgan's Acura.

Jon rings the doorbell. He can see Katherine through the door window. She opens the door with a frown.

"You're late," she says.

"I'm sorry, Kathy."

She walks toward the kitchen. He shuts the door and follows. She stops at the granite countertop and turns around. Even in sweats, there's something formal about her. Her hair, no longer dyed and highlighted, is dark, like Morgan's. Her summer color has worn off, exposing the creamy white skin underneath. Her eyes are blue, like the lake. She's not Morgan, but he can concentrate on her eyes or her hair or the slope of her nose and almost catch a glimpse of Morgan.

He holds up a stack of papers. "I made the edits."

"What about the rewrite of Chapter Thirty-Two?" she asks.

"It's in here too."

"I have edits for thirty-three and thirty-four to go over with you."

"I have to be somewhere tonight."

Katherine frowns. "I have places to be too. I agreed to do this, but I have limited time. I have two deadlines that I'm working on, while trying to teach *you* how to write."

"I can stay for a bit, and I can come by after, if you want."

"Let's just get it over with now," she says.

"So, what did you think?"

"There are a couple instances of lazy writing, where you're spoon-feeding the information. The reader has to be engaged, and, no matter how interesting the story, if they don't have to use their minds, they'll be bored."

"Was there anything you did like?"

"I like the interaction between you and Morgan. That feels real to me."

Jon smiles. "It feels real to me too."

"You still have a long way to go."

Jon nods. "I know."

"I was worried about the obvious disconnect where her writing ends and yours begins. She was much more poetic than you. Her words flowed like water. Your style is more blunt and choppy. But I'm starting to think that the disconnect adds to the story."

"She was really talented, wasn't she?"

Katherine looks away, her eyes downcast. "She was." She pauses and looks up. "We still have a lot of work to do."

+++

Jon parks behind his mom's Mercury sedan. He takes the concrete steps two at a time to the split level. The black labs bark in anticipation of his arrival. He pushes inside. The dogs jump on Jon with their tails wagging. He rubs their heads and necks, before walking on. He can smell spaghetti sauce, garlic bread, and a hint of dog urine.

"I'm sorry I'm late," he says.

Betsy glances up from her mostly empty plate at Jon bounding up the steps to the dining room table. A dab of greasy red sauce dribbles down her chins.

"It's okay," she says in between bites. "I'm gettin' used to eatin' alone."

"I know. I'm sorry. Morgan's sister was helping me with my writing."

"I still don't get all this."

"All what?"

"You doin' all this work but not gettin' no money."

"This isn't about money."

Betsy dumps her fork on her plate. "It is when you need stuff you can't afford."

Jon glances at her freshly dyed blond hair and her silver-sparkled Christmas nails. "It looks like you're getting by okay."

Betsy looks at Jon, tears squeezing out of the corner of the fatty slits covering her eye sockets. "I'm three months behind on the house."

Jon's eyes widen. "We did the budget. It all worked. What happened?"

She shrugs. "Everything costs more than you think. I can't

keep livin' like this. You gotta get a job. You ain't been workin' for six months now."

"I am working."

"It ain't no job if it don't pay."

"How much do you need to get up-to-date?"

"Six thousand."

"Jesus, Mom, I don't have that. Why don't you sell your car?"

"How am I supposed to go anywhere?"

"When was the last time you left this house for something important?"

She wipes her eyes with the sides of her chubby wrists. "Don't you worry about it. I'll figure it out. I always do. Why don't you sit down? Dinner's gettin' cold."

Jon sits. "I just need another month or two at the most to get this done, and I'll get a job."

She flicks her hand. "You can sell my car, but you gotta promise me that you'll buy me a new one, once you start workin'."

"All right, but you gotta stop spending on nonessentials."

"Nonessentials?"

"Yes, dying your hair, getting your nails done, ordering food in, pay-per-view."

"I can't live like you. I ain't no Jesus."

Jon exhales and concentrates on his food. The dogs sit on the floor next to him, looking up at him with sad eyes and drool spilling from their mouths.

"Could you get the pie?" she asks. "It's on the counter. And bring some paper plates."

Jon sets down his fork and pushes his dinner plate to the middle of the table, so the dogs won't snatch it. He strides to the kitchen; the dogs follow. He grabs two paper plates, utensils, and a store-bought apple pie in an aluminum pan.

"I heard Chad and Heather goin' outta business," Betsy calls from the table.

Jon returns, and sets the pie and the plates in front of her with a knife and a spatula.

"Who told you that?" Jon asks, as he sits down.

She cuts a quarter of the pie and heaves it onto her plate. "I seen Heather at Target. She was returning some big TV. She about ran away from me when I tried to say hi. She was big as a house. I never seen a pregnant woman move that fast. I was talkin' to Dusty about it, and he said they was havin' money troubles. Chad was drinkin' at the bar, tryin' to pick up some waitress, then his credit card got declined. He made a big scene about it."

"Money troubles doesn't mean they're going out of business."

Betsy takes a bite of pie. "That *is* good," she mumbles with pie in her mouth. "You forgot the Cool Whip."

"I didn't know you talked to Heather," Jon says as he stands.

"Sometimes."

Jon pushes his plate to the middle of the table again, walks into the kitchen with the dogs in tow, and pulls a tub of Cool Whip from the refrigerator. He returns, sits down, and slides the Cool Whip across the table to his mother. She opens it and shovels five heaping spoonfuls, completely covering her pie.

"Cool Whip ain't hardly got no calories," she says. Betsy dumps pie with whipped cream in her mouth.

Jon pulls his plate back and picks up his fork. "Are you friends with Heather?" He takes a bite of spaghetti.

She shrugs, her mouth full. She chews and swallows, "No, not friends, but we talk sometimes."

"Huh." Jon sets down his fork and rubs his chin. "Does she call you, or do you call her?"

"It ain't like that. I just see her sometimes."

"I thought you hated her?"

"Well, of course I do, for what she did to you, but sometimes I feel sorry for her. I don't think she ever got over you." She heaps pie into her mouth.

Jon stares at his mother, as if he's figured something out. "Do you remember the game when I hurt my knee?"

She chews and swallows. "I don't know why you always wanna bring up bad memories." She looks up, smiling. "Let's talk about somethin' fun, like what you want for Christmas this year?" She shovels pie and whipped cream in her mouth.

"But do you remember it?"

She chews, her chubby cheeks moving up and down. She shrugs.

Jon glares. "What does that mean? Do you remember it or not?"

"Some parts. Was a long time ago."

"Heather said something to me a while ago, about that night and about you."

"I thought you didn't talk to her?" Betsy takes a final bite of pie. "Um, um, um," she moans as she chews.

"I don't. She came to my cabin and told me some things."

Betsy swallows and frowns. "That lil' hussy's a liar."

Jon purses his lips. "I didn't tell you what she said."

Betsy moves her index finger around her empty plate, picking up the last remnants of apple pie filling. She sucks the sugary goodness from her finger.

Jon scowls. "Why would you say she was a liar, before I even told you what she said?"

She sighs and crosses her meaty forearms across her chest. "I don't wanna be messin' around in her gossip."

"She said you told her that I was cheating on her, before that game."

Betsy furrows her brow. "I did no such thing. I knew she was a schemin' lil' bitch, but this ain't right."

"So you never told her that I was cheating on her?"

"Of course not."

Jon narrows his eyes. "Do you remember how you had some boyfriends at the time?"

"Maybe one or two. I was single. Ain't nothin' wrong with that."

"You had four during my senior year football season. That's four over about three months."

Betsy frowns and places her elbows on the table. "I don't remember that."

Jon glares. "You did. I remember it like it was yesterday."

She shrugs. "If you say so, but I doubt it was that many."

"Do you remember how I asked you to stop bringing them to my games?"

"It was a long time ago, Jon. I don't understand where all this is comin' from. Are you tryin' to hurt me?"

Jon shakes his head. "I'm just looking for answers. Do you remember how I asked you to stop bringing them?"

"I really don't remember any of this."

"I do. I remember exactly. I did ask you to stop bringing your boyfriends to my games. For three games, you came alone, and then, on that game, the one when I got hurt, you brought your boyfriend and made a scene in the stands."

Betsy shakes her head and frowns. "I don't have to listen to this. Maybe I didn't wanna be alone all the time, but I sure as hell didn't make no scene."

Jon bites the inside of his cheek. "You were making out with him in the stands. I saw you. Kids were yelling stuff at me."

"I sure as shit don't remember any a that. Why you doin' this?

Do you wanna hurt me? Because, if you do, you're doin' a damn good job. I make you this meal, and this is what I get."

Jon exhales. "You never admit anything."

"Cause I ain't *did* nuthin'."

"Are you telling me that you've been the perfect mother to me, never made any mistakes?"

"I ain't sayin' that. Nobody's perfect. It's hard bein' a single mom. Unless you've been one, you just don't know."

"You didn't want me to get that scholarship, did you? You didn't want me to leave you."

Her cheeks redden. "You think my life was easier with you? You think you helped me? Hell, I didn't start gettin' fat until after I had you. You've been a drain on me my whole life. But I just give and give and give, because that's what I do. I sacrifice for you. It's all for you."

Jon stands up, his fists clenched. "What exactly is for me? Your house that I pay for? Your bills? You liked me a lot better when I was dropping off your weekly check. That's how our weekly meal started, right?"

Tears spill down her rosy, round cheeks. "I never knew you could be so cruel."

"Did you lie to Heather and make a scene with your boyfriend to fuck me up so I'd lose my scholarship?"

"If you can't play with a little pressure, then you'd never make it anyway. If I did that, and I didn't, it sounds like it was a favor."

Jon shakes his head with a smirk. "What if I said that I can no longer give you any financial support?"

"I don't know what kind of son would abandon his mother."

"I didn't say anything about abandoning you. I just said no more money."

Her eyes widen. "I'll be out on the street! Is that what you want?

I paid for you for fifteen years, until you could get a job."

"So that deserves payback?"

"Fair's fair."

"I was a child. I didn't ask to be born into this world. You were the one who raised me around abusive men, who left me home alone when I was way too young. You were the one who sabotaged me during that game. I don't owe you anything."

"You owe me everything! Without me, you wouldn't be here."

"I'm not giving you any more money. If you still want me in your life as your son, not as your ATM, let me know. Otherwise, I'm not coming back here."

Tears stream down her cheeks. "Please don't do this. I love you. I ain't got nobody else."

Jon pushes his chair in. "Thanks for dinner, Mom." He walks down the stairs of the split level to the front door; the dogs follow.

"Don't do this," she says. "You're puttin' me in an early grave."

He opens the door and looks up at his mother, still sitting at the table.

"If you walk out that door," she says, "you'll break my heart."

The dogs wag their tails, expecting Jon to take them for a walk. Instead he exits, shuts the door, and walks outside.

Chapter 19

El Patron

Jon clicks the Save button and prints his revised pages. He glances out the window at the melting snow. *It never stays long enough to appreciate the beauty.* He looks at the stack of mail, next to the laptop. He picks up the flyer on top that advertises Heavy Equipment Auction. Listed at the bottom is an address he knows well. He scans the thumb-size pictures of machines. He sees the first excavator he purchased. He grabs his keys, puts on his jacket, pulls on his knit hat, and exits the cabin.

He unplugs the orange extension cord attached to the front of his diesel truck. He climbs into the cab, and starts the engine.

He drives down the mountain over the suspension bridge to the industrial park. He enters the open chain link gate and drives past the tow yard, with junked cars stacked ten high, and the land-scapers, with their mountains of mulch. He pulls into the gravel parking lot and parks in the back, among a dozen lettered trucks. He strides across the parking lot to the office. Melted snow drips off the Stone Lake Excavating sign. A small crowd of men in work boots and jeans loiter within. Jon steps inside.

A couple dozen folding chairs are set up in neat rows and

columns in front of a podium. A small square table is just inside the front door. A young man sits behind the table, with a sign-up sheet and a box of auction paddles. He looks at Jon with a smile.

"Welcome, sir," the young man says. "Would you like a listing of the auction items?"

Jon takes the sheet from the man. "Thanks."

"You'll also need to sign in and take an auction paddle, if you plan to bid. We're gonna start soon, but you might have time to look at a few of the items, if you know what you want. Do you need help finding anything?"

"I won't be bidding."

Oscar and Victor stand in the corner, away from the crowd, speaking Spanish. Oscar holds an auction paddle with lucky number seven on it. Jon walks across the room with a respectful smile.

"*¿Hola, que pasa?*" Jon says.

Victor looks down. Oscar's jaw tightens.

"What are you doing here?" Oscar asks.

"I'm not really sure." Jon takes a deep breath. "I'm sorry, Oscar. *Lo siento*, Victor."

"I told you this would happen. I asked for your help. Where I come from, people help their friends."

Oscar turns his back to Jon. Jon stands in silence for a moment, before walking to the rows of folding chairs. A back office door opens, and Chad steps out, his face stubble-filled, his eyes blood-shot, and his button-down shirt rumpled. He scowls and stalks toward Jon with his fists clenched.

"Get out of my office," Chad says.

"Which part? Because 30 percent of it's still mine," Jon says.

Chad's wide nostrils flare. "Are you happy now? You fuckin' prick. This is your fuckin' fault."

Jon clenches his fists. "Let me get this straight. You married my ex-wife, took over half my company, after I gave you 40 percent to begin with. Then you fired me, and the company fell apart while I was fired. And that's supposed to be *my* fault?"

"You weren't even showin' up for work. I didn't have a replacement. You could have helped us transition, if you wanted to leave."

"Transition!"

Heads turn toward Jon and Chad.

"You fired me."

"You're the one who stopped doing his job, remember? It's for the best anyway. This hick town has been holdin' me back. Heather and I are movin' to northern Virginia. It's the wealthiest area in the United States. I'm gonna take my proceeds and build a new company there. Some of the guys are comin' with me."

"It's because nobody wants to do business with you here. And I don't blame 'em. Good riddance."

"You're just jealous," Chad says with a smirk. "You've always been jealous of me. I've got Heather. I've got a nicer house, nicer car. I could actually finish a football season without gettin' hurt, like a little pussy. People like me. I'm a cool guy. You're just this depressed douche bag."

Jon smiles. "I saw what you listed your house for. You need to knock off a couple hundred grand to sell it in this hick town. But you can't, right? Because you need to sell at list just to break even. Otherwise you gotta bring cash that you don't have. You'll be lucky to get two hundred grand from the business sale and auction. So I'm not sure how you're gonna start a business in northern Virginia where piece-of-shit town houses cost half a million, when you're broke, with bad credit, a newborn, and a materialistic wife. Good luck with that though."

Chad's smirk turns down. Jon walks away and sits in one of the last empty chairs, between a burly contractor and a thin man in a dark suit at the rear of the room. A middle-aged man with a white mustache steps up to the podium.

"Thank you all for coming on this cold January afternoon," the auctioneer says. "We're gonna start the bidding in order, right along with the list. If anyone didn't get a list, we still have a few on the table by the door." The man looks at Chad, standing off to the side, then back to the audience. "We're gonna start the bidding on the 1992 Caterpillar 312 Excavator." The auctioneer speeds up the rhythm and cadence of his speech. "Twenty thousand. Would ya give twenty thousand? Would ya go twenty thousand?"

A contractor in the front holds up a paddle.

The auctioneer gestures his open hand to the bidder. "Twenty thousand dollars, money bidder. Would ya give twenty-two five? Would ya go twenty-two five? Would ya bid twenty-two five?"

The thin man in the suit next to Jon raises his paddle.

The auctioneer gestures his open hand to the thin man. "Twenty-two five, money bidder. Would ya give twenty-five? Would ya go twenty-five?"

The contractor in front holds up his paddle.

The auctioneer gestures toward him. "Twenty-five, money bidder. Would ya give twenty-seven five?"

The man in the suit raises his paddle.

"Twenty-seven five, money bidder. Would ya give thirty? Would ya go thirty? Would ya bid thirty? Would ya give thirty for it?"

The contractor in front looks down at the floor, his paddle resting on his legs.

"Goin' once, goin' twice. *Sold* to the gentleman in the back for twenty-seven five!"

"The next item is a 1994 Caterpillar 301 Mini-Excavator. Ten thousand, would ya give ten thousand?"

Oscar holds up his paddle.

"Ten thousand, money bidder. Would ya give twelve? Would ya go twelve?"

The man in the suit holds up his paddle.

The auctioneer gestures his open hand toward him. "Twelve thousand, money bidder. Would ya give fourteen? Would ya go fourteen?"

Oscar holds up his paddle.

"Fourteen thousand, money bidder. Would ya give sixteen?"

The man in the suit holds up his paddle.

"Sixteen thousand, money bidder. Would ya give eighteen? Would ya go eighteen? Would ya bid eighteen? Would ya give eighteen for it?"

Oscar looks at the paddle, resting on his leg.

"Goin' once, goin' twice, *sold* to the gentleman in the back for sixteen thousand dollars!"

Midway through the auction, with the man in the suit buying every item for sale, Jon slips out the front door.

+++

Jon drives through Lake Landing, with the early harbingers of spring around him. The yellow blooms of the forsythia are about to open; daffodils are popping out of mulch, and chickweed and purple deadnettle are growing rampantly in the lawns. Jon parks his truck behind Morgan's Acura and walks up to the front door of the Stone Lake house, with a computer bag over his shoulder and a small printer in his arms. He turns and jabs the doorbell with his elbow. Katherine opens the door, blank-faced, in a sundress that flatters her soft, curvy features.

"You can keep the computer and the printer," she says. "I wasn't expecting to get it back."

"I just assumed," Jon says.

"I have three computers, and I hate inkjets."

Jon follows Katherine to the living room. He places the printer on the coffee table and takes the bag off his shoulder, leaning it up against the couch. Katherine stands in front of the panoramic windows, gazing down at the lake.

"Did you wanna go over the edits on the final chapter?" Jon asks.

"I've been coming here since I was a kid, but I never really appreciated the beauty," she says.

"It's never too late."

"It's too late for Morgan. It's too late for me to appreciate her beauty. I was such a jealous bitch. I always had to be the best at everything. Most of all I had to be better than Morgan."

"If Morgan were here, I think she'd forgive you."

Katherine shakes her head. "I watched her struggle through life with a sick satisfaction. Deep down I knew she was better than me. She was so … altruistic, to the point where it was annoying. Even in high school, when she had so much trouble, she was so beautiful. I used to *be* one of the beautiful girls in high school. I was popular, and I hung out with other beautiful, popular girls. We were all used to acting like little bitches and getting away with it. Morgan was never like that. And then, when she gave me her manuscript, I couldn't handle it. I had already published eight novels at the time, but her first was better than anything I had ever written. I just couldn't say that. I propped myself up as a literary genius and criticized her as inexperienced. She put her heart and soul into this book, and I did everything I could to ruin it." She turns around, gazing at Jon through red, watery eyes. "You said, 'If Morgan were here, she'd forgive me.' But I'm the reason she's not here." Tears slip down her face.

Jon walks to Katherine and puts his arms around her. She buries her face into his chest and sobs. He rubs her back, like he's comforting an infant.

"You can't put that on yourself," Jon says. "It wasn't just one thing or one person."

Katherine pulls back and wipes her eyes with the sides of her index fingers. Her pale face is blotchy and shiny with tear streaks.

"I was so wrong," she says. "I wish I could tell her that I'm sorry."

Jon walks to the kitchen; Katherine follows. He grabs the box of tissues from the counter and hands it to her. She pulls out two tissues and places the box on the counter, next to a 9x12 brown envelope. She wipes her face.

"I'm sorry, Jon."

"For what?" Jon raises his eyebrows.

"I'm sorry for the way I treated Morgan. I'm sorry for being an awful sister."

"You don't have to apologize to me."

"You're the only one who I can apologize to. She's gone, but you were the closest to her. If I can't say this to her, it has to be you."

"I think you should forgive yourself."

She waves her hand. "I'm sorry. I'm such an emotional mess these days."

"How's everything with Glen?"

She shakes her head with a smirk. "Morgan was right about him. He *is* a dick. I was so wrapped up in my career, that I didn't realize what was going on in my marriage."

"I'm sorry."

"Don't be. It's for the best. By the way, I have something for you." She grabs the brown shipping envelope. The front is blank. "My dad gave me this to give to you."

Jon breaks the seal on the envelope and pulls out a stack of papers with little red stickers poking out the sides. The cover page states:

Jon,

I've done as you instructed. I used Morgan's trust fund and every ounce of political capital I have toward clearing her name. I am not finished yet, but we will have national coverage and retractions over the next month or so.

Please sign the paperwork enclosed, wherever you see a red sticker, and mail it back to the address below, with a check to me for one dollar. I've taken the liberty of buying all your trucks and equipment at auction. I purchased your office from the bank, so you will no longer have mortgage payments.

I also purchased Chad's and Heather's stake in the business for a song. They were pretty eager to get out of there. It was one of the best investments I've ever made. I opened a new company bank account with three hundred thousand dollars, to help you until things are back up and running. Once your check clears, you will again be the sole owner of Stone Lake Excavating.

You and I both know that Morgan would have wanted this for you, so please accept this not as a gift from me but from her. Thank you for making the last moments of my daughter's life as happy as they could be.

Sincerely,
Richard Anderson

+++

Jon drives away from the lake, away from Lake Landing. He crosses the rusty suspension bridge and turns onto the highway. He passes the grocery store and strip malls. Farther out, the strip malls are populated with check-cashing places, liquor stores, dollar stores, and Latino markets. He turns down a battered asphalt road into a trailer park. He stops in front of boys playing soccer in the road. They pick up the ball and move to the shoulder. Jon drives by slowly. They wave with energetic smiles. He waves in return. The game resumes as soon as he passes.

Some of the trailers are well kept and freshly painted and tended to, with daffodils popping out of flower beds. Others are rusting, with broken cars and appliances in the front yards. Elderly couples sit in lawn chairs, enjoying the late-winter sun. Work trucks and Japanese economy cars are parked haphazardly in the cramped neighborhood.

Jon parks his truck behind a Honda Civic. He strides up to the front door of the trailer. Flower beds are freshly mulched. The house is bright white, with black shutters. He climbs a few wooden steps to the landing. He presses the doorbell. Victor answers the door in stocking feet, his brown balding head peeking out from his thinning black hair.

Jon raises his eyebrows. "*Hola*, Victor. *¿Que pasa? Estoy buscando a* Oscar."

Victor walks away, leaving the door open. The smell of grilling chicken hangs in the air. He calls down the hall. "Oscar, *el patron esta aqui.*"

Victor sits on the couch, watching television. Oscar marches to the door. Claudia sticks her head out from the kitchen, looking at

Jon with a frown.

Oscar stares at Jon, blank-faced. "What can I do for you, Jon?"

"I have a big announcement about the company," Jon says. "I thought maybe you could round up the guys and meet me at the office sometime tomorrow."

"There is no company."

"There is now."

"I'm not sure the guys would return, after everything that happened. I'm not sure I would even show up. The company going bankrupt hurt a lot of guys. Victor lost his apartment. That's why he's here. A lot of guys have had to double up their families just to get by. Now that spring is almost here, we're getting new jobs. I'm working at Jensen's Construction, for fourteen dollars an hour. I got a handful of other guys on there too."

"I'm not telling you guys to come back to work for me. I'm only asking that you'll hear me out. I apologize for leaving y'all hanging. It's been a tough time for everyone."

Oscar nods. "Do you wanna come in for lunch?"

+++

"I think that's everyone who's gonna show," Oscar says, as he scans the audience of workers standing in the office's reception area.

Jon looks out at the sea of brown and white haggard faces. He holds on to a clipboard. The hushed conversations stop; all eyes are on Jon.

"Could someone poke their head out the door and see if anyone else is in the parking lot?" Jon asks.

Karen, the former receptionist, opens the door and scans the parking lot. She returns. "I think that's it," she says.

"I guess we'll begin then. Oscar is going to translate."

"*Voy a traducir*," Oscar says.

"I think this business can be very special." Jon pauses.

"*Creo que este negocio puede ser muy especial.*"

"I would like to partner with each and every one of you."

Oscar translates.

"How we gonna partner with somethin' that's bankrupt?" a worker with crossed arms asks.

"The business was purchased by my friend Morgan Anderson. The equipment, the trucks, everything." Jon pauses.

"*El negocio fue comprado por mi amigo* Morgan Anderson," Oscar says. "*El equipo, los camiones, todo.*"

"She paid off the mortgage on the office and the truck loans. And she deposited three hundred thousand dollars in our account to help get us back in business. She gave it all to me."

Oscar translates.

"Oscar is going to be the boss. He's going to own 10 percent of this company."

Oscar's eyes widen. He translates.

"The remaining 90 percent will be divided among everyone in this room who wants to work here."

Oscar translates; the room is silent, the workers blank-faced.

Jon turns to Oscar. "I was expecting a bit more enthusiasm."

Karen raises her hand.

"Yes, Karen," Jon says.

"This sounds really nice. It's just kinda confusin'. I can't speak for everyone, but I don't really know what this means."

Heads nod in agreement.

"Does anybody know how many people are here?" Jon asks.

A handful of people look around and count as they point at each other.

"It's thirty-two, including you and Oscar," a worker says.

"Okay," Jon says. "What it means is that everyone does the exact same job that they were doing before."

Jon pauses. Oscar translates.

"Everyone gets paid what they were paid before, for whatever job they were doing."

Oscar translates.

"So everything is exactly the same. Does everyone understand that?"

Oscar translates. Heads nod.

"So what's the point of bein' a partner, if everything's the same?" another worker asks.

"I'm getting to that. The only difference is everyone is entitled to share in the profits."

Oscar translates. Smiles form.

"So, if we have thirty people who own 90 percent of this company, then each person would own 3 percent. Does anyone have a calculator?"

Oscar translates, while Karen brings Jon a calculator.

"With Chad and Heather gone, and without any debt, this company can be very profitable. If everyone works hard, together, you should be able to make about six hundred thousand dollars in profit this year."

Oscar translates, as Jon punches numbers on his calculator.

"That means, in addition to your regular pay, everyone would also receive a profit-sharing check at the end of the fiscal year of about $18,000."

Oscar translates.

The workers smile and look at each other. A few guys smack each other on the backs.

"There is one catch," Jon says.

Oscar translates; a few faces frown.

"You must work *here* to participate in the partnership. All partnerships will be returned to the company if you are fired or quit or retire."

Oscar translates.

"The partnership will then be given to the nonpartner employee with the most tenure."

Oscar translates.

"This will encourage new blood, and it won't allow partners to sit at home and collect profit sharing checks while they work somewhere else."

Oscar translates.

"What about you?" a burly worker asks, with his chest puffed out. "What's your percent?"

"Zero," Jon says.

The worker shrinks and lowers his head.

Oscar looks at Jon with his eyes wide. "I can't do this without you here."

Jon turns to Oscar and whispers, "Don't worry. I'm gonna stay until everyone's settled." Jon looks at the audience. "Everyone who wants to do this must sign this paper." Jon holds up the clipboard. "Put down your full legal names and social security numbers, so I can have my lawyer draft the paperwork. Can someone pass this around?"

Karen takes the clipboard.

"I don't know what to say," Oscar says.

Jon turns toward Oscar and holds out his hand. They shake. "You're already a good leader," Jon says, "You know this business inside and out, and this is something you really want."

Oscar grins. "How did you know that?"

"The auction. The look on your face when you lost the bid on the old mini-excavator."

Victor walks up to Jon and Oscar. The old man smacks Jon on the back and smiles, exposing a mouthful of silver. "*Gracias, el patron.*"

Jon smiles. "No, *eres el patron.*"

Chapter 20

Virtue

Jon gazes out the window into the darkness, listening to the click-clack of the tracks. He's broken from his trance by boisterous laughter. He turns and sees a group of young men sitting, dressed in Redskins garb, passing a flask. European tourists wearing fanny packs speak German. A young couple holds hands, their thighs touching. A dark-haired girl sits on her father's lap, enthralled by the story of her favorite picture book. Jon smiles and turns back to the window.

"Next stop, Smithsonian," the loudspeaker blares. "Next stop, Smithsonian."

Jon stands, the moving train unsteady beneath his feet. He grabs a pole and makes his way toward the doors. The train slows and stops. The metal-and-glass doors slide open.

The loudspeaker chimes and says, "This exit, Smithsonian, National Mall, National Gallery of Art, National Air and Space Museum."

Jon steps onto the subway platform, the lights on the edge flashing beneath his feet. He walks in step with the crowd of tourists. He pulls a rectangular ticket from his pocket and places it in the front of the turnstile. His card is devoured and reappears at the top. He grabs his card, and the plastic jaws open up, allowing him to pass through.

After crossing the turnstiles, the excitement of the crowd increases. Children skip and pull their parents ahead. Tourists talk faster and louder, with smiles on their faces. Jon steps on the escalator behind the dark-haired girl and her father. Her father holds her tiny hand. She stares at the hairy legs of the man on the stairway in front of her. She turns around, tilts her blue eyes up, and grins at Jon. Jon smiles back, and her grin grows to a wide smile.

Near the top of the escalator, sunlight blinds the riders. Jon slips on his sunglasses. The families and tourists step off the escalator and are greeted by a bright summer day and men selling maps.

"Anybody need a map?" an older man says. "Only two dollars. Air and Space Museum, National Gallery of Art, Museum of Natural History. Anybody need a map?"

The crowd passes, as if the men do not exist. Heads are firmly set forward, never wavering. The dark-haired girl flashes a grin at an older map salesman, as she walks by with her father. Jon approaches the older man. He's thin and fit. His dark skin and white stubble hides the wrinkles of a long life. He smiles at Jon, exposing a gap between his central incisors.

"Can I help you find someplace, sir?" he asks.

Jon pulls twenty dollars from his pocket. "Could I have one of those maps?"

Jon hands him the twenty and takes the map. The man reaches into his pocket and pulls out a wad of one dollar bills.

"Please keep it," Jon says.

The man looks up with a grin. "You sure about that?"

"It's not from me. It's from my friend."

"Well, you tell your friend thank you."

"You don't happen to know a Richard Anderson, do you?"

The old man smiles wide. "Everybody knows Dick."

"I was told he works down here on the weekends. Could you tell me where?"

He narrows his eyes. "And who might you be?"

"I'm a friend. My name's Jon Porter."

He stares at Jon, relaxes, and smiles. "I didn't recognize you in your sunglasses! I'm Chuck."

He holds out his hand; Jon shakes it. "It's nice to meet you, Chuck."

"I'm sorry for bein' doubtful. He been gettin' a lot a looky-loos since everythin'. He don't like bein' hassled when he's tryin' to work. We try not to send tourists over there. He's gotta lunch truck over by the Museum of Natural History."

"How long have you known him?"

"I've known Dick since …" The old man looks up at the sky, then back at Jon. "It must be damn near twenty-two years now. I'll never forget it. Morgan used to buy a map from me every weekend. She musta had a stack of 'em. Didn't throw 'em away neither. She'd always stop and show me on my map where they went. She would draw on it like a treasure map. Then one day, they just stopped comin'. I never forgot them though. I saw Dick in the food truck four or five months ago, and I recognized him immediately. I asked him about Morgan. I felt so bad, you know? I didn't know what happened. Damn near broke my heart."

Jon nods, his eyes downcast.

"It was a good thing you done, gettin' her story out. My wife loves your book. She's read it five times."

"Thank you, but it's really Morgan's book. The part I wrote

pales in comparison to her words."

"Well, I suppose everything pales in comparison to her."

"Truer words have never been spoken."

Jon waves good-bye and strolls along the tan gravel pathway, shaded by elm trees, toward the Museum of Natural History. Snack vendors and newspaper dispensers line the pathway as he gets closer. He stops and gazes at a head shot of Morgan on the front page of a gossip rag. The photo next to it shows the cliff, and the headline reads Did Her Rapist Push Her Off? A plain white lunch truck is parked on the curb. Folding chairs and tables are set up in the grass. Haggard men and women in tattered clothing eat in small groups. A few shopping carts filled with worldly possessions sit nearby. Children in dirty clothes eat together with innocent smiles.

Tourists steer clear of the outdoor dining area, often crossing the street before walking by, then crossing again once safely past. Richard Anderson hands plates of freshly grilled cheeseburgers and fries to outstretched hands. Beads of sweat sit on his bald head, and a perpetual smile is plastered on his face. He knows most of the patrons by first name. Susan Anderson flips burgers. She looks heavier, healthier, like the mother Morgan always wanted. Even without makeup, her face is radiant. Her gray and brown hair is tied up in a bun. Sweat droplets slide down her cheeks. The lunch rush dwindles. As the last patron is served, Jon strides to the window.

"You guys get quite a crowd," he says.

"Jon, what a surprise," Richard says. He turns to his wife. "Susan, Jon's here."

Susan steps out from the grill with a smile. She puts down her spatula. "Hey, Jon, I didn't know you were in town," she says. "I have a couple burgers left, if you want one."

"Why don't we all sit and eat? It's time for a break," Richard says.

Susan takes off her apron and steps out of the lunch truck. Richard follows. She hugs Jon.

"It's so nice to see you," she says in his ear. She pulls back. "I'm getting you all dirty. I'm sorry. I'm a mess."

"You look great," Jon says. "You both do."

Richard shakes Jon's hand with a grin. "Why don't you find a table, and we'll get the food."

Jon sits at an empty table under the shade of a majestic elm. The Andersons carry plates with burgers and fries, plus bottles of water. They arrange plates, water, and napkins before sitting down.

"So what brings you up here?" Richard asks.

"I have a flight to catch at Washington National this evening. I'm parked at the airport, but I came in early, so I could come down here and see you guys. I would have called, but I don't have your new number, and Katherine is unavailable for the next month or so."

"Did she tell you what she was working on?" Susan asks.

"She wouldn't say. She just mentioned she's going write in complete solitude until it's done."

"So where are you headed?" Richard asks.

"New Zealand. Well, first Chicago, then LAX, then Auckland. Morgan always wanted to go there."

"How long are you going to be gone?" Susan asks.

"I don't have a return ticket yet. I've never been outside the United States. I might visit a few other places. I've always been tied down to something. Maybe I'll see where the wind takes me."

"I hope you stay in touch," Richard says.

Jon nods. "I will."

"How are things with your mother?" Susan asks.

Jon shakes his head. "I have to be me with cash. She's not interested in just me."

Susan reaches out and grabs Jon's hand. "I'm so sorry."

"Don't be. It's probably for the best."

"I hope it's not strange for you," Susan says, "but we consider you part of our family now."

Jon blushes. "Thank you."

"We're serious about that, Jon," Richard says.

"And we hope you meet someone," Susan says. "Morgan would want you to find love."

"She showed me what to look for," Jon says.

"I looked up love in the dictionary the other day," Richard says. He glances at Susan. She flashes a grin. "It said that it's an intense feeling of deep affection, and I thought … that's bullshit."

Susan frowns. "Richard."

Richard laughs. "Sorry, honey. It's just that coming here and helping people with you made me realize that love is simply the result of goodness." Richard looks at Jon. "That's what you had with Morgan. She loved you because you're a good man, and you loved her because she was a good woman. It doesn't get any more pure than that."

Dear Reader,

I am thrilled that you took precious time out of your life to read my book. Thank you! I hope you found it entertaining, engaging, and thought-provoking. If so, please consider writing a positive review on Amazon and Goodreads. The more five-star reviews I receive, the more my book will vault up the sales charts. The review doesn't need to be long and detailed, if you're more of a reader than a writer.

As an author and a small businessman, competing against the big publishers, every reader, every review, and every referral is greatly appreciated.

If you're interested in receiving my new book releases for free, please subscribe to my author blog at www.PhilWBooks.com. If you want to contact me, don't be bashful. I can be found at Phil@PhilWBooks.com. I do my best to respond to all e-mails.

Sincerely,
Phil M. Williams

Made in the USA
Las Vegas, NV
25 May 2021

23630368R10152